Advance Acclaim for *Angel Eyes*

"*Angel Eyes* has everything I look for in a novel—gorgeous prose, a compelling heroine, humor, and an intriguing plot—and two things I dream of finding—permission for brokenness and the promise of hope."

—MYRA MCENTIRE,
AUTHOR OF *HOURGLASS*

"*Angel Eyes* is a fine debut. A touching and exciting romance with celestial implications."

—ANDREW KLAVAN, AWARD-WINNING
AUTHOR OF *CRAZY DANGEROUS*

"Stunning. A captivating read with all the intensity necessary to keep me turning pages well into the night."

—HEATHER BURCH, AUTHOR OF THE
CRITICALLY ACCLAIMED *HALFLINGS*

"Shannon Dittemore gives us a classic tale of good versus evil with an authentically contemporary feel – and the assurance that beautiful writing is back."

—NANCY RUE, AUTHOR
OF THE REAL LIFE SERIES

ANGEL EYES

ANGEL EYES

SHANNON DITTEMORE

THOMAS NELSON
Since 1798

NASHVILLE   DALLAS   MEXICO CITY   RIO DE JANEIRO

Published in Nashville, Tennessee, by Thomas Nelson. Thomas Nelson is a registered trademark of Thomas Nelson, Inc.

Scripture quotations are taken from the NEW KING JAMES VERSION. ©1982 by Thomas Nelson, Inc. Used by permission. All rights reserved.

Thomas Nelson, Inc., titles may be purchased in bulk for educational, business, fund-raising, or sales promotional use. For information, please e-mail SpecialMarkets@ThomasNelson.com.

Publisher's Note: This novel is a work of fiction. Names, characters, places, and incidents are either products of the author's imagination or used fictitiously. All characters are fictional, and any similarity to people living or dead is purely coincidental.

Library of Congress Cataloging-in-Publication Data

Dittemore, Shannon.
  Angel eyes / Shannon Dittemore.
      p. cm. -- (Angel eyes ; 1)
  Summary: Just returned home to tiny Stratus, Oregon, after finding tragedy instead of success as a ballerina, eighteen-year-old Brielle discovers she has a destiny with new neighbor Jake--to join a battle in a realm that only angels, demons, and Brielle can perceive.
  ISBN 978-1-4016-8635-2 (pbk.)
[1. Supernatural--Fiction. 2. Angels--Fiction. 3. Demonology--Fiction. 4. High schools--Fiction. 5. Schools--Fiction. 6. Fate and fatalism--Fiction.] I. Title.
  PZ7.D6294Ang 2012
  [Fic]--dc23

                                        2012004556

Printed in the United States of America
12 13 14 15 16 17 QG 6 5 4 3 2 1

For Matt, who chose me
And for Justus and Jazlyn, who had no choice in the matter

"Do not fear, for those who are with us are more than those who are with them."

ELISHA, THE PROPHET

Dothan, Israel—2500 years ago

*T*he boy trembles. Fear wraps him tight, rattling his callow frame.

He sees an army arrived in the dead of night. He sees soldiers flooding the canyon floor, flanking them on every side. Cursing, spitting soldiers, here for his master. The boy sees horses fogging the morning air and chariots pulling men with bows. He sees spears with bronze tips and swords of iron glinting in the predawn light.

And he imagines.

He imagines his master hauled away in chains. He imagines his own blood glazing one of those swords. He imagines death.

Fear does that to the imagination.

"Master," he asks, "what shall we do?"

The prophet wrestles silently with a truth. He knows things the boy does not. Sees things the boy can't see.

He sees the enemy. Oh yes, he sees them. But he sees their forces surrounded. He sees an angelic army. Great winged men with swords of light and halos of gold. He sees them lining the mountains that hem together this canyon. He sees horses emerging from fiery skies and chariots with wheels of sunset cloud. He sees riders with bows drawn and arrows of flame fixed on their adversaries.

And he knows. He knows they're here to protect him. To protect the boy.

Truth does that to the heart.

And the prophet knows this: There's no room here for fear. Only truth.

The boy needs to know it. He needs to know there are things unseen, forces for good and for evil. He needs to know there are more fighting for them than for their enemies.

Day breaks over the horizon, and the prophet lifts up his voice. With a cry to rival the snorting horses and the irreverent soldiers, he prays for his servant.

"Lord, give him eyes that he might see."

And God answers the prophet. By the hand of an angel and a halo of gold, he answers him.

And for the first time in his young life, the boy sees.

1

Brielle

*T*he knot in my throat is constant. An aching thing. Shallow breaths whisper around it, sting my chapped lips, and leave white smoke monsters in the air.

It takes them nine seconds to disappear. Nine seconds for the phantoms I've created to dissolve into nothingness.

How long till the one haunting my dreams does the same?

The absence of an answer makes my hands shake, so I slide the lambskin gloves out of my book bag and put them on.

If only it were that easy.

Like glacial masses shoving along, ice travels my veins, chilling my skin and numbing my insides. Three weeks of this biting cold outstrips the severity of my nightmares, but I haven't suffered enough and I know it.

"Miss, isn't this your stop?" The man's voice skates atop the frozen air.

I want to answer him, but the words don't come. A single tear thaws, escapes the confines of my lashes, and races triumphantly down my cheek. It soaks into my knit scarf—an invisible trail marking its life.

"Miss?" he tries again. "We're here. We've reached Stratus."

My legs are stiff, refusing to stand. I just need a minute. I should say something at least—answer him—but the knot in my throat refuses to budge. I raise a gloved hand to wrestle it away.

"I'm sorry, dear, but the conductor is impatient today. If you don't exit the train, you'll have to ride back to Portland with us."

I turn toward the aisle and look at the poor man. He's sixty at least, with a tuft of gray hair and an oversized bow tie. The kind you only see in the movies. He, too, is wearing gloves, and it's a small comfort to know I'm not the only one chilled. His face wrinkles into a million lines, and the corners of his mouth lift.

"Of course, if you'd like to return with the train, you're more than welcome. I could use the company." He gestures to row after row of empty seats.

"No," I murmur, standing quickly. I cannot return with this train. Not now. Not to the place where it happened. "You're right. This is my stop." I gather my bags and sink deep into my parka before stepping onto the platform.

Why is everything so cold?

I wrap my scarf around my neck once more and think of Hank, a coworker of my dad's, who climbs Mount Hood every year. He's lost all the toes on his right foot to frostbite, and one year a companion fell on the south side of the peak and slid into a crevasse, sacrificed to the god of adrenaline. After losing so much, how can such a journey be worth it?

The train pulls away from the station. It's empty now, but I stare after the steel snake as the heaviness of *good-bye* squirms inside my chest, locked away in a cage of frozen bones and tissue. Will I ever thaw enough to say the word?

The parking lot is small, but as I cross it I cast a flickering gaze at the man standing by a pickup. Six foot five and burly, my father waits with a stubborn smile as I trudge toward him. *Don't come*, I'd said. *I can take a taxi.* I knew he'd be here anyway.

The heavy load falls from my hands. It crunches into the frozen blacktop, and I lean against his truck, counting silently to fifty-eight before he says a word.

"I know you didn't want me to come, Brielle, but you're not in the city anymore. There's just the one cabbie. Didn't want you standing here all night waiting for the guy." He stretches his long lumberjack arms around my shoulders awkwardly. "Plus, I couldn't wait to see you. It's been too long."

He adds the last sentence very quietly, and I pretend not to hear it. The knot in my throat is a traitor, though, and explodes in a gush of air. The sobs that have bruised me from the inside out finally break free as my daddy wraps me in his arms and tucks me into his flannel coat.

He lets me cry, his grip so tight I have to struggle out of it when I'm done. Still snuffling, I wipe my face on my sleeve and crawl into the truck. The scent of wood chips and spearmint gum tickles my nostrils, and I settle back, breathing it deep. Dad drops into his seat, and I have to brace my hand against the door to keep from sliding into him on the sloping bench-seat.

"Sorry," he says.

The engine revs, and we leave the parking lot behind us. From the train station it's just three miles to the house I grew up in. The distance flies by, leaving me feeling like an outsider. I can't point out a single change, but it all feels foreign. The mixture of evergreen trees and cow pastures are a bizarre juxtaposition after the city's skyscrapers and manicured parks.

I don't want to be back here, but the oak tree in our lawn

comes into sight and the pain ebbs a bit. The house isn't anything to get worked up over, though I've always been happy to call it home. Ranch-style, white with yellow trim, it sits nestled in a jumble of evergreens. Within, everything about the furnishings is supersized to fit my mountain of a father.

We pull into the long gravel driveway, and I cringe at the ridiculous mailbox that's been added in my absence.

"Where did you get that?"

"I made it," he says, proud of his handiwork. The mailbox is ghastly: a ten-gallon bucket, our last name scrawled across it, perched atop the old post. "Whatcha think?"

"What happened to the old *normal* mailbox?"

"I backed into it with the trailer." He chuckles, and the elastic bands around my heart ease up just a millimeter.

"Well, at least I know what to get you for Christmas."

Dad parks the truck, and a small sigh escapes my lips. I hadn't planned on living here again, ever, and the sting of disappointment jabs at my gut: I did not finish what I set out to do. But I can't go back. I can't. I need this house, and I need my dad.

"Who's living in the old Miller place?" I ask, nodding at the only other house in sight—a farmhouse situated about a hundred yards to the east.

He cranes his neck to look past me. "Don't know. Somebody just moved in."

Several of the windows are alive with light. The truck rattles with the sound of a stereo, and my heart slows to the rhythm of the bass line. Like a metronome, it's soothing, and I lean back against the headrest.

"Ah, heck. I'll go over there after dinner and tell 'em to turn it down."

"No. Don't. Please."

His shoulders sag, and I realize he'll do anything to make me comfortable tonight. We sit in the cab, the rattling truck and bass guitar filling the silence.

"You know, kiddo, you don't have to talk about it. You don't. You don't really need to *do* anything for a while." He's rehearsed this little speech, I can tell. "Just *be*, okay? Be here, and maybe one day you'll see it really wasn't your fault."

I choke a bit and look into his big teddy bear face. He can't know. He's my dad. He sees only what he wants to see. He'll never understand that I could have stopped it. I look out the passenger-side window, over the dead grass and the brown leaves scattered on the ground. I look out at the coming winter and the setting sun and say all I plan on saying about it.

"Ali was eighteen, Dad. My age. A little bit younger, really." My body—my skin, even—feels so heavy with the icy weight of it all. "I could have stopped the whole thing. There's no way around that, but you said it yourself. I don't have to talk about it."

I turn to face my father. He needs to know how serious I am. This subject is off-limits. Until the trial—until I'm sitting on that witness stand—there isn't another soul who needs to hear my story. I look Dad straight in the eye. Tears gather there, they run down his face and sparkle in his beard.

"Okay. We just won't talk about it," he concedes. He kisses my nose. "Some guy named Pizza Hut made us dinner, so let's get to it."

He climbs out and throws a hostile look at the old Miller place. Then he grabs my bags from the bed of the truck and stomps inside.

"Pizza Hut, huh?"

I follow him into the house. His boots leave muddy prints up the porch stairs and across the linoleum floor. I used to reprimand him for stuff like that, but not today. Today, I simply ghost by.

Weaving around the mud splotches, I make my way through the kitchen and into my old room. It's been vacant for two years, and still it looks the same. I pick at a loose thread on my jeans, uneasy at the lack of change. This ancient town is tightfisted with her diversions, and it's quite possible I've had my share. The idea hurts. Like that dingy penny in the bottom of your pocket—the one that must be eighty years old. You scratch away the gummy muck and are horrified to find how new the coin is. Much newer than you ever would have guessed.

How did I get so filthy, so damaged in just a few short years?

I'd been given the chance of a lifetime, and now, two years later, my own inaction had ruined not only my dreams but the life of someone I'd loved. Broken dreams I can handle, but I'd give anything to go back and make things right for her.

That isn't possible, of course. Some things you have to do right the first time. If the past three weeks have taught me anything, it's that.

You don't always get a second chance.

The doorbell rings, mercifully pulling me from thoughts that can only lead to tears.

"Brielle! Company."

An unnoticed, quiet transition back home was too grand a thing to hope for. I realize this only now as I reenter the kitchen, followed by several of my old friends. It's a diverse group I've collected through the years: there's the softball player, the cheerleader, my first lab partner, a girl I've known since Girl Scouts, and two dancers from Miss Macy's studio on Main.

I'm the outgoing one. The ballerina, the model.

My place has always been the clubhouse. The home without a nagging mother. Without chores to do. Without pestering siblings. We've grown up together, all of us. Their mothers made me cookies and hemmed my dance costumes. Their fathers kept Dad company while I was away at summer camp. These girls and their families will always be the players on the stage of my childhood, and I can tell by their optimistic, chipper faces that they assume we can pick up where we left off.

They're wrong. Nothing will ever be the same.

I try to smile and nod at the right times, but I'm cold and slow. Eventually their smiles fade. They ask a few questions about the train ride home, about my school in the city. No one approaches the tie-dyed elephant in the room, but their eyes avoid mine, and I know they're scrutinizing the poor beast in any case. Mostly they fidget uncomfortably. After half an hour the entire huddle smiles politely, mutters garbled apologies, and leaves one after the other. Only Kaylee, my childhood sidekick, stays long enough to grab a slice of pizza and attempt to wring me from my melancholy.

"Brielle, you've got to let this go," she says, picking the pepperoni off her pizza. I wonder if this attempt at vegetarianism will last longer than her emo phase.

"If it's all right with you, Kay, I'd rather not talk about it," I say from across the kitchen.

"I know, but one day you will, and I'll be here, okay? I'll be right here." She stares at her pizza as she speaks, and for that I'm grateful. "This pizza's great. I mean, I know I'm a vegetarian, but if I pick it off like this"—she waves a pepperoni at me—"the cheese still tastes like meat." She flashes her teeth at me, marinara coating her braces.

A giggle hiding somewhere inside my gut wriggles its way north and surprises both of us.

"Well, you're not spewing soda out your nose yet, but it's better than the face you had when I got here. You'll be at school tomorrow?"

"Yes, of course. What else is there to do around here?"

"I heard that." Dad's recliner moans, and a second later he lumbers into the kitchen. He's been pretending to watch some Japanese reality show and now leans heavily on the island, studying my face. "You don't have to jump back into things so fast, kiddo. Thanksgiving break's just ending. Take a week for yourself. Adjust."

"It's. Stratus."

"Brielle . . ."

"The bucket outside doubling as a mailbox—that's the only thing that's changed, Dad." I tweak his nose, trying to cram my lively past-self into the gesture.

He takes my hand and folds it into his. "But *you've* changed, baby. You've had to."

I tug my fingers free and turn away. "School is fine."

Actually, I dread it. All those faces staring at me. Knowing. All the questions stirring behind sympathetic expressions. Yes, I dread it. Absolutely. Suddenly the pizza seems like an awful idea, and I'm sick to my stomach.

"Brielle? You're white as a sheet. Maybe you should listen to your dad."

"I just need to lie down. I'll see you tomorrow, Kay." I run from the room, bleating the last few words as I go.

I make it to the bathroom before I start throwing up, but only just. Dad brings me a glass of water and a rag. I send him to bed and tell him not to worry—it's probably just the greasy pizza. He isn't convinced, I'm sure, but he understands I'd rather be alone in my misery, and he's kind enough to give me that.

The rest of the night passes—uneasily, but it passes. I don't sleep much, and when I wake, my hands are shaking violently. My dreams scare me now. Not because they're always about Ali, but because I'm always afraid they will be. Fear is the real spook haunting my dreams. When I'm awake, though, it isn't fear that makes me shake. It's guilt. Frigid and ever present.

The sound of tire chewing gravel tells me Dad's truck is backing down the driveway. I yank the cord on my blinds. They fly up and away, and I rub my hands together as the sky brightens moderately behind a canopy of gray clouds. My sheets and blankets have balled up and settled in a wad on my stomach. I kick them off and step into the shower, cranking the knob hard to the left—so hard the pipes squeal in protest. Hot water, sputtering and steamy, washes over my skin. Still, I wash quickly.

How it can scald my flesh and still leave me chilled, I have no idea, but the past twenty-three days have brought one disappointing shower after the next.

It's too early to head to school, so I start a load of laundry for Dad. I unload the dishwasher and unpack quickly, cramming away shirts and pants before I'm forced to remember why I bought them or who I bought them with.

Wrapped in a blanket, I wander through the empty house. It's pretty clean, but I suspect Dad has paid someone to do that. There are no cobwebs on the white walls, the flat-screen TV is void of dust, the thick brown carpet has been vacuumed, the blue recliner and sectional smell like Febreze. An afghan is folded neatly and draped over my favorite reading chair. A collection of books adorns the leather ottoman, and the bathroom has a new addition: a plug-in air freshener.

Yeah, he's paying someone.

Pictures of my dead mother doing things I have no recollection of litter the walls and tables: holding my pudgy toddler hand as we walk through a park, wearing a flowery bathing suit and splashing in the surf, kissing my father under the mistletoe. I stop at a picture by the front door. It's a family portrait taken outside Miss Macy's dance studio on the afternoon of my first recital. Dad looks nearly unchanged: ruddy complexion, mussed beard and hair, flannel shirt. I think he was happier then.

In the photograph Mom's holding me tight. My legs, in white tights, wrap around her waist. The tiny bun on top of my head is pulling loose, but there's no mistaking the resemblance to my mother. Even at three years old I favor her. Blue eyes, red lips, fair skin. Her golden-blond hair sits in waves upon her shoulders in a way I've never been able to replicate. Instead, mine hangs long and straight. Still, I have her soft round cheeks and small chin. I run a finger over her face. I don't remember her at all.

Dressing as warmly as possible, I pull on my parka and gloves over everything else. I step onto the porch and fumble in my bag for the car keys I haven't needed in two years.

We live on a fairly empty stretch of road. The view from our porch shows a spattering of trees, the highway, and then acres and acres of abandoned farmland. The old Miller place sits to the east, and a mile or so beyond is the Stratus cemetery. There's also a road leading back to the interstate. The rest of the town sits to the west.

With an anxious sigh I climb into my hand-me-down Volkswagen Beetle. She's a 1967, black with a rack on top, and we call her Slugger. Slugger was Mom's, so Dad's always taken good care of her, but she's not allowed out of town. Too old, Dad says. Too slow, I say. Either way, Slugger's a piece of Mom, and I love her.

Stratus High isn't far: just a short drive up the highway and across Main Street. Almost everything in Stratus involves a drive across Main. When you see the neon grape jelly jar towering above, you know you've arrived. Jelly's, the closest thing Stratus has to a café. Across the street is the small theatre. An old-fashioned clock sits out front, surrounded by metal benches. We call this the town square. A quick glance at the clock tells me I've still not reacclimated to small-town life. Everything here starts so much later than in Portland.

I'm twenty-five minutes early.

The stoplight marking the center of Main turns red, and I consider flipping a U-turn. A cup of something hot from Jelly's doesn't sound half bad and would kill some time. But there on the corner, just past the stoplight, is Miss Macy's. The dance studio I all but lived in until two years ago.

I danced there. I taught.

I sweated.

It'd be nice to sweat again.

The windows are dark, but I've still got my key. It rattles against my steering column with a handful of others. By the time the light turns green, I've decided. Slugger putts through the intersection, and I park in front of the studio.

My hands are safe inside my gloves, but they tremble. It's been a long time since I danced just for myself.

The glass door is clean. I imagine the teacher who closed last night sprayed all the tiny fingerprints away. I unlock it and step inside. Leaning against the door, I breathe deep, expecting familiarity, but it smells different than I remember. New paint maybe?

The reception area is small and mostly unchanged. A small wooden desk, blue binders stacked on one corner, a white vase with plastic roses on the other. Eight folding chairs line the front window and the adjoining wall in a tidy L-shape. Pictures of students, past and present, fill the room, on shelves and in cases. Younger, warmer versions of myself smile back from many of them. It's like walking into a scrapbook of my life.

I step through the connecting doorway and into the studio. There's just the one. The wintry daylight outside does little to brighten the room as it trickles through the wall of windows looking out onto the street. I flip the switch to my right, and the studio fills with warm, yellow brightness. It spills across the wood floors and reflects off the mirror on the far wall.

Beyond the window, beyond my car parked at the curb and across the street, three old men sit outside a doughnut shop. They're bundled in flannels, jackets, and scarves—coffee mugs fogging the air, but still they sit.

Same thing they were doing when I left two years ago.

One of them, a thin stick of a man wearing an aviator cap—Bob, I think—catches me staring and waves. I wave back, but he's already turned back to his friends. I shake my head and crouch at the CD player sitting just inside the door. Against it leans a white CD sleeve. Purple writing loops across the front.

BRIELLE, it says. WELCOME HOME.

I run a gloved finger over Miss Macy's winding script and am ashamed of myself. I could have written. I could have called.

But, happy to move on, I soaked up life in the city and pushed Stratus and the ever-constant Miss Macy to the back of my mind. Still, she knew I'd find my way here, and she left this for me. A CD she probably mixed herself.

My chest tightens as I insert the disk into the slot and push Play. I don't bother removing my gloves or jacket. I'll just be a minute. My feet find the center of the floor as the music begins. The selection is very Miss Macy. Floaty. Flowery even. I don't recognize it. Sounds like a movie soundtrack. Jane Austen or something.

The mirror's in front of me, but I close my eyes. I know what I'll see there. A skinny girl disguised as a marshmallow. Parka, gloves, hat, boots.

Still, I dance.

And I cry. The music pulls my arms out and up, pushes me onto my toes and into myself. For three or four minutes I'm lost. Just the music. Just me. I move across the floor, my boots squeaking, my jacket swishing. I pause just long enough to turn the music up, tune out my mountain girl apparel. And then I rise on my toes and begin again.

The music fades away, and my body settles into first position. I rest, waiting for the next song.

When it begins I snort. Good thing I'm alone. The song is from my fifth-grade dance recital. A ridiculous ditty about jungle animals. The thumping drums and twanging guitars couldn't be more different from the gentle piano and flute duet of the first number.

But I can't help it. My feet tap to the rhythm. The music grows louder, and I stomp. My back curves out and in, out and in. My arms swing over my head one after the other, and when the animal noises start, I beat my chest like a gorilla, just like I did when I was eleven. I tip my head back and howl.

And then I catch my reflection in the mirror. I'm not the only one howling. Outside, standing just inches from the glass, leaning against a blue mailbox, is a boy. A boy I've never seen before.

And he's laughing. At me.

I lurch and turn toward the window, my hair flying. The boy jerks upright. Caught staring and he knows it.

His bright hazel eyes are what catch my attention first—green with a russet flame bleeding from the center. I take a step toward the glass. Brilliant hazel eyes trimmed with thick black lashes—the kind women buy and glue to their eyelids. His brows are dark, too dark for the sandy hair falling around his face.

And there's something very . . . tan about him. He looks out of place standing on the sidewalk in our frozen town, but I can't imagine him in the city either. Not part of the eclectic sect I hung with: ambitious dancers, plastic models, tragic actors, cutthroat talent agents.

I can't imagine an appropriate setting for him. Somewhere tropical maybe. Somewhere hot. He's wearing a long-sleeved T-shirt advertising some band I've never heard of, distressed jeans, and Chucks—an outfit so incredibly understated that every bit of my attention returns to his face.

He just looks warm.

I shove my hair over my shoulder and smooth my parka. Blood rushes to my face and neck. I'm mortified, but I stand really, really still. That's what you're supposed to do to avoid a bear attack, right?

Does it work with boys?

Apparently not. His hands come up in the universal gesture for *Whoops,* and his full-body guffaw is replaced by a pair of penitent puppy-dog eyes. But it seems he can't stifle his amusement for long. His face cracks, and a smile slips through.

At least he has the decency to cover his mouth.

Then his hands fall away to reveal a grin. A stupid, stupid grin. He steps toward the window and presses a hand to it. The glass fogs over immediately, and his mouth opens like he's got something to say. I cock my head, waiting.

Apology? Hello!

But his mouth closes, and he pulls his hand away. With his index finger he carves a single word into the misty fog his hand left behind: *Sorry.* It's backward, of course.

I can think of no adequate response, but for some reason my hands land on my hips. He turns away, that stupid grin still smeared across his face. He disappears beyond the frame of the window, leaving me huffing and puffing. Out of breath, embarrassed, and, if I'm honest, warmer than I've been in forever.

Across the street the old guys wave their coffee cups at me. Bob stands and claps. His friend whistles—a piercing sound I can hear even inside the studio. It seems they've enjoyed the show as well. I'd curtsy, but my jungle animal routine sucked all the snark out of me.

I creep to the window and press my face against it. It's cold, but the boy is gone. The town square juts out from the sidewalk like an octagon-shaped peninsula, and the clock catches my attention again.

I groan and zip my jacket.

Now that I've humiliated myself on Main Street, school should be a breeze.

2

Brielle

Stratus High looks cold. It's always looked this way, I guess, but after my morning . . . workout, I was hoping for something balmy. At least temperate.

Metal roofs top the white, weather-resistant structures: a gymnasium, two classroom buildings, and a multipurpose room. Against the white sky and the white, functional buildings, evergreens grow in abundance: holly, pine, cypress.

My first class is advanced calculus, or so says the schedule I've been handed by a well-informed, excessively sympathetic secretary whose name I can't remember. The calculus teacher, however, is new and apparently uninformed.

I nearly lose it when he introduces me to the rest of the class. My hands shake so fiercely I have to shove them into my pockets to keep them from becoming a point of attention. I'm sick again but force myself to swallow it down. As fast as humanly possible I take my seat at the back of the room and lay my head down on the desk. It's pathetic but necessary.

I'm dizzy. Very dizzy.

Two-thirds of the kids in this classroom have passed

through each grade with me, and every single one of them saw the news story three weeks ago. A fact utterly apparent by the pained looks on their faces. After my impromptu dance performance this morning, I've had quite enough attention. There's no need to point more of it my way. Not when I'm convinced there's some cosmic spotlight trained on my biggest failure.

I tell myself to keep breathing, to relax. Focusing on the teacher's voice helps. Monotone and austere—I wonder how many kids will be asleep by the time the class is over. I keep my eyes shut as he begins the lesson, reviewing material I can't make myself focus on or care about. Half the period passes before anything he says registers, and then his drab little voice surprises me.

"Ah," he says, absent inflection. "It appears you're not the only new student, Brielle. Everyone, meet Jake. Jake, everyone."

Without lifting my head, without looking, I know who it is, and I burrow deeper into my parka. Two new students at Stratus High in one day?

It has to be him.

"There are a few open seats in the back near Miss Matthews. Take your pick."

Mr. Calculus gestures haphazardly, and I duck into my parka. The entire class turns in my direction, but they're not looking at me. Not this time. They all seem captivated by the boy sliding into the seat next to mine. An entire row—all girls—cranes around to get a better look, and a couple jersey-clad football players nudge one another as they size up the new kid.

The teacher trudges on, but the atmosphere in the room feels downright awkward. Don't get me wrong, I'm glad the class's attention is no longer focused on me, but I feel bad for the guy.

On principle, I refuse to join the stalkarazzi as they giggle and bat their eyes, but their worship has me curious.

Did I miss something spectacular about the kid this morning? Does he sparkle in the sunlight? Does he have fangs? What?

The teacher raps his ruler against the blackboard to garner attention, and I roll my head sideways to get a better look.

Yeah. It's him.

The boy with the front-row seat to this morning's jungle-girl routine.

In the confines of the classroom, though, he looks even more out of place than he did on the sidewalk. His skin looks darker, his shoulders broader, and his eyes have an intensity to them—both dark and light at the same time.

For the first time in nearly a month, my hands stop shaking. I pull my gloves off a finger at a time and do my best not to stare at the stranger who so openly stared at me this morning.

Here in the classroom his demeanor is more formal, more stoic. He keeps his face on the blackboard until the lesson is over. He ignores the girls flipping their hair and sneaking glances at him from the front row. He ignores the posturing football players.

And he ignores me.

The bell rings, catching me unprepared. Most everyone is packed up already, but I'm still staring at an open calculus book.

The new kid, Jake, slides from his seat and reties his shoe. "That was cool this morning. The dancing." His voice has a boyish scratch to it. I can't help but think he's been laughing too much. He snatches my glove from the floor and places it on the desk in front of me. "You're good."

I close my book. "You—yeah."

There were words there. I swear there were. He chews his lip. Just like he did outside the studio.

"It's rude to stare," I blurt. "Your mom told you that, right?"

His face changes. It's sadder somehow.

"I've heard it around. And I didn't mean to stare. Right place, right time, I guess." He stands and throws his bag over his shoulder. "You've got skills."

He's mocking me, I'm sure of it. I mean, jungle dance doesn't exactly scream "mad skills." I've got a comeback. Something about monkeys and boys. It's just . . . stuck. Frozen on the tip of my tongue.

With a slight tilting of his head he walks out the door, and I'm left chewing on the icicle of another thing unsaid.

Learning to speak again is now priority one.

It's a minute before I realize my hands are shaking. So severely this time it takes a good thirty seconds to pull my gloves back in place.

If I could stay embarrassed all day, I might just thaw.

But this biting cold is well deserved, so I blink away the tear offering me its salty consolation. I flip up my hood—a shield against prying eyes—and make my way across the rime-freckled quad.

I don't think about the new kid.

I don't.

The rest of my classes are uneventful: literature, government, French. Advanced photography is the only class I've actually chosen, and my steps fall faster as I make my way there. It's been forever since I've been in an actual darkroom.

Austen—my school in the city—doesn't offer a traditional photography class. Instead they offer digital imaging, which focuses primarily on photo manipulation using computer software. No need for film. No need for a darkroom. Just digital cameras and a Mac lab. And while I enjoyed that class as well, there's just something about manually processing and developing film that's fully immersive. You touch it and see it. You smell it, for goodness' sake. There's an ebb and flow—a rhythm. Like dance, I guess. Maybe that's why I like it so much.

Admittedly, it's a dying art form. And while a jump into the modern world is exactly what our little town needs, I'm glad I'll be long gone before traditional photography vanishes from Stratus High.

I duck into the darkroom, catching a wink from the photo teacher as I go.

Mr. Burns is an eccentric old man and does not run a formal classroom setting. Once a week he lectures on a technique or piece of equipment, and on Tuesdays he holds a class-wide critique. Everyone submits a photo and everyone has a vote. There are award ribbons and everything. During the rest of the week, we're free to work on whatever projects we have going.

The darkroom is small, and though there are only two other students in the room with me, it feels crowded. This doesn't help the claustrophobic tendencies I've developed, but John Mayer croons from the radio in the corner and it's warmer than the outer classroom.

I drop my stuff at the corner station and set to work developing the film in my camera bag. Without a darkroom at my disposal, I've been hoarding it. Half a dozen rolls tumble out when I unzip the front flap, but I don't mind. It gives me something to focus on.

The mindless repetition is cathartic. Even my numb fingers cooperate while crammed inside the black bag. I slam the small container on its end to release the filmstrip and wrap it around the reel carefully to avoid leaving fingerprints. My fingers move quickly as I come up with a plan for the next couple days. Today the focus will be getting all this film developed and hung to dry. Since I've just returned, I'll bow out of the critique tomorrow and sort through the strips, make contact sheets, and see if I have anything here to work with.

I place the reel in the canister and unzip the bag while my thoughts wander. I think about the general solitude I've been granted by the other students. By now, the last period of the day, I'm pretty much ignored. My chill must be contagious, because the girl next to me in government actually shivered when she brushed my arm.

I'm glad this room is dark. If my hands do shake, I don't have to try too hard to hide them. But Mr. Burns must have turned the heater on, because for the third time today, I'm warm. Relieved to be free of the chill, I slide out of my sweater.

I feel a little more normal this way: Without the gloves, without the parka and the sweater. Just a long-sleeved white T-shirt over faded blue jeans.

My thoughts continue to wander. With some effort I pull them away from three weeks ago, away from the city. There are other things to think about. Other people. People from here. People with no connection at all to that place.

People like Kaylee. It's strange I don't have a single class with her. I want that fact to disappoint me, but I don't feel much about it at all.

And there's the new kid.

Jake.

Where did he come from, anyway? Did the teacher say?

I turn to grab the developing solution from the table behind me. Alone with my thoughts, I slam into someone, the metal canister in my hand smacking the person hard in the stomach.

"Oh, I'm . . ."

I am sorry, and I should tell him so. But I don't. I'm distracted by the hand holding my wrist.

It belongs to Jake. My stalker, apparently.

"Hey," he says. He steadies both my wrist and the canister against his chest. His heart pounds evenly against my hand, and mine speeds up.

It seems I'm destined to make a fool of myself in front of this guy.

"I didn't realize we had this class together," he says.

"I . . . me either," I stutter. "I didn't know either."

He smiles. Up close it's crooked, mischievous, and I think of that Pink song, the one about the pills and the morphine. I think how dangerous attraction is. How dangerous it was for *her*.

I take a step back and then realize he's still holding my wrist. I try to gather my thoughts and put together a coherent sentence, but nothing occurs to me. The door opens behind Jake, and Mr. Burns comes in.

"Jake, can I bother you for a second? I need some help bringing in the new enlarger."

"Sure, Mr. Burns." His eyes are still on my face, that lopsided grin mocking me, and it's a second or two before he releases my wrist and follows the teacher from the room.

"Elle, could you hold the inner door open for us? Grace has the door out here."

Between the darkroom and the classroom is a short hallway with heavy doors at each end. This area has no light at all and serves as a transition space protecting the darkroom from the white light of the classroom.

"Of course . . ." I run the canister back to my workstation and hurry back through the door to wait for them. I arrive just as Jake and Mr. Burns come through the first door. The bright light from the classroom beyond allows me to see them scooting past Grace, a redhead I've known since kindergarten. She's holding the classroom door open, and as Jake passes her, she fakes a swoon only I can see.

Grace is being friendly. I should wink and swoon back, and we can giggle like girlfriends. But for some reason her attraction to Jake irritates me.

Mr. Burns and Jake stop.

"Hey again," Jake says.

He's standing so close.

I clear my throat.

"Okay, Grace. We're through. Go ahead and close that door," Mr. Burns says.

"Have fun, Brielle." Her door shuts, and we're engulfed in darkness. It's for the briefest of moments, but I'm thankful Mr. Burns is here. I don't trust myself alone with this stranger. Who knows what I'll say. What I'll do.

Fumbling, I open the darkroom door, and they squeeze past me, Jake first, carrying his side of the enlarger with ease, and then tiny Mr. Burns, huffing with the strain of it. They place the enlarger in its new home, secure some cords, and plug things in. Mr. Burns thanks Jake and scoots out the door, cursing quietly under his breath and rubbing his shoulder. The two other students using the darkroom crack up at something I've missed and file past me into the classroom.

We're alone now: Jake and I. And that doesn't bode well for me. I could do an Irish jig or maybe run into him again?

Decisions.

But Jake sets up on the opposite side of the room, his head hunched over the enlarger, his back to me. Which is just fine. Preferable, actually. I have a ton of film to develop, and I can do that all the way over here. On this side of the room.

When Grace bounces through the door, my hands are trapped in the black bag, but I force a smile in her direction. She winks back at me and hops up on the counter next to Jake, all energy and charm.

"Hey," he says, looking up. "It's Faith, right?"

"Grace. Grace Middleton, silly. We have Spanish together."

Jake straightens up. "That's right."

Grace giggles and leans into him, brushing his bicep with her plastic fingernails.

Oh gag. I turn back to my station.

Grace has always been a flirt. It's never bothered me before, and there's no reason it should bother me now. Especially since she's keeping the stalker occupied. Still, she goes on and on, being all cute, chatting him up. Her verbal pawing fills the room, and I stare longingly at the radio in the corner.

As soon as my hands are free of the bag, I tromp over to it and crank the volume up.

Grace casts me a disparaging look, but I ignore her and melt into my work.

No one needs to listen to this.

3

Damien

An invisible form sniffs the air.

Despair.

A favorite of his. It smells of salt and rust. Of tears and corrosion.

Damien flies low, his eyes pinched against the light. He can't open them completely here. Not anymore. The light of this realm—of the Celestial—burns and singes. His fallen form is not as impenetrable as it once was.

Still, he'd suffer a thousand burns to feel the freedom of flight.

He soars over cow pastures, over farms rotting in the dampness of late autumn. He regards them all with distaste. Everything about this world and the humans who inhabit it disgusts him.

Except pain.

Fear.

Their duty lies with darkness and its Prince. As does his. And they draw him, a gigantic moth to the flame of human desperation.

The town ahead comes into view. Small, like the others he's scouted, but the name is familiar and he can't place it. Dozens of small cities, townships, and communities skirt Portland, a city he's haunted for so many years. And while he's not ready to abandon all he's accomplished there, he needs a new base of operations. A new home to destroy.

That idiot boy and his girlfriend ruined so much.

He allows himself a long, luxurious blink as he soars through the Celestial sky. What he wouldn't give to have his sight fully restored.

Though he was created for immortality, his Celestial eyes won't heal any more. Not completely. He traces their weakness back to the days of Elisha. Back to Dothan.

An ancient loss, but one with lingering consequences.

The prophet and his child-of-a-servant had been traveling alone. They camped in the open, on a much-used road. Just a tent. No soldiers, no weapons. If this was just any prophet, Damien might not have bothered, might have passed the man by. But this was Elisha. And Elisha carried a grace in his hands. He healed. He did miraculous things. Things that stifled darkness.

And every attempt to corrupt him had failed.

How could Damien not act?

He found a willing accomplice in the Syrian king, who also courted a fiery hatred for Elisha. A mere suggestion from Damien, and the king sent an entire army to Dothan. They arrived before dawn, surrounding the prophet and his lone tent.

Victory was imminent.

But then . . .

Ah!

Defeat had appeared in the form of an angelic army. Out

of the bright Celestial sky, the forces appeared. Invisible to the humans, but present all the same. And with the stealth of a whisper, an invisible legion of light surrounded the Syrian king. Surrounded his horses and their riders.

Damien did what he could to warn them off, but he was one against so many, and it was too late.

His wings twitch at the memory. Some wounds never close.

Elisha lifted up his hands that day, and he asked his God, the Creator of the universe, to blind the Syrian army. And the Creator answered his prayer.

But the physical blindness the Syrians suffered affected their escorting demon in a way Damien could not have anticipated. He, too, was struck dim.

The last thing he saw, stationed invisibly before the Syrian king, was the prophet's Shield: an angel named Canaan. One he knew well from his days around heaven's throne.

Outnumbered as he was, fleeing would have been in Damien's best interest, but pride moved him forward to meet his adversary.

His former friend.

He drew his own sword, a scimitar of ice and stone forged in the dungeons of outer darkness. And as he swung his blade, he caught sight of the child. The prophet's servant. Such an inconsequential being, but as Damien's smoking weapon met the angel's, the child flinched visibly.

He flinched!

Could he see the warring angels gathered about? Could the boy see Damien?

And then blindness. A darkness he'd never experienced swallowed Damien whole.

He'd never been blind in his Celestial form. But it didn't last long. In the moment that followed, he was thrust through. Canaan's sword, no doubt.

And as the light of Canaan's sword ate away at him, he considered the devastating possibility that humans could see through the Terrestrial veil. That they could see darkness for what it was.

If that was true and they could see fear and despair as weapons, as tactical warfare, evil didn't stand a chance. And though the thrust of a Shield's sword could not kill Damien, it flung him to the pit. The abyss of eternal light and fire. A chasm where the Creator's glory reflects and increases. The light of the Celestial multiplied exponentially.

For those who have rejected the light, the pit is torture unrivaled. Their spiritual forms, created for immortality, are burned by His radiance again and again, only to spontaneously adapt and scar, healing in their own twisted way to be singed and charred once more.

In short: it's hell.

After a time, when the Prince deemed his punishment sufficient, Damien was summoned and returned to the front lines. To earth. To humanity. To steal, to kill, to destroy.

And yet, the momentary blindness he experienced at Dothan damaged his eyes in a way that would not mend. They pained him constantly, and he was a weaker fighter for it. His only escape was to take on his Terrestrial form.

His human form.

Something he would do as soon as this scouting expedition was over. As soon as he identified the source of such mouthwatering despair.

Damien searches, flying low over a small stretch of a community. Shops on a run-down street, the town hall and a post office, a diner with violet neon lights.

He continues out over the highway. Everywhere he sees empty barns, farmhouses abandoned. Vacant plots of land. The economy has taken its toll here. So many empty places for darkness to hide.

A current of wind brings him another tendril of despair, and he follows it, inhaling, savoring the fragrance. Despair is everywhere, of course, but like all delectable dishes, some despair is more appealing than others. And this, whatever it is, is deep and dark.

He speeds his wings.

And there it is. Below him. An ordinary human house, not large, not small. Fear leaks from its windows and doors, black and thick. It oozes into the street, searching, searching for other souls to latch on to.

He slows his wings and descends, touching down next to a strange-looking mailbox. *Matthews*, it says.

The fear here is thick. The despair fresh.

He forces his eyes to focus on the wall in front of him. As it peels away, he sees her, the source of the fragrant ache.

So broken. So vulnerable.

And he decides. This town, this Stratus, is a good place to start again. It's far enough from the city not to attract attention and small enough to destroy single-handedly. And this girl, this Matthews girl, is too ripe to be left alone.

4

Brielle

eyond the bay window, the sky is a smudge of black and gray. Night shrouds the yard and wind sweeps through, diluting the canvas in gusty blows of rain. The shutters rattle, and the wind dislodges the front door screen, leaving mangled hinges in its place.

I watch for falling snow or ice—anything to signal a continuing dip in temperature—but am mildly relieved that November seems content with rain. Central Oregon can get nasty cold, but we usually have until January before the snow and ice take over.

The night makes me anxious. Dad's been called away to remove and cut up a tree that fell onto the roof of the Presbyterian church in town. The dread I feel as he walks out the door nearly pulls me after him. He's all I have now, and watching him fade into the night is torture, but the plea dies on my lips. My dad is the strongest, most able person in the world, and he's managed to survive these past few years without me. I'm just selfish and don't like being alone at night anymore. I have all sorts of new phobias these days.

I take sanctuary in my favorite reading chair and tug an

32

old quilt over the afghan resting on my knees. I yank both up to my chin and watch the storm grapple with the shadowy oak tree in the yard. I'm not sure how the victor is declared in such a battle, but the tree takes quite a beating: branches torn from their home, flung up and down the road.

But by dawn the storm has blown itself out and the old tree is still standing.

I haven't slept much, here in the chair, but the oak's survival inspires me, and I slide to the floor. Shoving aside the blankets, I settle my elbows into the thick carpet and lift my knees to my chest, rotating first my left hip and then my right. My turnout muscles stretch with a familiar ache, and I keep at it until the sleepiness falls away. For years, stretching has been a morning ritual of mine, but in the past three weeks I've shoved it aside.

Even now, as I consider how long it's been, the why stirs in my gut, and I abandon my exercises for a bowl of cereal. I run a brush through my hair and quickly dress, nearly panicking when I can't find my left glove. At last I spot it beneath my night-stand, and I'm out the door.

I reach my poor mud-splotched car as Dad pulls up the drive. He parks next to me and hops out, his door still wide open.

"Hey, baby girl."

"I left you some Cocoa Pebbles," I tell him, leaning in for a kiss. I never could cook.

"What would I do without you? Enjoy school, all right?"

He's distracted. His cell's ringing, and he can't find it. He empties his tool belt onto the floor of the truck and shakes out a wet jacket. The battered BlackBerry falls onto the seat just as the call goes to voice mail. He hits Redial and starts repacking his tool belt.

"What are you doing, Dad? Go get some sleep."

"No time. I need a shower and some food, but not the Cocoa Pebbles, thank you very much. Those are all yours."

Whoever he's trying to reach must not be answering. He ends the call and shoves the phone into his pocket.

"I won't be back until late tonight. There are trees and power lines down everywhere. If we don't get the trees moved, life in Stratus will grind to a complete standstill."

"It hasn't already?"

"Well, aren't you feeling better? Mocking our quaint little town and giving me cheek. You never should have left me for that big city."

I swallow hard against the lump that has magically reappeared in my throat. I haven't thought about Ali this morning at all. Not really. I'm an awful, horrible person.

Dad must know he's misspoken. He drops a socket wrench and draws me into his arms.

"It's okay, Elle. I can't believe I said that. You gotta remember, I'm just a stupid lumberjack. These big ol' boots jump into my mouth faster than I can salt 'em." He pushes my face back, looking into my eyes. "I'll work on it, okay?"

I don't know what to say, so I just nod and wipe away the tears.

"Okay. We should get a move on, both of us. You'll be late to school. Go on."

I sink into Slugger and twist the steering wheel in my gloved hands.

Ali's face swims before my eyes, and I bite down hard on my lip to control the trembling. I am lost again, my mind back in the city, the detective asking questions I can't answer, expecting a testimony I don't want to give.

"You said she had bruises on her arms, right?" Detective Krantz *drags a manila folder across the stubble on his chin. "The kid con-fessed, Miss Matthews. He's not worth protecting. Marco James is a monster."*

Dad knocks on the window, and I jump, fumbling clumsily as I attempt to roll it down.

"Avoid 13th if you can. There's a huge pine blocking the road. Take Main over to the school."

Again I nod.

"Love you, kiddo."

"Love you too, Dad."

I take a deep breath and cram away images of the detective's pursed lips and furrowed brow. A strange feeling sneaks up on me, and it's a minute before I can squash it. It's a craving almost. To be back in photo. In the darkroom. And now I cram away another face. A younger face. With bright eyes and dark brows. I pretend thoughts of him don't press my foot to the accelerator. I tell myself I just don't want to be late to calculus. Because being late will attract attention.

Well, it will.

But as I settle into Slugger once again, I realize both Dad and I have clock issues. Slugger says I'm running a good twenty minutes early.

I'd kill for a caramel macchiato, but Stratus isn't grown-up enough to have a Starbucks.

We do have Jelly's, though.

Jelly's is a greasy spoon that predates me by at least half a century. They specialize in all the normal stuff—omelets and waffles, questionable coffee and apple pie—but ever since Kaylee's Aunt Delia took over the kitchen a decade ago, Jelly's serves carved gyros alongside their fried eggs. You can ask for bacon or sausage links, but you'll get a sneezeburger if you do.

Slugger eases off the road, and I throw her into park against the stainless steel wall of the diner. Jelly's is busy this morning. Maintenance workers taking a breakfast break from their post-storm cleanup, it looks like. Dad should've eaten here.

The door jingles shut behind me, and I grimace at Jelly's version of a winter wonderland. Red garlands loop from anything and everything within reach of a staple gun. Candy canes hang here and there, and vintage ornaments dress a lopsided Christmas tree crowding the pint-sized entryway. Fake snow, stained with coffee cup rings, lines the counter. And though the scene is over-the-top gaudy, the pins pricking my heart have nothing to do with the mechanical Santa shaking his booty by the cash register.

Christmas without Ali.

I hadn't considered it until now.

"Elle, honey, you're back." Aunt Delia leans over the counter and pulls me in for a quick hug, smashing a Rudolph figurine against my chest as she does.

"Brielle!" Kaylee's here, behind the counter. "Hot chocolate?"

I nod. You're taking your life in your hands if you order the coffee this early.

She disappears, and I catch part of Delia's conversation with a mailman shoveling spoonfuls of oatmeal into his mouth.

"The boy called me *Jelly*, Frank." She plants two thick hands on her round hips. "I mean, honestly, do I look like a Jelly?"

The mailman cuts his eyes at me, and I look away. Poor guy.

"Let's go," Kaylee says, appearing out of nowhere. She presses a to-go cup in my hands and tugs me out the door.

It's hot, thank goodness, and I scorch my tongue with an overeager first sip.

"Delia's all ticked off this morning. Can I bum a ride?"

"Sure."

"Aunt Delia's intuition's in hyperdrive these days. Makes me wanna move back in with my parents." She uses air quotes when she says *intuition*, and I almost snort hot chocolate out my nose. Delia depends on her "intuition" almost as much as Kaylee depends on her air quotes. These constants are reassuring.

"You working for her?"

"Just mornings. Kitchen prep and stuff. I'm saving for summer. Peace Corps."

"Really? That's awesome, Kay. So, your proximity to all that lamb meat not really a temptation?"

"Oh, barf," she says, pulling her curly brown hair into two low pigtails and then securing a multicolored beanie on top. "You ever see what she does to that stuff? If anything, she's convinced me that veggies are the only way to go."

The senior lot is nearly full when we arrive. I squeeze Slugger into one of the last open spots, kicking myself for the Jelly's run. It's a longer walk to the math wing from here. Not a big deal unless you're a veritable ice cube.

"Where you off to this morning?" I ask Kaylee, zipping my parka and flipping up my hood. Big splotches of rain are falling again, and the wind is getting grumpier by the second.

"Gym," she says.

"P.E. your senior year?"

"Yeah. I put it off as long as I could, but they won't let me graduate without two semesters."

"Well, be careful," I say, climbing out of the car. She does the same, somehow managing to get her foot tangled in the seat belt.

"I tell myself that every morning," she says, unwinding herself. "I have student government at lunch, or I'd meet you."

"That's okay. I'll see you after school."

The wind is loud now, making conversation hard. She kisses my cheek and turns to go. Her elbow clips a parked car's side mirror, and I wince. She jerks and knocks her hip on the bumper of a large truck.

"I'm okay, I'm okay," she yells.

I shake my head and follow Kaylee's lead, not quite running, but too cold to linger. Miss Macy would say I'm moving with urgency. She'd also tell me to knock it off, that it isn't graceful.

It would be good to see her. Maybe I'll stop by after school. Thank her for the CD.

Tell her to get shades for her front windows.

The wind kicks up, and I duck my head. By the time I reach the math wing, my eyes stream and my lips could use a thick coat of Blistex. The final bell rings just as I enter the classroom. I fall into my seat, grateful to be indoors.

"Morning," Jake says.

Ugh. On the mad dash to class, I nearly forgot he'd be here.

"Morning," I say.

It's not warm, not by any means, but my parka and scarf seem too much all of a sudden. I shrug out of them and let them fall against the seat. My gloves stay in place.

I look around the room. We seem to be short a teacher.

"Where's Mr. . . ."

Jake shrugs. "I was going to ask you the same thing."

"I just got here, remember?"

As the class realizes we're unsupervised, the volume level rises. There's talk about Friday's football game, about the chess club's devastating loss, something about a school-wide battle of the bands. The girl in front of me pulls out a bottle of bright orange nail polish and sets to work on her fingers. Five or six students disappear out the door, a cold rush smacking me in the face as they do.

"Whatcha think? We free to go?"

I look to my left, over the heads of my classmates and out the window. I can't see much, but it's snowflake white out there. Nothing says frigid like snowflake white. "Maybe."

"You dance this morning?"

I roll my eyes to his, expecting sarcasm, but they're so . . . inviting. Like a fireplace at Christmas. Stalkers have no business being handsome.

"Not today," I say, pulling a notebook from my bag. "You?"

He laughs. "I have two left feet. Three sometimes. You give lessons?"

I draw a doodle, a heart squiggle. "Mm-hmm, as long as you're willing to don a tutu."

He unzips his sweatshirt and hangs it on the back of his chair. "So if I wear a tutu, you'll show me how to do that monkey-dance thing?"

Monkey-dance thing. That's what he remembers?

"Sure," I say, "but no tutu, no dance."

"Shoot. I left mine at home."

"Maybe next time, then." I turn my face to the blackboard, but there's nothing there to see. The classroom is chaos now. Cell phones are out, spit wads are being shot at the ceiling, at the teacher's desk.

"You wanna duck out?" Jake says. "Grab a coffee?"

He's so uncomfortably comfortable with me. It's weird. He's weird. But coffee does sound warm. Of course, we'd have to freeze to get there.

"Come on," he says.

"You know, *this*," I say, swirling a leather-clad finger at him, "this is what we call peer pressure."

"Yes, I know. But you look like you could use a little peer pressure. And who knows, maybe we'll run into a tutu."

The door opens, and a gush of wind silences the room. Mr. What's-His-Name wrestles the door closed and steps inside. He's carrying a mangled umbrella under one arm and a worn briefcase in the other. "Sorry, sorry, sorry," he says. "Open to page fifty-six."

"Rain check?" Jake whispers, digging his book out.

Someone who could use a little peer pressure, he'd said. I look at my doodle. At the heart with a crack down the middle.

"Tutu first," I say.

"You have something to share with the class, Miss Matthews?"

Every eye in the room is suddenly on me, on my face. I shake my head, hoping they'll all look away, but they don't.

"No, I . . ." I don't know what to say, so I drop my head. A tear falls onto my notebook—that fast. It smudges my doodle, my broken heart.

The teacher puts a hand to his ear, mocking. "What was that?"

"It's nothing, sir," Jake says. "I was just asking Brielle where I could find a tutu. Maybe you know?"

The class laughs, all of them, and their attention shifts to Jake. Even the teacher cracks a smile.

"No, no, I don't. But good luck with that. Class, you're opening your books, yes?"

A murmur makes its way across the room—yes, books are being opened—and the teacher launches into his lesson, scraping spit wads off the board with a ruler.

My eyes swim hot in my chilled face. I hate that my emotions are so extreme. Hate that I can't control them. Hate how weak it makes me. The teacher is a jerk, sure, but I've dealt with jerks before. It's just now . . .

I stand and push my way into the hall. But I'm not far enough away from the embarrassment, so I keep going. Before I know it I'm standing outside the math wing. The wind shoves against me, loud as it storms between the buildings, my hair like tiny whips as it lashes my face. The door slams behind me, and I'm alone.

I should just leave. Dad wouldn't care. But I've left my stuff inside. My car keys and my bag.

My scarf and my jacket.

Tears spill down my cheeks. Selfish, stupid tears. They're not tears for Ali. Not tears of guilt. They're tears of embarrassment. Of frustration. Tears I don't deserve.

I can't leave. I don't want to stay.

So I stand and freeze.

When the bell rings, I'm numb. I walk away from the doors, away from the steady stream of my peers and their curious eyes. An empty planter box stands between the math wing and the gymnasium. I stare at it, wondering if flowers once lived there. Had the cold killed them too?

"You decided to cut after all." It's Jake. His voice is quiet, but it slices through the wind all the same. He slides my parka onto my shoulders and steps in front of me. "I'm jealous."

"Thanks," I say. "You didn't have to . . . I mean, I could have . . ."

Kids rush around us on the right and the left. They look at

me, at us, and I try to ignore them. Being scared of people—
of their stares—is ridiculous. I'm a dancer, a model. People are
supposed to look at me. I tell myself these things, but my hands
tremble all the same.

"My bag," I say, straining to keep my voice steady.

"I have it." He touches the strap that hangs over his shoulder.
"Can I walk you to your car?"

"No," I say, my voice hoarse. "I'll stay."

"You sure?"

I nod.

"Your next class, then? Can I walk you there?"

I squint at him. "Do I look like I'm going to fall over?"

He shifts his weight from one foot to the other. "No, but you
look like you could use a friend."

I flick one last tear from my eye. "Thanks, really, but I got it."

He hands my bag over, his face reluctant. "Okay."

"I'll see you in photo." I turn and walk away, toward senior
lit. I don't want to go, but I've got to. I'm tired of being afraid.

○

After the debacle in calculus, the rest of the day is cake. Pop quiz
in lit class and a clueless substitute in government. At lunch I
grab a hot sandwich and take it to my car. I'm not hiding. Not
really. It's just warmer with Slugger. Honest.

French soars by in a blur of conjugated verbs, and soon
enough it's the last period of the day.

Photo.

When I arrive, the room is empty save Mr. Burns. He's sitting at his desk eating a bowl of steaming noodles.

"Elle," he says. "Come on up here before you get started."

His fringe of gray hair is disheveled, and he's already dripping noodle juice onto his thinning button-down, but he's always been my favorite teacher. He could give the artsy fartsy professors in Portland a run for their money.

When I reach his desk, I lean my hip against it, trying to appear nonchalant.

His bifocals sit on the brim of his nose. "You doing okay?" he asks, peering over them.

He has one, two, three film containers on his desk. I stack them one on top of the other. "Sure, Mr. B. I'm good."

He pulls another film canister from beneath a stack of prints and adds it to my tower. "You're a good actress, Elle. You always have been. It's one of your many talents. But you don't fool me."

I purse my lips. I don't want to cry anymore. Not here. Not now.

He pats my hand. "When you're ready to talk, you will. I just hope it's soon."

I nod and meet his gaze.

He squints up at me, his spoon halfway to his mouth. "It's okay to be broken. You know that, right?"

A tremor in my hand sends my tower toppling. One of the containers falls into Mr. B's soup.

How could broken ever be okay?

I don't have the answer, so I tip my chin up, hoping Mr. B does. His eyes widen.

"Oh, you *don't* know that."

Squishy, squeaky footsteps make their way into the classroom. I look around, pre-panic.

"Could we maybe talk about this another—"

"Go," he says, looking around. Understanding. "I've got a critique to run. We'll talk later."

I move to the far wall and grab the filmstrips I developed yesterday. There are several of them hanging on hooks, dried and ready to be viewed. Before I duck into the darkroom, I give Mr. Burns another look, but he's mopping the noodle juice from his shirt and doesn't see me.

It's okay to be broken?

I'm guessing the darkroom will be fairly empty today, with the critique and all, but before anyone else can stake a claim, I drop my bag at the station in the far right corner. I spread out the filmstrips and remove my gloves. One after the other, I lift the filmstrips to the yellow light.

I don't want to think anymore. I just want to work.

But unless I've been sleep snapping, one of these filmstrips does not belong to me. Snow-covered trees and lovey-dovey couples skating on a frozen lake? Definitely not mine. I return to the classroom, ducking past Grace, who's draped over our starting quarterback, and rehang the film.

By the time I get back to the darkroom, a couple of the workstations are occupied. Jake's sweatshirt hangs on the stool next to mine, but he's hovering at my station.

Of course he is.

He's fiddling with the enlarger, looking at a negative. My negative. Feigning a confidence I don't feel, I walk over. His fingers turn a knob, and before I can object, we watch a picture come into focus.

Two girls smile back at us: night and day. The image is black-and-white, but I see it as it was—as we were—that day. My blond hair straight to my waist, hers dark and cropped in choppy layers. My blue eyes smiling. Hers, chocolate brown and twinkling. My mouth curved into an amused grin, and her full lips wide open in a cackling laugh.

I can hear it. Her laugh. Her addictive, childish laugh.

My hands shake, and the lump returns so forcefully to my throat that I suddenly realize I've had a short reprieve.

"Great shot," Jake says, enlarging the picture. "Where is this?"

I don't respond. I can't. I'm doubled over, holding my stomach.

I thought I destroyed all that film. Surely I had. There are four filmstrips lying at my station, ready to be viewed. How had he picked up the *one* that could gut me?

"Hey. Hey," he says quietly.

I'm hyperventilating. Jake helps me into a sitting position on the floor and places two blazing hands on my shoulders. My breathing slows a bit. After a minute or so I'm able to think again.

"I'm so sorry," he says. "Again. I shouldn't have touched your stuff."

"No, it's . . . I just . . . I forgot about that picture. About that day."

I look up at him, my eyes moist with tears, and for the first time I wish I could explain. What I'm thinking. Why it hurts so much.

"It really is a great shot. But I'm sure most of your shots are great." The attempt at bravado does not go unnoticed. "Would you like me to get rid of it for you?"

"Yes. Please."

Good shot or not, I can't look at her right now.

My body shakes.

"Hey," he says again. He places both hands on my knees heavily, and they obey his touch. I can't breathe, but at least I'm not shaking.

"You'll destroy it?"

"Absolutely."

He tears the filmstrip from the enlarger and shoves it into his pocket.

"Better?"

I swipe at my eyes. "Yes. Thank you."

My left leg stretches out next to his right leg, just inches shorter. My gaze bounces around, finally settling on my hands. I *should* say something, explain myself maybe, but my tongue is heavy and confused. The other students work around us. We get a look or two, but it's funny, no one says a thing about the idiots on the floor.

The bell rings and Jake stands. He reaches down for my hand and I take it, pulling myself up beside him. I can't believe how warm his hands are.

"So, two days," he says.

"Huh?"

"That's how long I've known you, two days. And I've had to apologize on both of them."

I find my gloves and slide them on. "Maybe try not to be so consistent."

"Right." He chews his lip. "No more staring, no more touching your stuff. Tomorrow there will be no need for apologies."

"It's a good goal," I say.

He throws his sweatshirt over his head and moves me out of the way, against the wall. He busies himself packing up my photo supplies.

Making amends, I guess. I let him.

When he's done, he slides the strap of my camera bag over my shoulder and lays it softly against my hip. I nearly hyperventilate again. His skin radiates heat. Literally.

"What were you doing out that early anyway?" I ask. "And on Main Street? Stratus doesn't open till at least noon."

He swings his own bag over his shoulder. "The doughnut shop was open."

Big fat liar. "So you were getting doughnuts?"

He shrugs.

Maybe he really is a stalker? I narrow my eyes. He's not off the hook, and I want him to know it—he was staring at me, for crying out loud!—but he seems content to ignore my suspicion.

He jerks his head to the door. "Shall we?"

"Uh-huh."

"I really am sorry," he says as we leave the darkroom.

"Sorry you got caught creeping."

He laughs. "I meant about the film."

Of course he did.

"Just promise me you'll destroy it, and we're square."

"I can do that."

He smiles, and I can't help it—I smile back.

"I'll see you tomorrow," he says. "Calculus?"

"Sure."

I watch him walk away and wonder what *she'd* say. What my best friend in the whole wide world would think about my new stalker.

Never mind.

I know what she'd say. *Run, Elle*, she'd say. *Hide*.

I'm an idiot. Letting a guy affect me like this. Like she did.

I do my best to fight the cold and the ache, but they creep back in. It's only fair. How can I have hope when she has none? My hands resume their tremors, and I pull the lambskin gloves back in place. I duck my head and walk to my car in the senior lot.

The wind is picking up, and I can smell the coming rain. I crawl into the driver's seat, lean over the dash, and peer out the window. The clouds are black now and heavy, queuing up, like waves waiting to crash. Raindrops the size of lemons smack my windshield—the firstfruits of a massive storm. I flex my gloved hands and start Slugger.

I'll never sleep tonight.

5

Brielle

The rest of the week passes, and Jake keeps his word.

No more apologies.

He sits next to me in calculus every day, still hovers in photo, but he doesn't touch my stuff. I make it through my classes and spend my lunch hours with Kaylee and Slugger.

On the downside, my nightmares are getting worse. I'm not sleeping much, though I pretend to, for Dad's sake. Every few hours his mammoth feet set the floorboards squeaking and my bedroom door bumps open. I know he means well, but worrying about him worrying about me makes everything harder.

The weather's getting vicious too, and I'd give anything for a drop of sunshine. I've never hated the cold like this, never hated winter or fall, but my muscles ache, always clenched against the cold, and I can't figure out how to stay warm. I wear thermals under everything.

Still, it's Friday, and I survived the week. My first week back. There's some kind of victory in that.

I haven't stopped by Miss Macy's, haven't thanked her for the CD. Getting out of the car does not sound appealing, but on the drive home from school, I cave. Miss Macy's always been so good to me.

The studio comes into view, and I park. Slugger hasn't had time to warm up, and white smoke monsters climb from my nose and mouth. I wrap my scarf around my face, leaving the tiniest slit possible for my eyes. I glance at myself in the rearview. I'm a cable-knit ninja. A cashmere-wrapped mummy. But I've killed the smoke monsters—another small victory.

Now I glare at the wind. I can't see it, but I know it's there. Brown leaves spiral down the street, and brave shoppers wrestle with glass doors that don't want to close. The green and red holiday banners lining Main swing and snap. I hear them over Slugger's rattling windows.

Armed against the wind, I lunge from the car. Like a Band-Aid, right? Fast, fast. The wind yanks at my scarf, tugging my ninja wrappings from my face, but I reach the door and shove inside.

It's not warm in here, but at least it's not windy.

Three of the chairs in the reception area are filled. Moms waiting for their daughters.

Dad always stood. He's never been one for faith, and trusting the strength of a small folding chair is far outside his comfort zone.

The moms look up from their magazines, tiny sparks of recognition on their faces. I move past the empty desk before they can offer condolences.

I stop in the doorway and watch. The afternoon class is young—kindergarten, first grade maybe. Bedazzled in wings and sequins, they spin and twirl to Miss Macy's floaty music. Colorful tutus and tiaras litter the floor. Miss Macy is lovely, dressed in a simple pale-pink ensemble: leotard, skirt, and tights.

In the corner of the studio an older student, junior high I'd say, works on a solo. I recognize it, a simplified number from *Swan Lake*.

The girl is good. Very good, actually, but she's struggling. She stops a time or two and turns to Miss Macy, but the teacher is distracted with the little ones and doesn't notice.

I take pity on her and cross the floor.

She sees me and drops back on her heels.

"Go ahead," I tell her. "I'll help."

She blushes, but resets and begins again, moving through the choreography. Here and there, I reach out and adjust her body position. She's a quick learner and makes the corrections with ease. "Your turnout is beautiful," I tell her. "Really. For someone your age."

Her blush deepens, but she continues. Her skill is evident. Her poise inspiring. When she finishes, I clap lightly. "Beautiful."

"Thank you," she says. "I couldn't figure out what I was doing wrong."

"If you're careful not to collapse your torso, it'll help. But really, it was wonderful."

"And you couldn't ask for higher praise than Brielle's." Long, thin arms wrap my waist from behind.

I turn into Miss Macy and squeeze. She smells of soap and roses. It's the familiar smell I was expecting to find on Monday, and I choke at the comfort it brings. "Thank you for the CD."

Her face is perhaps more lined and her eyes darker than I remember, but she looks much the same. "I'm glad you got it. The question is, did you dance it?"

"I did," I say. "Just ask the guys at the doughnut shop."

She laughs and waves out the window. "I've given them a show or two myself over the years."

"Yes, well." I turn to see the men waving back. All three of them.

And Jake.

Only Jake's not across the street. He's just outside the window. Again.

He's got that stupid grin on his face, and he's pointing at the bright orange tutu lying on the floor, pressed against the glass.

"Oh my," says Miss Macy. "You know him?"

I turn back to my mentor. "Tell me about the studio. Who's teaching?"

"Well, I just hired a new instructor. Helene something. Nice girl. So graceful she puts a butterfly to shame. You two would be quite a team. I'd love for you to meet her."

"That'd be great," I say. I'm distracted. Out of the corner of my eye, I can see Jake bouncing up and down like a kindergartner.

Miss Macy peers over my shoulder. "I think he wants the tutu," she says.

"That's exactly what he wants."

"Well, my goodness, take it to him." Miss Macy lifts her foot and nudges me with her leather slipper. "Handsome boy like that. My goodness."

I rub my eyes. "No. If I take it to him . . . Just . . . No. But thank you."

Eventually Jake stops pointing and motions me outside.

"You best go," Miss Macy says. "Never keep a gentleman waiting, Elle. Best manners, remember."

Best manners?

"I'll just . . ."

"Yes, yes." She kisses my cheek and pushes me toward the door. "Bring him by. Tell him I have purple tutus as well."

The room fills with giggles, and I slip out onto the sidewalk. The wind smacks me, and my mouth fills with my own hair. I spit it out and shove it from my face.

As I stalk toward him, I do my best to disregard the tiny ballerinas lining up along the glass, but they tap and point.

I'm a fish. In a tank.

In Antarctica.

I retreat into my jacket. "What are you doing here?"

He smirks and holds up a half-eaten doughnut.

I kinda want to punch him.

"Really," I say. "Really?"

"Where's my tutu?" he asks.

Fifty fingers press against the glass—foreheads and noses too—and though I'm outside, I'm suddenly claustrophobic. I push Jake away from the window and down Main Street. Anything to get away from our miniature audience. He's wearing another sweatshirt, but I can feel the heat radiating through it. Through my gloves, even.

I'm dragging him now, his sweatshirt balled in my hands. The theatre ahead has a recessed entryway, and I step into it to escape the wind.

"So, doughnuts. At three thirty in the afternoon. Explain."

He tugs his sweatshirt from my grip and readjusts the hood. "Actually, I was picking up a job application. The doughnut was just a plus." He shoves the rest of it into his mouth and dusts off his hands.

"You want a job at the Donut Factory?"

I wait while he chews. And swallows. At least he's not talking with his mouth full. Miss Macy would approve.

"The photo supply store next door."

Still skeptical. I'm sure I look it too.

"You seem to need proof." He huffs and pulls a crinkled piece of paper from beneath his hoodie, holding it up for me to see.

"I don't need proof," I say, scrutinizing the page.

It's an application for Photo Depot. Fine. We just keep running into one another. Whatever. My eyes are watering and my nose is running. I sniff and flip up my hood. I've got to get out of this cold.

"You okay?" he asks, tucking the application away.

"Just cold," I say. "Good luck with the application."

I step out of the entryway and turn right, intending to head back to my car. Movement snags my peripheral vision, and I turn my head. A man exits the real estate office across the street. He lingers on the stairs, watching. He's tall. Taller than Dad, even. His hair is black, cropped short. Olive skin. Deep, shadowed eyes. His clothes are dark.

Really, everything about him is dark. I think that's what keeps me looking. Against the white sky and the weather-faded storefronts, he's a gigantic blotch of darkness.

I've taken a single step when his eyes meet mine. I just have time to shiver before I'm roughly, and very suddenly, yanked backward into the recessed doorway of the theatre. My elbow knocks the wall as I'm pressed against it. Jake's hands grip both my biceps, holding me tight, but his face is turned away. He looks past me.

"Hey!" I wrap my fingers around his wrists and shove, but he's stronger than I am. "What . . ."

"Shh," he says, leaning around me. "Hang on."

I groan in protest, but I obey. He peers down the street, and I hang on. He's so warm. The heat in his hands bleeds through my jacket, through my sweater and my thermal shirt. It spreads across my chest and slides into my gut. I'm a snowman melting in the sun. I'm butter in a sizzling pan.

The wind sneaks into the entryway and brushes our faces, blowing a hot, almost summery breeze from his skin to mine. It smells like sugared doughnut. The globe lights flicker overhead. Or maybe my eyes are closing.

"Brielle?"

Yes, definitely closing.

I force them open and find myself staring into Jake's eyes. Something I try to avoid.

"What was that?" I ask. It's possible my words are running together.

Jake doesn't answer. But there's something in his eyes, and I have no idea how to decode it. It's not fear. Not anger. It's . . . fire.

"Jake, who was that?"

"Someone you don't want to meet in a dark alley."

I turn my head to the right and look across the street. Whoever it was, he's gone. "A bad guy? In Stratus?"

"Apparently."

Jake steps back, releasing my arms. I can't make myself let go of his, and his eyes search my face. I can't fathom what he sees there.

"I just need to send a text," he says.

"Yeah. Sorry." I let go of his wrists and wrap my arms across my chest.

Can I trap the heat? Keep it locked inside?

He pulls a phone from his back pocket and sends a message. His jaw is clenched, his dark brows drawn together. I've never seen him so serious.

His eyes are still on his phone, his fingers still. Waiting, I guess. "I didn't hurt you, did I?"

I rub my elbow. "I'm all right."

His phone vibrates in his hand. He reads the screen and then tucks the phone back into his pocket.

"It's okay now," he says, turning his hazel eyes back to mine. "We can go."

The heat in my chest is fading, but I resist the urge to step closer.

"'Cause the little man in your phone said so?"

His face relaxes. "Something like that."

I want to argue, trade jabs with him, ask about the "bad guy," but really. The longer we stand out here, the colder I'm going to get. And it's Stratus. How bad can the guy be? I turn on my heel and walk back to Slugger—Jake two or three paces behind.

I know he's there, but I've got to get out of this wind. I drop into Slugger, turn the key in the ignition, and jam my fingers into the vents. No heat. Not yet.

Jake's standing at the passenger door, his eyes pleading.

Leaning across the seat, I unlock it and he climbs in. He fills up my car. He's got that tall, lean, muscle-y thing going on. But it's more than his size. I'm used to big. Dad's big. Jake's different. Jake's got stage presence. It's one of those things—hard to teach, hard to learn. You either have it or you don't. And Jake has it. In spades.

"Can you do me a favor?" he says.

The car's warming up, and there's no way it's Slugger. I shake my hood off and loosen my scarf. "I'm not stealing you a tutu."

"Can you put my number in your cell?"

I squint at him but dig my phone out of my pocket and hand it over. "That's the most unoriginal pickup line ever."

He laughs. "I didn't ask for *your* number. I'm giving you mine."

Can't really argue with that.

He hands my phone back. "One more favor," he says.

"If it's as painful as the first one . . ."

"Call me if you see that guy again."

And suddenly we're serious. I feel it.

"Where do you know him from?"

"My ride's here," he says, reaching for the door handle.

"Where?"

He nods out his window, back toward the theatre we just left. A tall, silver-haired man stands in the town square. He leans against a bench, examining the theatre marquee. Strong jaw, same tawny complexion as Jake. At least I know where he gets his looks.

"So you're not going to tell me about the bad guy?"

"I don't want to keep Canaan waiting," he says.

"Canaan?"

"My guardian."

I look past him again. "You're not related?"

He shakes his head.

"Wow, I'd never guess. He could be your dad."

"He raised me. For all intents and purposes, he is my dad."

He's quiet, his smile soft. There's no mischief there. No pretense. Another round of wind beats at the car, and Jake waits it out. I'd rather he stayed. It's comfortable. Talking like this. No games. No snark.

"You'll call me?"

"Sure."

He pushes the door open and steps out. The wind slams it, and I wince. I look down at the phone in my hand. His name is still on the screen.

Jake Shield.

When I look up, he's gone. His guardian's gone. Swept away by the wind, I guess, like everything else today.

He's interesting, this Jake Shield.

And he's warm.

I tuck the phone away and slide Slugger into reverse.

I think I'd like to know what else he is.

6

Damien

amien leans against the warehouse. With human eyes he stares—at the burned-out church across the street, at the dark stretch of road before him, at the abandoned half-built skyscraper covering the site in shadow.

This place was perfect.

If it weren't for that idiot Marco and his girlfriend, he wouldn't have to relocate. But as it is, the warehouse is too conspicuous, too attached to what happened with the girl. Sooner or later the authorities will trace its ownership. And by the sound of it, later seems to be creeping up on him.

The man next to him has a cell phone to his ear. In many ways the two resemble one another. Same dark hair, dark eyes, olive complexion. And though Horacio's not nearly as tall as he is, they both wear cruelty as a second skin.

Horacio Santilla.

His voice is silk, flattering whoever's on the other end of the line. Despite his irritation, Damien chuckles.

The guy has a gift. Charisma. Likeability.

It's a gift so easily corrupted. A flaring temper, greed, lust.

Any of these will serve. Eventually, what was once charisma is transformed into a slippery, manipulative flair.

And Horacio's been corrupt for years. Like the rest of his kind, Damien's an opportunist, and when he stumbled upon Horacio, the youth was just begging to be manipulated. Charming, yes, but unpredictable and explosive. At seventeen, an argument with a sibling led him, ruthless and unrestrained, to light his father's guesthouse on fire. Before it could be extinguished, half the property was destroyed and Horacio's younger sister killed.

That was a decade ago, and Damien had been just an observer. A silent, invisible observer. But when the time was right, he made himself available to Horacio. Fixing things. Ensuring the investigation went awry. Laying the blame elsewhere.

Soon he had an ally. A human ally. The most valuable kind.

Of course, Horacio knows nothing of Damien's true nature. Just that he shares a penchant for cruelty and has the means to carry out his whims. And as long as Damien keeps him clothed and fed, housed and moneyed—as long as shiny things are dangled before his eyes, he doesn't ask for details.

A valuable partner indeed.

Horacio ends the call, and Damien raises his dark brows.

"The detective says they're understaffed. The investigation's moving slowly. Nothing to worry about for another week or so," Horacio says.

"We'll be cutting it close. We've a buyer coming next Friday—Henry Madison. After that, we pack up shop and move. Who we got inside?"

"Mostly young ones. If it's Henry, we'll need a few older girls."

Damien scowls at his man. "I'm aware of that. I meant who's *watching* them?"

"My mistake." Horacio dips his head in apology. "Eddie. Eddie's watching them. He and Juan are taking it in shifts."

"Fine," Damien says. "Tell Eddie I'll have another girl for him."

Horacio pulls out his phone, opening it to the calendar he keeps carefully updated. "When?"

"Soon," he says. "Before Henry arrives this weekend."

His fingers move quickly over the keys. "I'll tell him." Horacio tucks the phone away and pulls a cigarette from his jacket, lights it, and hands it to Damien.

Damien takes a puff, looking left and right along the road. "He's late."

"Baby Joe's always late."

"What's he got?"

"Redhead."

Rubber chews asphalt as a brown Cadillac moves up the road. Finally.

Horacio disappears into the warehouse. A second later the door next to Damien rolls up, and Baby Joe pulls his car inside. Damien follows and the door is shut.

He watches the transaction, leaning against the door. Damien hates this kid. Baby Joe. He never, ever stops talking.

They lift the girl from the car. Her hands and feet are wrapped in duct tape, her head covered with a dark pillowcase. That, too, is taped shut.

But something's wrong.

There's no fear here. He can't smell it. He can't taste it.

He strides toward the Cadillac. "You drug her?"

Baby Joe answers, "Na. Knocked her with my piece. She's awake now."

Then she should be afraid. She should be very afraid.

Damien yanks at the tape on the pillowcase.

"I got it, boss," Horacio says, pulling a knife from his boot. He cuts through the tape and pulls the pillowcase away. "We don't want to damage the merchandise."

The girl stares back at him. Brown eyes, auburn hair. Petite. Attractive. A good fit for Henry Madison. But there's something wrong with her. She's not afraid. He can see it in her eyes.

"What's your name?" he growls.

She lifts her chin, defiant.

"Helene."

"We can't use her," he says.

"What do you mean you can't use her?" Baby Joe says.

"We need girls, boss, and she's perfect."

"I've got another girl coming. We're not using this one." He pulls the sidearm from his belt and shoots her in the stomach.

The shot throws her against the car, her eyes wide, blood spreading across her shirt.

"Whoa! Whoa!" Baby Joe backs away.

"Boss . . ."

Their indignation builds as Damien watches the girl, completely collected, disappear and reappear within the span of a second. As she rematerializes, she plants the controlled power of both her fists into his sternum. He flies backward several steps, landing in a crouch.

Her shirt is unmarred. There's no evidence she was just shot.

"Like I said, we can't use her."

Horacio just stares. His eyes wide, his lips curled. Baby Joe's hysterical. He curses and backs away. Damien points his gun at the boy, anything to shut him up.

But Helene moves fast, stepping in front of Baby Joe.

Damien laughs. "You think he's worth saving? You're a fool. I've had my claws in him for years."

She doesn't answer. But Damien knows. He's encountered this ridiculous optimism before. A sadistic soul like Baby Joe's still has potential, they think—can still be saved.

She steps toward Damien with an air of authority. "You won't touch him again."

Rage shakes him. His natural desires are taking over, and he'll have to transfer soon. He needs the release of flight, but how strong is this little angel challenging him?

"He's been bought with a price," she says. "It's a gift I pray he lays hold of."

And then they're gone, Baby Joe's cries disappearing with the rest of him.

Instinct pulls Damien into the Celestial. He can't afford to be blind to this realm while there's a Shield about. His black wings unfurl and push him back several paces, away from her last position. But she's gone already.

Her wings sound high above, and he turns his face to the sky.

The height to which Helene has already risen is a challenge for Damien's tarnished eyes. He can barely see her, and the odds of catching her are diminishing with each second. But he wants that boy. He wants Baby Joe. Not because the kid has value, but because the boy belonged to him. Belonged to darkness, and now light is staking a claim.

Next to him, Horacio curses. Panicking as those around him vanish. Thick, gooey globs of fear bubble out of his nose and ears. They leak slowly from his eyes and mouth, running down his chest.

Damien knows the Shield won't let a man die, not if she can

prevent it. Not even a man like Horacio. The optimism of the Shield is sickening, but it is certain and steadfast, making it, above all else, predictable.

Damien is nearly on top of Horacio when he transfers back to the Terrestrial. His sudden reappearance causes the man to trip and fall. Damien pulls his gun from its holster and without ceremony shoots Horacio in the gut.

He sputters something and gropes at his stomach in an effort to catch the life-force as it leaks out of him. It's a futile attempt, and Damien turns away, transferring back to the Celestial. Without question, Helene has heard the gunshot and will return. The demon leaps into the sky, flaps his wings just once, and lands on the roof of the crumbling church across the way. If the Shield acts as expected and lands at Horacio's side, he'll be out of her immediate reach here.

His ears pick up the thrust of her wings before she comes into view, at last wrapping her outer wings tight to her frame and tunneling like a sniper's bullet to the earth. Tucked against her core, enveloped in her sinewy, transparent inner wings, is the frightened Baby Joe. His knobby arms and legs are balled up—a ridiculous spectacle.

The force of flight notwithstanding, Helene lands softly, hugging Baby Joe to herself. She glares up at the demon, enraged, as though he hasn't played fair, as though he's cheated. Damien savors the compliment, waiting for the perfect moment to act. He watches as she kneels next to Horacio, reaching her hands out to his wound.

Suddenly, too suddenly, she stands and shoots into the sky. Away from him. Away from the dying man on the ground. Flustered and bewildered by her abandonment of Horacio,

Damien takes flight, quickly gaining on her forsaken position at the man's side. Only the whites of Horacio's eyes are visible as they roll back and forth in his head. His face is moist and gray beneath the sludge of fear.

Death is close. Damien can taste it.

He can conceive no reason for the angel's desertion of a human facing certain death. As much as it angers Damien to do it, he needs Horacio. He'll have to heal this dying man.

Damien reaches out, placing his hand on Horacio's abdomen.

A current of electricity shoots up his arm. The pain is raw, excruciating. He tears his arm away in horror—horror at the pain coursing through his body, and then more devastatingly, horror at his mistake.

He'd forgotten. Neglected the obvious.

Although Celestial beings can deliver both life and death, their finality does not rest with the angelic. Like a violent dog on a short leash, he howls.

From high above, the sound of frenetic wings draws his attention. Helene hovers hundreds of feet up, her face pointed toward the heavens. Damien cannot make out her expression, but he has no trouble hearing the words her soul cries.

"Thy kingdom come. Thy will be done!"

The demon curses and spits. As much as He allows their rampant intrusion, life and death rest solely in the hands of the Creator. If Horacio's end has been determined, death will not be permitted to give him up. Damien pulls out his scimitar and drives it through the man's heart, sending his tortured soul into darkness. Years and years of work on this man, training him, corrupting his gifts. All wasted.

With Horacio's soul added to his cosmic scorecard, his lips

curl and he snaps both sets of wings, taunting the angel still hovering above the warehouse. She cries out again.

"Holy! Holy! Holy is the Lord of hosts! The whole earth is full of His glory!"

The sound of her voice is a grainy, acidic salt in the wound of his mistake, and Damien cringes.

Her anthem continues to echo across the heavens, and he remembers a time when his mouth, too, sang the Creator's praises. It was like an impulse, a compulsion, like there was nothing more imperative than declaring the holiness of the Almighty. An overwhelming sense of gratitude and awe continually flood the angels of light—an awareness impossible for them to ignore in the Celestial. Whether intended or not, opening their mouths in that realm sends nothing but praises into the atmosphere.

If it weren't for the innate ability of Celestial beings to share thoughts at will, the angels of light would be unable to communicate anything but God's holiness in their angelic form.

Damien tries to remember what it's like to be grateful to Him, to feel indebted to the Creator. Instead, as Helene's cries fade, hatred stirs in his spirit—hatred for what he is, disgust for the limitations of his kind, and resentment that one decision long ago numbered his days.

It's no wonder the voices of the Fallen can do nothing but rage like beasts in the Celestial. When *their* mouths open, it's their vile hatred that is thrown into the atmosphere: guttural cries and howls, snarling hisses and roaring growls. These are the only sounds their Celestial lips can make.

He transfers to the Terrestrial and pulls out his phone, finds the contact, and dials.

"Our position's been compromised. We need to move the merchandise. Today."

The idiot on the other end of the line rattles off question after question. Logistics Horacio would have been happy to work out.

Damien looks down at the man's empty body, and he curses.

He needs a new right hand.

Someone to corrupt.

And he needs him now.

7

Brielle

Saturday morning arrives, and I haven't slept at all. The storm last night was brutal. Rolled in by the frigid winds of the past few days, rain and ice fell, pummeling the roof and keeping me wide awake.

Dad's up just after dawn. He has to work today. It's like this in the fall. He has to get in as much work as he can before the weather makes it impossible. I'm showered and eating a bowl of Cocoa Pebbles when his crew arrives. They joke and mill around the driveway while he packs his lunch.

"You call Kaylee or something, Elle. I don't want you moping around all day by yourself."

"I'll do something," I tell him. "Dishes or laundry. Movie marathon, maybe."

"Fine, but get that vegetarian over here to do it with you, all right? Bribe her with some carrots or lettuce or something."

I scoop another spoonful of chocolate-y yumminess into my spoon. "She's not a rabbit, Dad."

"Might as well be."

"I thought you liked Kay?"

"Oh, I do. I love that kid. She's good for you. But no meat? Come on. How she lives with Delia and her lamb fetish is beyond me."

He slams the lid of his lunch box—an ice chest, really—and cups my chin. "I mean it, kiddo. Alone time is off the table today. Promise me."

I want to remind him that I did perfectly well in the city without him, but that's not entirely true, is it?

"I gotcha, Dad. I promise."

"I'll be back late. Call if you need me."

My mouth is full, but I ask anyway. "You get cell phone coverage up there?"

"Not really."

"So, you're useless, then."

"Pretty much."

I kiss his cheek. "Love you, Dad. Be safe."

"Love you too, kid. See you tonight."

He loads into his truck with his ice chest and tool belt. Four or five other guys and their trucks back out and follow him onto the highway. A roughneck car club.

My Cocoa Pebbles are gone, so I rinse my bowl and put it in the dishwasher. I mean it when I tell Dad I'll stay busy. The idea of spending an entire Saturday with nothing but my memories for company tastes bitter, and I decide firmly against it.

I think about calling Kaylee—it'd make Dad happy—but can't imagine passing the day while she mitigates my failures. No, I'd rather be alone with my guilt than listen to an ignorant someone tell me it wasn't my fault. There's got to be something I can do to get the blood pumping. Something that doesn't require me to wear tights and a leotard. Something active.

But this is Stratus.

Honestly.

What is there to do?

I scrounge the quilt from the living room and step out onto the porch. The sun has disappeared behind a layer of gray clouds, but the wind has mellowed and rain hardly seems imminent. My camera is in the backseat, and the storm is sure to have left some fabulous wreckage all over Stratus. I think about the old horse stables at the back of our property. Did they survive the wind and rain?

We don't own horses, never have. But Dad hadn't cared enough to tear down the stables when he bought the place years ago. In fact, he rarely ventures that far onto our property anymore. He just likes having distance between himself and the neighbors. He says if he wants to run around naked on his own property, he should have the freedom to do it. So with the money Grams left him, he bought a chunk of land southeast of town in case the inclination ever strikes.

Of course, this is a man who wears two pairs of socks and Timberland boots at all times. He isn't running naked anywhere. He just wants the option.

I grab my camera bag from the car and head out. It's a good five miles to the stables. There's a magnificent creek about halfway there, and when I was a kid, Dad hung a swing from one of the large oak branches dangling over it. I wonder nostalgically if it's still there.

The hike is easy, nothing but flat land and trees the entire way: some barren oaks and some of the evergreen variety. In the spring, tall grasses will grow here, as high as my waist. Green and yellow strands blowing in the wind. But the rain and cold have them cowed. They shrink from the icy white sky, bowing so low the mud claims them.

I pass through an overgrown apple orchard, snapping several pictures of downed branches and uprooted trees. I even manage to stay quiet enough to capture a doe rooting around the orchard floor looking for apples. The cold air stings my face, but today I ignore it. I get lost in the quest for a great shot, and each time I think I've snapped one, I remember Jake's earlier compliment and press on looking for another.

I have so many great shots to make up for. Rolls and rolls of them, actually. Silly pictures of our adventures in the city. Of the life I sabotaged with negligence. I don't let my mind wander too far down that path. When I do, my hands shake and photography becomes impossible. I allow tears only once and quickly regret it. It takes forty-five minutes to regain my composure.

By midmorning I reach the creek. The *shick-shick* of my camera's shutter sends a sparrow flying through the branches of a great red oak. Shouldn't he have flown south by now?

Ghosts from my childhood seem to pass across the lens as I snap away. Like the sparrow, the images are out of place, but welcome. I've let so many things slip from remembrance. The shed, for instance, that sits not far from the creek bed. It's a rickety old thing that cozies up to the eastern edge of our property and belongs to whoever's living in the old Miller place these days. Why Jeb Miller built a shed way out in the middle of nowhere is anyone's guess—fishing supplies, maybe—but Dad's particularly fierce about land rights, and though it's the perfect size for a fort, I was never allowed to play in it.

I get as close as I dare and take several pictures. The swing is gone, but I snap a shot of the branch it hung from. Like friendship bracelets littering the arm of a junior high girl, the remnants of several different ropes decorate the limb now. Someone else has hung their swings here—maybe many someones. I wonder who's been on our land and then decide I don't care. This creek and the missing swing filled hours of childhood history. Everyone deserves memories like that.

The creek is calf-deep, but I avoid getting wet by crossing it stone by stone, grasping the hanging branches above to steady myself. I continue across the flattened grasses, snapping shots here and there, but the hike's taking longer than it should. Longer than I remember anyway. When I reach a series of rolling hills, I'm certain. I've gotten turned around somehow. I reach into my back pocket, thinking to call Dad, but my pocket's empty. My cell's at the house.

Dang it.

I scrabble to the top of the nearest hill and look around. Ah! In the distance I see the stables. I must have crossed the creek at the wrong place, because now a soggy field lies between me and my destination. I'll have to go around.

It takes considerably longer than I thought, and what should have been a couple hours of hiking has turned into a day-long affair.

But at last I reach the stables, my face chafing with exertion. I feel alive, which is more than I can say for the stables. The years of wear and tear and harsh weather have taken their toll, and there isn't much left. Only the north face of the aging structure remains standing; the rest leans precariously south or has fallen altogether. I begin snapping pictures and continue for over an hour. When I run out of film, I pull the digital camera from my bag and keep going. Finally, when my legs begin to ache and the camera feels heavy, I seek out a dry place to sit. It takes some looking, but I finally settle on a large, flattish rock. I climb up and lie back, looking up at the clouds. They're getting darker. I'll have to head back soon.

I practice my yoga breathing and replay yesterday's conversation with Jake. The comfortable one. The one in the car.

It's foolish to entertain thoughts of this guy. He's . . . I don't know . . . mysterious, I guess. And hot—yeah, there's that. But I know better. This is exactly what *she* did.

There's just something different about him.

I snort at myself. I'm ridiculous. Surely I'm not the first girl who's thought that about a guy.

Probably not even about Jake.

My eyes close against the fleecy white sky as I banish thoughts of him.

I should have brought my cell. If Dad calls . . .

It's so cold.

Something hurts.

My forehead stings.

My lips.

My neck.

My hands fly up to defend the onslaught, and my eyes snap open.

Man!

I've fallen asleep. The sun has already set behind the gushing clouds, and if there's one thing I'm more afraid of than being alone at night, it's being alone at night and lost in the dark. Hail bounces off the large rock, off the ground. I stand and zip my parka, flipping the hood up to protect my head. I grab my camera bag and turn toward the house.

At least I think I'm turned toward the house. The light is fading and I can't really tell.

Stupid short winter days.

I turn left and right looking for something familiar. This is right, isn't it? It has to be. My feet pound through the slippery grass as panic curdles in my stomach and turns it sour.

I don't have time to be sick.

I don't have time.

I break into a sprint. I won't be able to keep this pace up, but I have to get home before night falls. Of that I'm certain. My legs burn, and I trip over a rock. Or a tree root? I fall and scrape my hands. The camera bag smacks me in the face, but at least it keeps my head off the ground. Mud splatters my chest and neck.

I get up. Fast. Fast. I count my footfalls, my breaths, any-thing to keep my mind off the encroaching darkness. Three hundred and eighteen strides later, the creek comes into view. The clouds shift just enough for me to catch the moon's light bouncing off the rushing water.

Halfway there.

Almost home.

I can do this!

It's completely dark now and my lungs ache. Every breath is a sharpened needle sewing stitches into my side. Ten more footfalls and doubt begins to eat away at the encouragement I've given myself. The moon has hidden again behind black clouds, and the hail has turned into a soaking rain. Visibility is dimin-ishing quickly. A sob rips from my chest, and I can't find the energy to fight back the tears.

Even through the wind and rain, I can hear the creek ahead—its water splashing over the rocks I'd crossed so easily this morning. I slow to a walk. The creek has risen and nearly overrun its banks. I have to cross now. I walk up and down the rushing water, looking for the narrowest way across. When I find something that seems acceptable, I take three giant steps back and then run as fast as I can. I cross my fingers and launch off the muddy ground.

There's a moment of relief as I clear the creek bed, but my boot catches something on the way down and I lurch. That's when I hear the crack. I don't feel the pain until a second later, when I'm sprawled in the mud. I scream and try to curl into a ball, but whatever's caught my boot still has hold of it. My first thought is that something, a stick maybe, has skewered my leg. I reach for my ankle and find it's tangled in a mess of roots jutting from the mucky ground. With shaking hands, I work it free. It's been skewered, all right, but from the inside out. My ankle's broken—bone straining against skin.

Panic turns to hysteria, and my body shakes. I know full-blown shock is not far off, and I fight to keep it at bay. The wind whistles, louder and louder, calling my name.

"Brielle!"

I fear I'm losing my mind. And then I see him, running through the mud and sliding at my feet.

"Brielle!" he cries again. "Here. Put your arm around my neck—no, don't stand. I've got you."

It isn't the wind at all. It's Jake. The fire in his eyes demands my attention, but I vaguely note the white beam of a flashlight bouncing around. He shoves it into his back pocket, and we're shrouded in darkness again. He pulls me tight against his chest and stands. I turn my face into his neck to avoid the rain forcing its way into my nose and mouth.

He smells like coffee—hot coffee—laced with chocolate.

"You're okay. You'll be okay." His voice is thick with emotion—an emotion I can't define.

A thawing blaze roars through my body, and my breathing slows. His speed and agility are impressive, and before I've had much time to digest his presence, we're inside, out of the rain. I feel him adjust me, hear the squeal of hinges and the slam of a door. He kneels carefully, placing my weight on his knee. I tighten my arms around his neck. If I don't, he'll let me go, and I'm not ready for that. Not yet.

He's patient and waits several long moments for me to loosen my grip and look up at him. He's staring back at me with those eyes. They scour my face so deeply I look away.

"Will you be okay if I set you down?" He frees one hand and pulls the flashlight from his pocket. In the white light I see the concern etched on his face. And something else: blood.

I'm not the only one injured.

"Of course. I'm—Yes, I'm so sorry," I blurt. He's cut. Rain and blood run mingled down his face and drip onto my jacket. He sets me down on the moist earth. "Your face," I say.

"What?" Jake reaches for his cheek. He pulls his hand away, and his fingers are fresh with blood. "I didn't even realize. A branch must've caught me." He swipes a dripping sleeve across his face and turns his attention back to me. "What about you? Let me see that foot."

He repositions himself and slides my dripping pant leg up over my calf. "Oh man. Yeah, it's broken."

His words shatter some sort of delusional barrier, and the shock starts to wear off. I feel pain again. More physical pain than I think I've ever felt. My body tightens as he sets my foot on his knee.

"Don't move. I know it hurts, but give me a minute."

Careful not to jostle my foot, he removes his sweatshirt and hands it to me. He tugs off his undershirt and tears it into strips.

"What are you doing?" I ask, struggling to keep my attention on his face. His certainly isn't the first bare chest I've seen, but the emotions running through my veins have charged the moment, and I twist the sweatshirt in my hands nervously.

"I'm going to splint your ankle so you can't move it around," Jake answers.

"Don't you have to set it or something?"

I don't know a thing about broken bones, but it seems like something I'd heard in Girl Scouts. He flashes a smile at me. Just a hint of patronization there.

"No, this will be okay."

It takes him no time at all to wrap the shirt soundly around my ankle, shoe and all. Then he pulls his sweatshirt on and leans back against a stack of rotting boards, holding my foot tightly. I keep my eyes on his hands as the stabbing sensation recedes and my breathing slows. I can't believe how hot they are.

Or maybe I'm just that cold.

"Where are we?" I ask. The heat soaks into my foot and seeps up my leg. My body is starting to relax, like sliding into a hot bath.

"A storage shed, I think. I hope this roof holds."

We glance at the rotting boards above. The decaying wood is already letting streams of rainwater through in places. They splash in mud puddles and soak the ground.

"Oh. Right. The shed." I lean my head against the wall at my back. It hadn't even crossed my mind to take shelter somewhere other than home.

I used to be so savvy, so smart. Now it seems all my actions are motivated by fear. This revelation depresses me, and again my hands begin to tremble. Even with the poor light, Jake notices.

"Are you warm enough?"

He tightens his grip on my foot, and heat floods my body.

"How are you *doing* that?"

"What?" he counters innocently. He *has* to know what I mean. I'm incredulous, but he just flashes me a smile again and shrugs. "Body heat works wonders."

"I've never known anyone as hot as you."

I've spoken without thinking, and he raises an eyebrow at me in response. I feel the blood rush to my ears and we laugh, embarrassed. Broken ankle aside, this isn't the worst way to spend a stormy night. It's been weeks since I've enjoyed the company of another human being. Except Dad, of course.

Oh, sheesh. Dad.

"You don't have a cell phone, do you?"

"Sure." He pulls a phone from his pocket with one hand, his other secured around my ankle. One look at the fogged-up screen and I know water has made its way inside.

"Yeah. I don't think that thing's gonna work," I say.

He presses the On button for good measure and then chucks the phone to the far corner of the shed. "Is someone going to worry about you?"

"My dad. All this rain has him working late, though, so I'm probably all right for a bit."

"That's good. We should stay here a little longer. Let your foot rest."

We sit in silence as the rain pounds on the rickety shed, and the wind does its best to tear the rusty nails free. The bright but narrowly focused beam of the flashlight is hardly ideal for such a situation, but it casts enough light for me to see around the tiny shed.

We're both soaked through, that much is apparent. I yank off my gloves, saturated and useless, and cram them into my jacket pocket. My hair drips a river down my back, so I wring it out, braid it into a long plait, and throw it over my shoulder. I'm sure I should be concerned about my appearance after the rain, the mud, and the hail, but I can't make myself concentrate on any of it.

Jake breaks the silence. "You grew up here?"

"Stratus, Oregon. Born and raised."

"So, why did Mr. Whatever-his-name-is say you were new?"

"Misinformed, I guess."

"Maybe he's new too?" Jake ventures.

"Maybe," I concede. "Though that's a lot of new blood for a cow town."

Jake smirks. "And yet I haven't seen a single cow."

"Smelled them?"

"*That's* what that was."

I smile. "I went to Stratus High my freshman year. Just moved back here from the city."

"Ah." He has that look—like he's figured it out. Figured me out. "Parents divorced?"

I wish.

"No. My mom died when I was young. It's just me and Dad."

"I'm sorry," he says.

It's an apology I've heard a million times—an unnecessary one.

"It's okay. It was a long time ago."

He waits for me to go on, and to my utter amazement it isn't difficult to continue.

"Toward the end of my freshman year, a talent scout spent the weekend here at the bed-and-breakfast on Main. Behind Jelly's? Anyway, she wasn't here to scout, just taking a weekend, you know, but the only entertainment options in town that night were a Kung Fu movie and the high school dance recital."

"I'm guessing you were at the dance recital."

"Maybe I'm a Kung Fu junkie?"

"My apologies." He laughs. "Continue."

I grin. But just a bit. "Yeah, so she attended the spring dance recital. I'm a ballerina. Well, I was a ballerina." I pause, but I can see what his next question's going to be, so I hurry on. "Anyway, before the weekend was over she'd secured me a scholarship at a prestigious boarding school in the city: the Austen School for the Arts."

"That's very—wow. That was very generous of her."

"Yes, it was," I agree, remembering my first impressions of Susie Slade.

A woman dedicated to her clients and married to her iPhone, Susie is one of the best in the business. She took Dad and me out after the recital and promised to change my life forever with modeling jobs and commercial auditions. Sure, I could continue to dance. Several prominent dancers had graced the halls at Austen. Was I interested in theatre? I didn't know. Could I sing? Absolutely not. But when she told me Austen was located in the heart of the city, far from the quiet life of Stratus, she became my savior.

"Susie was very generous, but moving me served her needs as well. She's very hands-on, and the commute to Stratus isn't exactly ideal," I tell him. "So when the summer ended, I moved to the dorm at Austen."

"Wow."

Yeah, wow. Very few girls get such an opportunity, and the

story starts out just like a fairy tale. The ending, of course, is more Brothers Grimm than Disney, but it comes pouring out of me nonetheless.

"It was the chance of a lifetime—a dream come true and all that—but I couldn't imagine leaving Dad. We don't really have anyone else, you know?" I pick at the mud drying on my knees, remembering. "But he wanted me to go and promised to visit often. Which he did. Nearly every weekend that first year."

"Just the first year?"

I pause, expecting my hands to resume their tremors, but am pleasantly surprised. Still, my voice is soft.

"My junior year passed easier, and I didn't think I needed him as much. I had made friends. A friend."

"The girl in the picture?"

"Ali," I confirm. "Her name was Ali."

A tear runs down my cheek, but it isn't an icy, numbing thing. It's hot and fierce, and it gives me courage. I want to tell him this story. I want to talk about my friend.

"She died three weeks ago," I say, brushing away the tear. I want him to know what everyone else knows, but for once, I want to be the one telling the story. The fake excuses and pardons everyone gives me are tiresome. This mistake is a part of me as nothing else ever has been, and I want him to know how badly I wish I could undo it all.

"Oh man, Brielle. I'm so sorry," he says. Without letting go of my injured ankle, he moves himself closer to my face. I bend my knees so he can sit right in front of me. The heat off his skin is intoxicating—its appeal frightening—but I force myself to go on.

"Me too," I whisper. "It was my fault."

He eyes me curiously but doesn't challenge my claim, so I continue.

"Ali was an actress. Easily the most talented girl at Austen. They had her tabbed for Julliard or the NY Film Academy. See, I had a fabulous talent agent who saw something marketable in me, but Ali was the shining star of Austen. *Everyone* wanted her."

I let my eyes focus on the wall behind him.

"She was picky, though, and wouldn't take on more than one project at a time. And she absolutely refused to do commercials. Not because they were beneath her, but because they kept her too busy. She liked the stage—a captive audience, you know—but she wanted to finish school before committing full-time to anything. She was always so grounded when it came to her career. I envied her that. Her agency was always begging her to take on this project and that. *You gotta strike while the iron is hot*, they'd say, but she didn't worry about it at all. The rest of us bought all the crap about youth and sex being the only thing in demand. Ali didn't. She figured if they didn't want her when she was ready, she'd just do something else."

I smile, remembering the day Ali dropped her modern dance class. The sigh of relief heaved by the rest of the class was resounding.

"She was good at just about everything, but she wasn't a dancer. She didn't enjoy it. It was a gift really. When she left the dance class, I became the envy of the other girls. She didn't mind giving up the spotlight. She was kind that way."

"She meant a lot to you."

"She inspired me. She made me want to excel at everything. She made me think I could."

I stop. The wind has picked up, and we sit listening for a while.

"She made me fearless," I finally say. "I miss that."

Jake's eyes rake my face now. When at last he focuses their brilliance on mine, he says, "Being fearless is overrated."

"But being afraid of everything isn't."

I know what he wants to ask, and though it surprises me, I find I'm ready to tell him. He pauses, but apparently recognizes the unspoken permission I've given him.

"And why, Brielle? Why are you afraid of everything?"

He raises a hand and runs his thumb along my cheekbone, where it leaves a trail of heat burning pleasantly. The action is unexpected, and it seems to catch him off guard too. He pulls his hand away and puts it back on my foot.

Is he blushing?

After a minute I take a huge, rattling breath and continue.

"I had the opportunity to travel abroad last summer. We performed in Rome and Paris, London, and a dozen smaller cities in between. It was a dance tour, so of course Ali didn't go. She'd taken a job on an indie film. The director was a guy named Marco James."

I gnaw on my lip at the memory of Marco. Tall, thin, dreadfully handsome, with a head full of shaggy black hair constantly veiling a pair of exotic green eyes. He was everything a young, independent filmmaker should be. One night Ali and I played rock-paper-scissors for him. I won—paper beats rock every time—but I let her have him. We were just goofing around, and it was obvious he was into Ali.

"We'd met him at an art show, and Ali stayed in contact with him, mostly through e-mail and online stuff. Our school and audition schedules kept us pretty busy. He'd graduated from film school the year before and had this screenplay he'd completed. An art patron agreed to finance the film, and Marco gave the lead to Ali."

Jake sits, hands still around my ankle, attentive and kind, patiently waiting for the rest—the tragic ending to this fairy tale.

"When I returned from Europe, she was just . . . so . . . different."

"Different?"

"She was quieter," I say, "and she had bruises on her arms that she tried to explain away. She told me they were from filming accidents. Tripping. Clumsiness. I wanted to believe her, but nothing made sense. Filming had wrapped weeks before, and dancing aside, she was the most coordinated person I knew. I'd never even seen her stumble."

Another tear, hot and scorching, rips down my cheek. Rainwater pings off a metal tackle box in the corner, sounding like another heart sharing the shed with us.

"The detective was right," I whisper, his words pressing into me, into my chest. "I didn't want to see. In so many ways Ali and Marco were perfect for one another. Both so talented, so passionate about their craft."

A memory surfaces, and though I despise the fresh round of tears it provokes, I'm helpless against them.

Marco was playing Hamlet with a small theatre company, and Ali and I had front-row seats. His performance was captivating, especially the famous "To be or not to be" speech. Polonius and Ophelia in the background, Hamlet talking himself in and out of a self-made grave, contemplating death as if it were a menu item.

I'd never really *felt* that speech before, never considered the words. But in Marco's performance I appreciated the draw of death. I understood Hamlet's internal battle: the sea of troubles he found himself drowning in, and the sleep of death that appealed to his misery but was sure to carry troubles of its own. I wonder how often Marco's thought of those words in recent days.

Jake interrupts my trip down memory lane.

"You couldn't have known, Brielle."

Even now, he can see where this is going. Why hadn't I?

"I *should* have known," I correct him. "The bruises got worse as the summer ended, and once I even threatened to drag her into the police station, but it was an empty threat. There was a part of me that couldn't believe he'd lay a hand on her, and she was such a fantastic liar."

"She was good at everything," Jake says, repeating my own words back to me.

"Yes, she was," I grant. "The school year started and the bruising continued, but it slipped to the back of my mind. We were busy, and her time with Marco was limited," I explain through heaving breaths. "Then one day three weeks ago, she went with Marco to show the finished film to the financier."

I let the tears flow now. They comfort me. Warm me.

"She never came home. They found her in an old warehouse where Marco often filmed. He was there too, they say. Sobbing, soaked in her blood. Even when the detective told me he'd confessed, I had a hard time believing it. He loved her. I know he loved her."

Jake tightens his grip on my ankle but says nothing. Words can't fix this.

"I should have known. I was the only one who *could* have known."

He lets me cry, his face inches from mine, until I have no more tears. It takes awhile, but eventually the tears slow and my chest stills. The night grows quiet, until the only thing I hear is the other heart in the shed, pinging away.

"I can't imagine losing my best friend," Jake says. "She sounds like an incredible person."

"She was."

He moves back against the wall, still holding my foot between his hands.

"Thank you," I say.

"For what?"

"For listening. I haven't been able to talk about it. The words have been"—I rub my chest—"frozen, you know?"

"I do know," Jake says. And he looks like he does. Like he really knows what it's like. "I'm glad you chose me."

"Me too." I wipe the tears from my eyes and take a breath. I feel better. Purged.

"So, you live with your Dad?" Jake says, lightening the conversation. "What does he do?"

"He owns a logging company. Dad's dad was a logger, *his* dad was a logger. Sort of a Matthews family tradition."

"You planning on following in his footsteps?"

"Um. No. Definitely not. I don't know what I'll do. I always thought I'd be dancing. And then the modeling opportunities came along. But it's just . . . it's too hard to think about that now."

"You might not always feel that way," Jake says. "You might change your mind."

"I might." Tired of all the attention, I suddenly realize I still know nothing about him. "What about your guardian? Canaan, you said? He's, like, a foster parent?"

"Kinda. That's probably a good way to describe him."

He's clamming up now? When I've just poured my guts out. Come on!

"Tell me about him."

"Well, Ali and I have a lot in common," he says slowly, watching my face. "Are you sure you want to hear this right now?"

I swallow. No lump.

"Yes. I do. If you don't mind telling me, that is."

He cocks his head and looks me in the eye, appraising my mental state, apparently.

"Well, my father was a drinker and my mother was a screamer. That's about all I remember of them. I was little when things fell apart. My father had a tendency to swing at anything and everything that got in his way when he drank, and I frequently got in the way."

A wave of nausea hits, and I stiffen.

"Are you okay?" Jake asks.

"Are *you*?"

"I am. I really am. I don't remember the details at all. Everything's very fuzzy. We were living in Portland and I was young, just six, when Canaan found me home alone. I had a broken wrist and a shattered collarbone. Maggots in the sink, cockroaches crawling on the floor, and absolutely nothing edible left in the apartment. Who knows how long I'd been alone? The first thing I remember with any clarity is Canaan carrying me out of the building. I've been with him ever since."

"So, Canaan's a social worker?" I ask, doing my best to focus on the story's happy ending.

Jake's eyes drop to his hands, still wrapped snuggly around my foot. He doesn't say anything for a long time—almost too long. I nearly ask again, but his chin tilts up, and he speaks in carefully measured words.

"Canaan works for a private party whose goal is to bring hope to those who have none."

His face is screwed up tight with the effort of putting the sentence together, and his blazing eyes dare me to contradict him.

"Oh. That's a lofty goal," I say as I digest this new change in his demeanor.

"I just know every memory I have before Canaan is saturated with alcohol and sadness. My parents weren't good people. They did horrible things to each other and to the people around them. I don't hate them," he says.

I can't help thinking it sounds more like a reminder to himself than anything.

"But they dug their own graves."

"So, they're dead?" Ugh. So many people buried around us.

"I don't know," he says, shaking off the acidic look on his face. "They never tried to find me, but if I had to guess, I'd say their lifestyle was certainly leading them in that direction."

There's angst in the hang of his shoulders, but he speaks of it all with such detachment, such distance. I wonder if I'll ever be able to talk about Ali without the pain.

"I'm so sorry, Jake."

He nods. He's heard pointless apologies as well.

"You're very lucky to have your father. Losing your mom must have been hard, but at least you have your dad."

"Dad has always been there for me, you know? Losing my mother was horrible for him, I'm sure, but I don't remember her at all. I mean, even less than you remember your parents. I have no recollection of my mother ever existing. I see pictures of her and hear stories, but nothing brings back even the slightest flicker of a memory. I think it hurts my dad that I can't remember, but I was even younger than you. I was three when she died."

"Does it bother you that you can't remember her?"

"All the time," I say. "But I sort of don't know what I'm missing, and Dad's always been so great." I think about all the psychological advice I've been given and regurgitate a sentence I've chewed on often. "Maybe forgetting was the only way I could move on."

"Maybe," Jake agrees. It's quiet again. The heart pinging away in the corner. "Do you ever wish you could forget about *her*? Ali, I mean."

It's a harsh, expected question. I have to look at his face to know he isn't asking to hurt me. He seems genuinely, painfully curious.

"No," I answer, and I know I mean it. "She made me a better person. She's a part of me. Maybe that part died too, but I don't ever want to forget it existed."

He smiles. "That's very wise of you."

Jake breaks eye contact, and we emerge from the intimate little bubble of emotion we've landed in. The army of raindrops has retreated, and the wind's symphonic efforts have ceased.

"Come on, let's get you home. It's getting late."

"Thank goodness," I say. "Will you help me walk?"

"If you need me, but I think you'll be fine now."

I look down to see him rolling my ankle—first one way, then the other.

I gasp.

It's not broken.

Not anymore.

8

Canaan

Canaan stands in the darkness beneath a weather-ravaged oak. Wet and windblown, but vigilant. The rain has slowed, and the terror he sensed has all but melted away.

And though the fear seems to be diminishing, there's something malevolent nearby. Something close.

He extends his wings the full width of their span—wings that are not visible in this realm—and with a snap his Terrestrial ears cannot hear, he wraps them around his body. Had anyone been watching, Canaan would have disappeared before their very eyes. But the closest humans are huddled away in a shed just beyond the tree line.

He closes his eyes and allows himself to be pulled from the Terrestrial realm—an impulse he fights every minute he functions as the human, Canaan Shield.

Instantly the moon's counterfeit rays are replaced by the ever-true, constant light that is his strength. He breathes it deep. Here, shadows do not exist. Light is his sustenance, and it is bountiful. Only the sludge of evil has any effect. It's a realm where every one of his senses is heightened, for this is his home. This is where he was created to live.

Whereas his Terrestrial eyes are limited and can see only the prosaic, his Celestial eyes see anything and everything for miles. Neither wall nor mountain can obstruct his view. And whereas his Terrestrial ears hear only the sounds of this globe, his Celestial ears hear the sounds of both the earth and the heavens, human and spirit alike. Only in this form is he truly equipped to protect his charge.

Instinct causes him to draw his sword. Its pure, white light is hot as punishing hellfire and radiant as the river flowing from the throne of the Creator. The darkness he felt in his Terrestrial state crouches atop the shed. A demon.

One he knows well.

An ache forms in his chest.

This is Damien. A former friend. An angel who served alongside him. Whose mouth once sang the praises of the Creator. His abandonment was felt personally, not just by the Father, but by the other angels, by Canaan. Damien and the others left so much for so little. It's a choice Canaan won't ever understand.

He's not seen Damien since Dothan, and Dothan ended badly for the demon. If Canaan had to guess, he'd say Damien spent several hundred, maybe a thousand years suffering for his failure there. For his defeat.

The Prince of Darkness forgives slowly, and he never, ever forgets.

Canaan watches as Damien salivates, the scene within the shed capturing the demon's full attention. Like the rest of the Fallen, he's learned to keep his muscular legs—once no different from a Shield's—close to his body, under the protection of his wings and away from the light, almost always drawn into this crouched position. His hands, once used for noble purposes, have been twisted by ill use and maltreatment of the gifts instilled in them. They curl now, around the corner of the shed, black talons piercing the wood. His skin and hair, once alight with the glory of the Celestial, have long since charred, and his wings, once snowy white, now hang like lifeless sails, their feathers singed black by the very light they have rejected.

His strength, however, is not to be underestimated.

And yet he's not noticed Canaan. Not noticed the drawn sword, the Shield ready to defend his charge. Whatever's going on in that shed has him transfixed, and he presses his face into the roof, his wings twitching.

Canaan focuses on the walls of the shed and they thin before him, fading from view. He sees rubble and loose boards. Rusted rakes and fishing rods. And there amongst it all is Jake.

He sits on the muddy floor, his hands wrapped around the girl's ankle. Her mouth gapes and her hands tremble. Fear breaks out in black beads along her forehead, running in thin, sticky streams down her face.

"How?" she says. "How did you do that?"

Canaan's eyes flash to Damien, whose fascination he's beginning to understand.

Jake must have healed the girl.

Damien must have seen.

Razor-sharp talons slip through the roof of the shed, reaching, reaching for his prey.

All four of Canaan's wings push against the air, and suddenly he's hurtling through the sky toward Damien.

9

Damien

Damien's ears pick up the sound of frenzied wings, and he turns, drawing his scimitar and shoving away from the shed all in one motion. His movement is sloppy, and the Shield's sword connects with his elbow. He opens his mouth and releases a cry of fury, but there's no time for self-pity. The Shield flies low, body extended, looping around for another pass.

Damien flies backward, squinting into the light. He encounters members of the Shield frequently—all of them strong, fast, capable. But even his dying eyes recognize this one.

He slows his wings and sets down, watching as Canaan draws closer and closer. He blinks and blinks, fighting the light, fighting his desperate need for darkness.

He can hardly believe what he sees.

His wings push him into the sky, and he raises his scimitar. The freezing weapon hisses against the heat of the Celestial, fogging the air with frigid smoke.

He waits for Canaan's attack, but the Shield doesn't advance past the shed. He hovers, his wings spread wide, his sword in his outstretched hand.

The temptation to attack is strong. Damien wants the boy. Wants him for his own. For his right hand.

The gift of healing is rare and so easily corrupted. Could be used to advance the kingdom of darkness. It takes so little to convince a human to do wrong. Especially a human who cares for others. In many ways, this one would be easier to destroy than Horacio.

And a human like this boy, his gift twisted to serve darkness, would surely garner favor. Maybe even earn him time at the Prince's stronghold, far from the light that picks at his eyes, vicious as a scavenger.

Damian growls with anticipation.

Yes, he will see this gift corrupted.

The boy and the girl, then.

The girl for Henry Madison, and this boy with the gift as his new right hand.

But is Canaan here to protect the boy? The girl? Either way, now that Damien's intentions are known, Canaan is sure to stay close. So Damien decides. He'll arrange two more buyers for Friday. Two more humans corrupted by his fallen brothers. And when the buyers show up next week, they'll be flanked by their demonic escorts. Brothers who will fight alongside him.

He can't face Canaan alone.

He needs the odds tipped in his favor.

When his brothers see what the boy is capable of, they'll agree Damien's done well. If he can arrange for Maka to be one of them, perhaps word will travel quickly to the Prince. And when the boy's hands have been corrupted, maybe, just maybe Damien's failures will be forgiven.

Dothan will be forgotten.

And Damien's eyes given time to heal.

10

Brielle

*I*t was broken! I saw it. You said it yourself! The bone was sticking out and . . . it was broken!" I'm rambling and clutching at my ankle in disbelief. Jake moves his hands as I grab desperately at my foot. My ankle is hot to the touch but completely uninjured. Finally my mouth forms a question. "How . . . how did you do that?"

He looks away, narrowing his eyes at the ceiling. Such a bizarre response, and one that does nothing to untangle this knot of bewilderment. He seems to be thinking, considering something. At last he shrugs—very devil-may-care of him—but his tone contradicts his blasé posture.

"I'll make you a deal, Elle," he says, using carefully measured words again.

"What kind of deal?"

"You keep *this* between us," he says, indicating my ankle, "and I will tell you how."

I can't think. I don't know what to say, how to answer him. I don't understand what's happened, but I do believe him.

"I won't tell a soul."

"Good," he says, grabbing my hands. They've grown chilled, and the heat in his causes me to yank them away.

"Sorry," he says, grabbing my biceps instead and lifting me to my feet.

"It's fine, I just . . ."

I can still feel the heat through my parka, but it's not uncomfortable. I stomp my foot on the muddy ground, dubious at the lack of pain. He grins at my display and walks out the door.

"Wait," I say. "Aren't you going to tell me?"

I run after him, sloshing through the mud. He turns back to me, but I can't stop fast enough and I run into him. My forehead smacks his chin. He steadies me and laughs at my frustration.

"Tell me something," he says.

"I thought it was your turn to tell me something." I'm starting to feel a little like my old self. It isn't so hard to think, to breathe. Sarcasm itself may be reviving.

Jake rolls his eyes. It's incredibly endearing, so I nod, giving him permission to ask.

"Is Brielle your full name, or is it short for something?"

"Gabrielle," I say, thrown by the question. "How did you know that?"

"So why Brielle? Why not Gabby?"

"Mom called me Gabby, I think, when I was small. At least that's what Grams said before she died. But Dad liked Brielle. Once Mom passed away, there was only Dad, and everyone followed his lead, I suppose."

"Do you have a preference?"

"I don't know. I like Brielle, I guess."

He grabs my sleeve and pulls me a step closer.

"Brielle," he says very deliberately. "This thing, your ankle, it's not something I can just 'explain.'"

"But you said—"

"Spend time with me. There are things you need to see first."

Things I need to see?

"If I spend time with you, I'll understand how you magically fixed my ankle?"

"I didn't say you'd understand. But I will explain."

His request is fair, I suppose, but spending time with him has the butterflies in my tummy all manic. And that's dangerous. I'd rather he just tell me now.

"You don't trust me?"

"That's not it," he says, starting back toward the house, towing me along. "This is really all about me. It's something I'm still getting comfortable with. Is that okay?"

I consider forcing the issue, but he genuinely seems uncomfortable, and I deflate.

"I guess."

The clouds part slightly, and we're favored with a glimpse of the stars. Just a sliver of the inky night sky is visible, but it's enough. Enough to remind me that storms are temporary, that the cottony billows high above are little more than vague substance.

I speed up, falling into stride with Jake.

Glimpses. That's what this night has been about. Whoever Jake is, whatever he can do, I've caught just a glimpse of it tonight. In a run-down shed in the middle of nowhere, something happened that even George Lucas and his special effects team would have trouble simulating.

His hand is still latched on to my cuff, but the heat travels up my sleeve, something I could definitely get used to. But the thought brings a small moment of panic. How much longer till Jake disappears?

Like my mom. Like Ali.

Are brief glimpses all I'll ever get?

When Jake and I arrive back at the house, Dad's truck is already parked in the driveway. I leave Jake standing on the porch and hurry inside. I hate making Dad worry. There's been enough of that lately, and he deserves better. As expected, he's a bit of a mess. He drops the boot he's struggling to pull into place and collapses on the nearest kitchen chair.

"You gave me a heart attack, kid. I just called the sheriff."

"I'm sorry, Dad," I say, kissing his scruffy beard.

He asks me about my day and then stops me before I have a chance to answer. "Let me call the sheriff's office and tell 'em you're home. They're sending a deputy out."

While he phones the authorities, I duck onto the porch.

"Everything okay?" Jake asks.

"Yeah, but he'd already called the sheriff."

"I should've gotten you back sooner."

"It's okay. Dad's been known to overreact. Only child and all. He's very protective."

"Canaan's the same way. I should go." He tugs the braid that's settled onto my shoulder and backs down the stairs. His eyes are the last thing I see as he disappears beyond the illumination of our porch light.

I don't sigh. I don't. That would be too cliché. But Jake's taken all the heat with him and I'm soaked, so I retreat to the safety of the kitchen and give Dad a brief overview of the day—omitting the broken ankle, of course. He raises his eyebrows when I tell him I ran into the new kid from school, but he doesn't ask questions. He's just relieved to have me home and grateful I had company and a place to stay dry when the storm kicked up. Or so he says. He's suspiciously unsuspicious, but I follow his lead and choose to be grateful.

"You look better, Elle," Dad says over his shoulder, turning in for the night. "I'll have to thank that boy. Where does he live again?"

"I have no idea, Dad. We didn't get around to that."

Without Jake to distract me, the wet clothes chafe and itch. I throw them in the wash and pull on a pair of sweats. I wander around the house again wrapped in the quilt and afghan. I touch pictures of my mom and wish I could tell her about Jake. Ask her if I'm crazy for being preoccupied with a boy I know so little about. Would she have been that kind of mom? The kind I could talk to?

There's no way to know, I guess.

After the wash is moved to the dryer, I switch off the lights and pad through the kitchen to my room. I burrow into bed, aware sleep is still a ways off. Tonight I don't mind. There are countless things to think about now—some of them wonderful, pleasant things. The pain of losing Ali, and my role in it, is still sickening, and there isn't enough distance yet, but maybe time really does heal.

I sit up and examine my ankle. Moonlight slips through the Venetian blinds and falls across my leg in silvery stripes. There's no sign of a break. I can't help but compare the complete absence of injury to the lingering pain of Ali's death. They are different in so many ways, but brokenness is something they share.

My fingers press at the bone, at the soft muscles in my foot.

I find no hint of injury. Without proof, without a scar of some kind, I'd have trouble convincing anyone it had once been broken. Certainly no one would believe Jake's hands did what they did. I run my thumb over my foot and up my calf, trying to recall the heat of Jake's touch. I'm sure I didn't imagine the whole thing, but it would be nice to have some sort of proof, something to remind me of our evening in the shed.

I tuck my feet back under the covers and try to recapture the earlier warmth. My hands shake slightly, so I rub them against my thighs. They remind me that, unlike my ankle, I'll forever carry evidence of Ali's death. She changed me. Changed the way I think, the way I dance. Ali taught me about bravery. She gave me resolve. Her death may have bloodied that resolve, but it can't kill it. It will scab and scar like other wounds. But my life will forever bear witness that the pain existed. That she existed.

My hands may stop shaking and the chill may leave me, but I'll never forget. And I don't want to. Losing Ali was hard enough. Forgetting her would be like walking through life without a scar, without proof of her existence. And that would kill me.

I have Jake to thank for that revelation.

Maybe he's one of those Catholic saints? Like the one on the medal Ali wore around her neck. She was never without that thing. You have to perform a miracle to become a saint, right? And that thing he did in the shed—whatever it was—was definitely miraculous. Imagining Jake's face carved onto a little golden medal makes me grin at the darkness.

The *clump-clump* of Dad's bare feet shuffling outside the door sobers me.

Once, years ago, I got a small but rather bitter taste of Dad's opinion on religion. It was late and I was supposed to be asleep, but I'd had one too many Dr. Peppers. I took care of business and then stuck my head into the living room to stay good night. The sight of Dad huddled on the floor in tears, bowed before the big screen, shook me.

The volume on the television was low, so low I could barely hear the jumpy organ music. At the front of the carpeted stage were a purple-suited man and a woman in a wheelchair. The man had a big leather book in his hands, and he waved it around like a magic wand. I knew it was a Bible. My mom's old Bible held a place of honor on my nightstand.

I watched from behind the sofa as the purple-suited man threw his arms in the air and the woman rose from the wheelchair. The crowd erupted in celebration as she danced around the stage, flapping like a chicken. I was young—ten or eleven, maybe—and I didn't understand what I was watching. But Dad stood, took a mad swipe at his eyes, and snapped off the television. He grabbed the beer sitting next to the lamp and took a swig.

Then he turned and caught me staring.

"Sorry, Dad. I just . . ."

"Get to bed, Brielle." His voice was gruff. Angry. "And don't you believe a thing you just saw. Why would God heal that lady and not your mom? God's cruel, kid. He doesn't exist."

He had a point, I guess. Why would God heal some people and not others? Not my mom?

I tucked Mom's Bible into my sock drawer that night. To say God doesn't exist feels like betraying the beliefs of my dead mother. But I've yet to be convinced either way. I guess the idea of Jake as a religious healer would require me to come to some sort of conclusion.

The next morning I wake late. My body must be rebelling against my lack of sleep, because I don't even hear Dad leave. For the first time in weeks I enjoy the process of getting ready. I take a long shower, feeling the heat warm me through, and then sit in front of the mirror for ages doing my makeup and hair before sliding into my favorite jeans.

I let myself be picky, taking forever to select a top. It's one of Ali's old shirts that grabs my attention. With some reservation I pull it from the closet and drape it over my desk chair, then I back up to my bed and sit. I stare at it, picking through my muddled feelings.

It's just a T-shirt. Black with pink swirly letters that say *Prima Donna*. The O in Donna is the mask from *The Phantom of the Opera*, Ali's favorite show. Her mother, Serena, insisted I take it, along with some of her other things. At the time I only took it so I wouldn't hurt her feelings, but now I think I'd like to wear it.

Just staring at it gives me some of Ali's courage, and today I want to be this new person—a girl who is healing instead of one who is constantly dying.

I stand and cross the room, picking up Ali's shirt. One hand makes it through the arm hole before I have second thoughts. It smells like her, like her fruity perfume. My chest heaves. I drop to the floor and press the shirt to my face.

And I cry.

11

Canaan

It's noon before Canaan makes his way home. A church bell in town rings loud and clear, calling to the believing and unbelieving alike. He sends his own call up. To the Throne Room. To the Father. He prays for direction, for insight.

He receives peace. Nothing more.

But it's enough. Satisfied Damien's left town, Canaan returns home, dropping through the ceiling and into his bedroom.

At the foot of the bed is an incredibly old piece of furniture. It's one of only two possessions in his home that carries with it the supernatural: a black chest, cut from onyx. He kneels before it and lifts the lid, setting it next to him on the faded carpet.

Two items reside within. The first is new. It's a copy of *Hamlet*, an early edition by the looks of it. The middle of the book bulges; there's a stack of paper shoved between the pages.

He opens up the book and pulls out the papers. They're real estate forms of some sort. Warehouse listings. He'll have to look more closely.

"Thank you," he whispers, resting his head against the tome.

Answered prayer. There's nothing quite so sweet.

It's not the first time he's wished for omniscience, but knowing it isn't necessary to complete his task, he replaces the lid, shutting away the singular item residing inside.

And then a figure is before him.

Her hair flames auburn as she hovers above. Instinct pulls Canaan's hand to the sword at his hip, but by the time his fingers reach the hilt, he knows she is an ally. Her hands are spread wide in a gesture of peace, and the selfless white light pouring from her eyes is distinguishing. Her wings slow, and she alights on the bed. He pushes to a stand and finds himself at eye level with another angel.

"You are Canaan," her mind says.

It's been some time since he's conversed with his own kind, and the opportunity is most welcome. He considers her elfin form. Smaller, faster angels spend much of their time in the role of a messenger, a courier of sorts.

"I am. And you? You're a Herald, it seems?"

"I was. For many centuries. Four years ago I was reassigned to the Shield."

"What does the Creator call you, little one?"

"Helene."

"*Light* He calls you. And light you are. What brings you to Stratus?"

"A charge."

"Yes?"

"Your neighbor. The girl with fear bleeding from her chest."

"I was under the impression she was my charge."

"Haven't you another charge? A young man?"

Canaan nods. "Jake. The Throne Room has indicated their futures will entwine."

"That may be. I've no instructions regarding the boy, but the Throne Room has suggested you may need to leave for a time."

Canaan considers the book in his hand. If what she says is accurate, the papers within will lead him from Stratus.

"I'm to remain here," Helene continues. "I can keep watch over your charge as well, if leaving him behind seems best to you."

"No," Canaan says. "He's caught the eye of the Fallen. I'll keep him with me for now. Though I don't imagine he'll want to leave Brielle for long."

"Also, I've had a run-in with one of the Fallen—an encounter that will certainly interest you."

"Tell me."

12

Brielle

O
h good. You're ready."

After my sob fest I've finally got my makeup reapplied and my breathing under control. My eyes are a little puffy, but there's nothing I can do about that.

"Afternoon, Kay. What are you doing here?"

"You're kidding me, right? Didn't you get my text?"

I open the door a smidge wider, and she shimmies past me.

"I need new seat covers," she says.

I yawn. "You don't have a car."

"Text, Elle, text. I sent you all this in a text," she says. "Shoes, girl. Move it, and I'll explain."

She shoves me through the kitchen and back into my room. I've rehung Ali's shirt, choosing instead a long-sleeved sweater. It's blue. Cozy. Smells like Tide. Before grabbing my shoes from the closet, I run a hand over the raised details of Ali's tee and promise myself something: one day soon, I'll wear it.

I'll be brave. Like she was.

"So Auntie sold me her old Honda, but the seats are disgusting. Brielle, are you listening?"

"Of course."

"Okay, and this guy who works at the Auto Body said if I came by during his shift, he'd give me a discount. But Delia has to work, so she dropped me here."

"Jelly's is on Main. She couldn't have just dropped you on her way?"

My Uggs are in place now, and my scarf is around my neck. Where's my jacket?

"Okay, okay. I'm not using you for your wheels. I need your opinion too."

"You need my opinion on seat covers?"

I take a second and actually look at her. She's got her hair all Princess Leia'd out—cinnamon buns on the side of her head. Adorable, actually. Except she's scowling at me.

"You *so* weren't listening. Seat covers I can choose. It's the boy selling me the seat covers I'm not so sure about."

"Oh, yes. The boy. 'Cause I have so much experience."

"Yes. Well. I'm ignoring that. You ready?"

I can't find my jacket, but—I peek out my bedroom window—maybe I don't need one today. It's not raining. And I'm wearing a sweater.

"Yes," I say, making my decision. "Let's go."

Kay skips through the kitchen and out the door. I see no need to skip but must admit her energy's a bit contagious.

Before leaving the house I glance at my lambskin gloves sitting on the kitchen table. I hold my hands in front of me and stare at them for a moment, but they remain steady. Not a shake. Not a tremor. With a deep breath I propel my legs toward the kitchen door and over the threshold. The door swings shut behind me, and I dig out my keys.

Before I can change my mind, I lock the gloves inside.

Braving the day without a jacket or gloves.

I'm a daredevil.

"Come on, slow poke," Kay says. "His shift ends at one."

Slugger's just cruised onto the highway when a horn yelps pathetically behind us. In the rearview I see a Karmann Ghia riding my bumper.

It's Jake.

And he's waving like an idiot. He pulls up next to us at one of the two stoplights on Main. He cranks his window down, and I do the same.

"You dry out last night?" he says.

"I did. You?"

"Barely."

"So you're a Volkswagen fan too?" I'm smiling far too much, I know I am. My teeth dry in the cold air and stick to my lips.

"Fan might be an overstatement." He laughs. "It was available."

"Yo, Matthews," says the voice next to me. "It's green."

It is. The light's green and I ease onto the gas, remembering I have a passenger. I catch Kaylee's eye and grin. Everything about her face is spread wide: her mouth, her eyes, her comedically flaring nostrils.

"You have been home for exactly six days. How did that happen?"

"What?" I try to look innocent. I do. I try.

"Gabrielle Matthews!"

"Kaylonice Kostopoulos!"

She shrinks in her seat. "You win."

How did I not know this was coming?

"Okay, look, we have calculus together."

"Uh, hello. That was so not an 'I-remember-you-from-calculus' smile." Air quotes.

"And photo."

A carefully manicured eyebrow disappears into her hairline.

"And I ran into him yesterday, okay?" I avoid her glare as I slide Slugger into park and climb out.

"Details, Matthews," she demands over the top of the car.

"Later."

"You're a big fat liar. You have no intention of telling me anything later."

Jake parks next to me, and I cringe. This is a conversation I really don't want to have in his presence. But Kaylee's giving me that look, like she might sic her air quotes on me again.

"Details. Now."

"Later," I hiss. "After we rate the Auto Body guy. I swear. You can come over, and I'll spill my guts. Every last one of them. Now go. Choose seat covers."

She grins, triumphant, and takes a cynical glance at Jake's car before prancing away, stumbling over her scarf.

Now that it's parked, I take a better look at his Karmann Ghia and understand Kaylee's wary glance entirely. The car is light blue. At least it was at one point. The paint is chipping, and the rear bumper nearly drags on the pavement. One of the back doors is missing a handle, and the other is red.

Jake climbs out and rounds the car.

"This was the only thing available?" I ask.

"I guess it was the *first* thing available," he says. "I'm not really a car person. Did I choose poorly?"

In his hand is a piece of paper. The application for Photo

Depot. He's wearing a black thermal shirt today with an army-green bomber jacket over it. Jeans and Chucks again.

"I spill something?"

"No, sorry," I say, embarrassed. "I just . . . You look warm."

Yeah. That didn't suck.

"Downgraded already? Last night I was hot."

Blood rushes my face, but I maintain my composure. "Your hands. Your hands are hot."

"Ah. Thank you for clarifying."

I'm smiling too much again, I fear. My shoulder warms at his closeness, and I'm forced to admit it's not just his hands.

"Has anyone ever told you that, though? How crazy your skin is? It's like werewolf hot."

He flinches at the *Twilight* reference, and I'm surprised at how much I enjoy the jab.

"Well, I rarely howl at the moon, if that helps."

"I can teach you. It's part of the jungle dance."

"Do I still need a tutu?"

"Afraid so."

He's dodged the question altogether, but my curiosity is not dissuaded. We have a deal, though. He's promised that understanding will come with time, so although I was hoping for some first-person insight, I'll just have to enjoy this strange sensation without understanding it—something that seems perfectly within my capacity this afternoon.

"I'd better go," he says, lifting the application. "Interview."

"Cool," I say. "Good luck."

"You haven't—haven't seen that guy again, have you?"

"Not since Friday."

"But you'll call, right? If you do."

"Cross my heart."

Am I flirting?

He smiles. "See you tomorrow," he says.

"Yeah. See ya."

Four steps take me into the Auto Body, Stratus's only auto parts store. Kaylee's been watching me through the glass.

She attacks me in the aisle with all the scratch-n-sniff trees.

"Sooooo, where is he?"

"He?"

"He, him, the man-child-appeared-out-of-nowhere. The hot guy with the crappy car."

"Oh, him."

"Yeah, him. Where in the world did he apparate from?"

She smacks a wad of neon-green gum while she waits for me to answer. I can't help but squirm.

"Oh, oh, oh . . . there he is."

At first I think she's talking about Jake, and I spin toward the door. "No, at the register. What do you think?"

A roundish, dimpled boy is ringing up a customer. He's cute in a just-saw-*The-Phantom-Menace*-for-the-hundredth-time kind of way. "He's . . . endearing."

She groans. "You mean geeky."

"Aren't you leaving anyway? Peace Corps and all that?"

"I'm not looking for *forever*, Elle. I'm looking for prom."

"Oh well, then. I think he's a dream. Put that guy in a tux, give him a boutonniere, and you've got yourself a pretty picture."

She glares at me. "You could always ask Hot Boy if he has a friend."

I grab a handful of strawberry-scented trees. "You pick out your seat covers?"

"Wuss."

She flits to the counter and bats her purple eyelashes at Dimples. He gives her a 20 percent discount on a pair of leopard-print seat covers, and she promises to call him later. When we leave the store, his number's still on the counter.

She's shameless.

"That poor boy really thought you were going to call him, Kay."

"Did he?" Her faux innocence isn't fooling me, and she knows it. "Ah, well. You have a hot guy. I want one now."

I'm about to argue her premise when I notice something pinned under Slugger's windshield wiper.

"What's that?" Kay asks.

"I don't know." I lift the wiper and pull the paper free, open it, and read.

Brielle,

Had to cancel my interview. Emergency. Leaving town for a few days, but I have something for you at my house. The door's unlocked. I hope you smile when you see my address.

Jake

Below his name is the address of the old Miller place. I draw in a slow breath. He's my neighbor. He sleeps less than a football field away from my bedroom window.

13

Brielle

on't tell me!" she squeals. "It's from Hot Guy, isn't it? Isn't it?"

I almost forgot Kaylee was here.

"Your shoe's untied," I tell her, diving into the driver's seat.

"Oh, that's how it is. We're keeping secrets now. Fine. But just remember, Twinkle Toes, you promised me details."

Parked in the line at Burgerville, I try to devise a plan to ditch Kaylee and come up with nothing. Kaylee gets a salad, and I order a burger.

"How can you possibly fit into a leotard after eating like that?"

"Ah, but I don't have to fit into a leotard anymore." Although truth be told, I have an incredibly high metabolism. I could eat a burger a day and not worry about it. The downside: no boobs.

"You're really not dancing anymore?"

"I don't know, Kay." Two days ago I would have sworn that the stage was completely off limits, but today I wonder if I might, one day, feel different. "Not now anyway."

"That's fair. It is, Elle. It's fair. But you have a gift, right? You know that. A gift that got you outta here. A gift every senior in Stratus would kill for."

Her choice of words makes me flinch.

"A gift that led me to a very dark place, Kay. I'm not saying it's entirely off the table, but can we just let it go for now?"

She shrugs. "I guess."

Faster than I can cram a fry into my mouth, her frown turns into a huge cheesy smile.

"Besides, you have something else to dish about."

"And what's that?" I throw Slugger into park. We're home.

"Oh, come on!" she squeals, jumping out of the car.

"Well, um . . . we have calculus together."

"Uh-huh."

"And that's sort of where we met."

"Sort of?"

"Well, we didn't really get a chance to talk until photo on Monday," I say.

"So that's it? You meet in calculus, hung out in photo, and now you're . . . what? You're dating?"

"No, not dating," I say. "Not dating."

I figured I'd have to whip out the story about the storm, and I do, recounting the same version I told Dad and omitting anything about my injured ankle. As far as they know, Jake and I both got caught out in the rain and hail, and at his invitation we weathered the storm in the relative safety of the shed. Kaylee hangs on every word and, unlike Dad, asks question after question about insignificant, miniscule details—details I was sure to have missed, given the reality of the situation.

We cover the lighting, Jake's wardrobe, the state of my hair, the leaky shed, and my poor choice of rainy-day activity, and then Kaylee pops one last cherry tomato into her mouth.

"You totally need something like this. Nothing too intense, you know. A fling. A fling with a hot guy." Air quotes around the word *fling*. She tosses her salad container across the kitchen, aiming pathetically for the trash can.

She misses, and the plastic box clatters to the ground. I force myself to smile as I pick it up, wishing more than anything it was Ali sitting across from me, balanced on the kitchen counter. She would have known that a "fling" isn't at all what I need.

Much to my chagrin, Kaylee stays until Dad gets home. He drops his tool belt on the porch and pulls me into a hug. I can see he's pleased to find I have company. In my absence, work and his crew of roughnecks have become his life, and I wonder if these quiet nights at home with me bore him now.

Kaylee kisses my cheek and trips out the door, winking conspiratorially at Dad. I should have known he'd ask her to keep me company. I feel like a prisoner, being transferred from one guard's custody to the next. I'm dying to find out what Jake left me and was counting on having a chance to run over there before Dad got home.

That certainly didn't happen.

Dad makes his famous spaghetti and meatballs, and I pick at my food while he tells me about his day. I alternately nod and shake my head when he tells me how the economy has affected logging and about all the damage the recent rain has caused Stratus—all the while praying he has some evening plans. I stand and rinse my plate, stacking it in the dishwasher.

"So what do you want to do, kiddo? Movie night?"

"Sure, but do you mind if I make the trip to the video store? I don't think I can handle battling robots tonight."

"Whatever you want to watch is fine with me. Just nothing with that DiCaprio guy." He drops his plate into the sink and stretches loudly. "Gimme a sec to change and I'll come with you."

He's exhausted. Why doesn't he want to grab a beer and crash on the couch? Maybe he thinks I'm suicidal?

"Umm . . . would it be okay if I went alone? Kaylee's been here all day, and I could use some peace and quiet."

It's the truth. After an afternoon with Kaylee, some time alone would do me good.

"Are you sure? I can be real quiet when I try," he says, pretending to lock his lips and throw away the key. I walk over and wrap my arms around him.

"It's not you, Dad. Really. I'd just like some time alone, and I'll come back with a movie we can both live with. I promise."

He squeezes his assent—begrudgingly, I can tell—and I wait until he's safely in the shower before I take off.

I drive the hundred yards to Jake's, parking on the far side of the farmhouse so Dad won't notice Slugger if he steps outside for any reason. Jamming the keys into my pocket, I jump out of the car and make my way up the three steps onto the wrap-around porch.

The Miller place has been here for ages. It has that old, sturdy feel about it—I imagine it was built by contractors who felt the best way to ensure stability was to use as much wood and as many nails as possible. I lean against one of the wooden posts on the porch, a square column that's easily bigger around than two of me. It's cool to the touch, and a shiver runs down my back.

I'm . . . excited.

I need to be quick. Dad will be waiting for a gender-neutral movie, and it would be unfair to make him worry two nights running. Still, as I open the screen door, my calves tighten.

Out of habit I knock on the door twice before placing my hand on the knob and turning. I stick my head and shoulders inside as the door squeaks open.

"Hello?"

No one answers. I flex my hands to stop the shaking and step inside.

Not only has Jake left the door unlocked, but the living room light is on. Like Jake, the room is warm and bright. Boxes are stacked thigh-high throughout the room. The only thing that looks unpacked is a gigantic entertainment system. Flush with all the trimmings, it covers an entire wall. The ridiculously oversized speakers are impressive. Dad would go into cardiac arrest if he knew the potential volume of noise this house could generate.

Like Jake, the entertainment system looks out of place in Stratus, but the rest of the house is remarkably conservative. Beneath the boxes is a sparse collection of older furniture. Nothing presumptuous. Nothing expensive. And there, in the center of the room, is a shabby cherry-wood coffee table with a dictionary-sized cigar box as its only ornament.

It couldn't be more obvious: this is what Jake left me. The table sits wrapped in a swell of heat, the cigar box rippling like a desert mirage. I walk down a wide aisle made by the unpacked boxes. The uneven patter of my footsteps against the hardwood floor and the blood pounding in my head make the silent room seem noisy.

Now I'm standing directly in front of it. Waves of heat emanate from the box, warming my legs. I sink to the floor and reach out hungrily, pulling the box onto my lap. Feeling all the drama of a good mystery, I flip open the lid.

And scratch my head.

I have no idea what I'm looking at.

If forced to call it something, I'd say it was a gold ring, but that doesn't even begin to explain it. Though it resembles Dad's wedding band, it's far too large to be worn on a finger. It's the width of my thumb, all the way around its twenty-inch circumference, give or take. If it *is* to be worn, it would fit more appropriately on the head, like a metallic headband or a crown.

My face feels flushed with the heat radiating off the thing, and it looks so much like liquid gold that when I reach out to touch it, I half expect the creature Gollum to tackle me. I run my index finger along the top, in a circular fashion, and though fairy tale creatures remain safely in their books, the ring continues to impress.

I'm a bit more courageous now, and knowing it won't burn me, I lift it gently with two hands. The ring is hard and smooth to the touch. I spin it slowly, feeling the burnished surface. Every bit of light in the room seems both absorbed by it and reflected in it. I suppress an urge to place it on my head, and as quickly as the thought surfaces, the ring acts of its own accord. It contracts upon itself, twisting and flowing like molten lava.

I gasp and release it. It falls into the box, where it lands ever so lightly, having taken the shape of a two-inch-wide arm cuff—the liquid gold surging and flowing, finally solidifying.

As the heat washes over my face and neck, I gaze into the box, my distorted reflection staring back at me from the rounded cuff. It's a moment or two before I realize the cuff is reflecting something in the lid of the box: another note. I grab and open it in one motion.

This will help.

Jake hasn't addressed it or signed it, but both are unnecessary. His heat signature is all over the little piece of paper. I have no idea what this magnificent trinket is, but that it's something beyond technology, beyond human understanding, is entirely plain.

How did Jake come across it? Is this the source of the mystery surrounding him, or just another piece of the puzzle?

He intends me to wear it—that much is obvious—and I want more than anything to make him happy, to honor this borrowed gift by putting it on immediately.

Still, I hesitate.

Never put it on. Isn't that what Gandalf told Frodo?

Feeling reckless, and maybe a little brave, I pick up the cuff, fantastically surreal, and slide it onto my left wrist.

Amazing.

It's like Jake is holding my sleeve again. That same blaze of fire, calm and reassuring, travels up my arm and spreads to the rest of my being. The stress of the day vanishes. The grief that shakes my hands darts away.

I am at peace.

14

Brielle

I need to make good on my commitment to Dad, so I don't linger at Jake's house. Tucking the cigar box under my arm and snapping off the lights, I step onto the porch and lock the door behind me. According to Jake's note, he has no idea how long he'll be gone, and I can't imagine leaving the door unlocked one minute longer with that colossal entertainment system in there. Granted, someone would have to rent a moving van to get it all out, but I've lived in the city long enough to appreciate the passion of a thief.

The cuff is hidden under the sleeve of my hoodie, but as I go through the motions of driving to and from the video store, I wonder vaguely what I'll tell Dad if he sees it. I can't imagine. I'm suddenly grateful for the coming winter and the opportunity to wear long sleeves.

Without much thought I decide on a Steve Carell movie. It's fairly middle-of-the-road. Not at all bloody, in case I happen to actually catch some of it, and certainly not too girly. I grab some popcorn and am back home in a flash, having taken marginally more time than normal.

Still, Dad notices. He snaps my thigh with the towel he's using to dry his hair. "I was about to call the sheriff again, kid. What took so long?"

"You just got out of the shower. I could ask you the same thing." I do my best to sound exasperated, and he lets it go.

We sit side by side on the couch, munching on popcorn, our minds in two different places: his on the raunchy humor and mine on the fascinating turn my life has taken in the past three days. My body's reaction to the cuff has not subsided. On the contrary, not only is my body entirely heated and at ease, but I can literally feel my muscles relaxing. My shoulders and back unknot. My head bobs forward on excessively relaxed neck muscles, and I have trouble keeping my eyes open.

"Brielle, baby," I hear Dad say, "you don't have to stay up with me. Go to bed, little girl."

I mumble something and wander to my room, leaving him to turn off the lights. I climb under the covers, fully dressed. But somewhere between awake and asleep, I realize that the cuff is getting heavier and heavier on my wrist. Where before it felt light as air, it now feels like it weighs ten pounds and is gaining weight with each passing moment.

Irritated, I tug it off and set it on my lap, where again it feels more like steam, weightless and warm, than a piece of clunky jewelry. I'm not entirely awake, and the idea of parting with it and sinking into a freezing cold, numbing state of unrest does not appeal to me. I nearly break into tears at the thought of it.

Before I consider the predicament any further, the cuff begins to twist and coil and unravel. It's breathtaking, really—the liquid-gold shine and the precision with which it moves. I watch through sleepy eyes as it reforms into the crown-sized ring.

Should I wear it on my head to sleep? But what if Dad sneaks in to check on me? That could be an awkward conversation. Instead, I decide to try something. I take the ring in both hands and slide it under my pillow. I force myself to stand and leave it, just long enough to change into a tank top and boxers. Then I crawl back under the covers, crossing my fingers that my experiment has worked.

Ever so slowly I lay my head down, and immediately breathe a sigh of relief. The ring has completely warmed my pillow. The reassuring heat moves down the mattress, down my back, my thighs, my calves, until even my toes are toasty warm. I succumb to the ridiculous serenity of it all and allow thoughts of Jake to pull me into unconsciousness.

My dreams are full of nothing but colors—like oil mixing with rain on the blacktop, they swirl in and out of each other, taking no specific shape and never ceasing in their movement. First a palette of dark blue and purple dances before me, and then a passionate wave of orange and red, followed by shocks of gray and black before a bright green and white wash my mind clear. Over and over again, the colors bow and curve. The heartbreak turning to passion, passion interrupted by mourning, mourning giving birth to new life. It is peace. It is joy. And when I wake ten hours later, I haven't moved an inch.

Lying in bed, I listen to the sounds of a fast-approaching winter. The wind rattles the trash cans outside, and leaden raindrops tap like Fred Astaire against the roof. What will it be like when I have to give this trinket back to Jake? Will I be able to sleep as naturally without it? Probably not, though I'd gladly trade the undisturbed sleep of this night for a day spent in his company.

I wonder if he'll be at school today.

I leave the ring under my pillow and shower quickly. Pulling on a sweatshirt and fleece-lined cargo pants, I run to the kitchen for a bite to eat. Dad's loading his lunch box when I walk through the doorway.

"Hey, baby."

"Mornin,' Dad." I kiss him on the cheek.

He turns suspicious eyes on me again, but I ignore him while I wait for my Pop-Tart to toast.

"I'm outta here," he says from the door.

"See ya, Dad. Be safe."

"You seem . . . happy today."

My Pop-Tart pops.

"Do I?"

"Uh-huh."

I don't really have an answer. I wrap my Pop-Tart in a paper towel, kiss him again, and dash back to my room. "Be safe," I call over my shoulder.

"You said that already."

A minute later I hear the door swing shut behind him.

I'm alone.

I reach under my pillow, feeling around for the ring. To my surprise I pull out the cuff. I have no idea how it knows what I need, but the prospect of seeing Jake hurries me, so I simply slide it on my wrist and run out the door. I chance a look at his house as I climb into Slugger, but there's no way of knowing if he's returned or not.

I'm the first to arrive in calculus, and I busy myself scribbling my name in the front of each of my books. The teacher looks half asleep still and ignores me. Each time the door opens my head snaps up, expecting. Finally the bell rings, and I'm forced to acknowledge that perhaps Jake hasn't returned.

I stare at the blackboard, at the teacher whose name I cannot remember, and pray for steady hands. Lately all my emotions have been so extreme. After Ali, everything was so dark, so sad, and then with Jake and this strange gold ring came excitement and peace. I don't trust my emotions to understand he'll return.

Calculus plods on, though, and I learn something.

Not about mathematics. No, nothing that tedious.

I miss Jake.

Probably more than I should, really.

But without the numbness that had overtaken me before, I'm able to think more clearly. I'm not in pain. I'm just disappointed. I'm not abandoned. I'm just alone. This I can deal with. I slide my right hand inside my left sleeve and grip the cuff. The effect is instantaneous, and my body is aware again of the heat that has not left me.

I eat lunch with Kaylee and allow her to drag me to the parking lot to show off her new seat covers.

I'm sure it has something to do with the strange little cuff buried under my sleeve, but I feel more and more like my old self today. I feel almost right again. For that, and for this borrowed gift, I owe Jake more than I'll ever be able to repay.

The afternoon rolls by, slowly for the most part. Photo arrives, and I hide out in the darkroom sorting through film. We have a critique tomorrow, and I've done absolutely nothing to prepare. Eventually I settle on a shot of a maple leaf—the last one left on the tree. In the background, out of focus, is the dilapidated mess of boards in which Jake and I weathered the storm.

I expose and process the picture and mount it on a golden-yellow backdrop. Using photo oils and a cotton swab, I paint the leaf burnt orange. As the final minutes of class tick by, I lay it out to dry next to several other pictures already in place for the critique.

Maybe Jake will be back by tomorrow.

But Tuesday arrives, and then Wednesday. Still Jake hasn't returned to school. His house, which I glance at more often than strictly necessary, looks the same as it did when I left it on Sunday night. I work hard to focus in my classes and spend both lunch and my after-school hours with Kaylee.

She's different from Ali, to be sure, but her friendship, I'm realizing anew, is something I need.

Ali forced me to think. Forced me to consider. Turned me into a better person because I had discussed life, discussed change, debated my thoughts and abilities. Whenever I was with her, I was always challenged to excel, to move forward, to make a decision. Not because she required it, but because her very presence drew it out of me. Certainly, we had fun, but it wasn't without growth, without change.

With Kaylee, I can just be. I don't have to consider anything other than the present. She doesn't challenge me academically or philosophically, and she is far too clumsy to be my physical equal, but she reminds me of the person I used to be—the person I was before some ballet shoes and a talent scout changed my world forever. She reminds me that I don't have to be so composed, so prodigious all the time.

And I've never slept better. This I can only attribute to Jake's gift. Each night I pull it off my wrist and watch as it transforms exquisitely into the ring. With it tucked safely under my pillow, my dreams persist just as they had that first night: colors and colors, over and over. Each morning I wake in the same position I'd curled up in, and when I reach under my pillow, the cuff is there, warm and waiting.

It's weird that it knows what I need. Strange that it transforms. It gets heavy at night, when it's time to remove it from my wrist. Light as air when it's where it's supposed to be. Like it's nudging me, reminding me to sleep, to rest.

I feel mothered.

What a strange, strange thing.

15

Brielle

Somehow Eddie got my number," Kaylee says. We're sitting across from one another at Jelly's. Cheese fries and hot chocolate between us.

"Eddie?"

"You *so* don't pay attention to me," she says, scowling. "Eddie. The guy from the Auto Body."

"Oh, Dimples."

"That is the worst nickname ever," she says. "Anyway, he asked me to a movie Friday night."

"You going?"

"I don't think so," she says, adding a handful of marshmallows to her mug. "You've inspired me. I'm not settling till I find my Jake."

"Kay . . ."

She waves me off. "You heard from him?"

I stab a cheese fry with my fork.

"And he didn't say when he'd be back?"

"Nope. Maybe today."

"Maybe," she says, showing me her crossed fingers.

We leave the diner and climb into her Honda. She launches into a story about her gym teacher and a ketchup-covered doorknob while I stare out the window and think about what she said. *I'm not settling until I find my Jake.* I remember feeling that way about Ali and Marco: jealous, in a you're-still-my-best-friend sort of way.

She was so adorably in love with him. I remember her disappearing behind that leather journal of hers after their first date. I remember how she smiled through their eternal phone conversations. How she repeated his name in her sleep. How she did his laundry in our tiny dorm washer when his broke. How she panicked when he ran the slightest bit late. She'd named their future children, for crying out loud.

Yeah, Ali loved him. Absolutely loved him.

Right up until he killed her.

It's something I still can't wrap my mind around: Marco killing Ali. If it weren't for the bruises . . . but there were bruises. Lots of them. Maybe if she hadn't trusted him so blindly, she would have seen the violence coming.

I shiver, and like a true friend, Kaylee turns up the heat.

She drops me at the top of my driveway, and I let her talk me into the movies with her and Dimples tomorrow night. Third wheel. Should be fun.

We did our homework at the diner, and Dad's out of town—he and his crew are logging in the mountains a couple hours away—so I have nothing to fill my evening. Maybe I'll upload my digital pics to the computer and mess around in Photoshop for a few hours. Dad won't be back till Sunday night. I bet I can get a collage together of the property before he returns. Kind of an early Christmas present.

Habit pulls my attention through the trees to the old Miller place. My breath hitches. Every window is full of light.

"Brielle? You okay?"

My head whips around. It takes my eyes a second to find him, but there he sits. On our porch swing, in the shade of the awning.

"You're home."

"I am." He laughs.

I tell my legs not to skip toward him, but they only sort of get the message.

"Finally," I mock, fumbling for a slice of pride.

"Sit," he says, sliding over so I can sit next to him on the porch swing. My arm presses against his, and I note with relief that he's still very, very warm.

"You missed the critique," I say. "In photo." I try to be nonchalant but fail miserably.

"What was your picture of?"

"A maple leaf."

"You win?"

"No," I say, forcing my gaze to the street and kicking my legs to get the swing moving. "Grace had a time-lapse photo of the storm hitting Main Street."

"Was it good?"

"It got my vote. I blame you for the loss, though."

"Me?"

"Yes, you. I lost by one vote."

"Oh, and you assume I would have . . ." He stands and raises his right hand, like he's swearing to tell the truth, the whole truth, and nothing but the truth. "I shall never be absent again."

"At least not on critique Tuesdays. I don't take losing well."

"Understandable," he says, turning back to me. He leans against the rail, his expression soft. "You got the box I left you?"

I slide my sleeve up and show him. "I did. Thank you so much, by the way. I have no idea how, but it really helps."

"What do you think of it?" he asks.

There's something about the way he says it, like it's the most important question he'll ever ask. I have no idea what I think but can't imagine that answer being adequate.

"It's beautiful," I say. There are just far too many adjectives to describe the thing. "Can you tell me what it is exactly?"

"Absolutely, but I'd like you to meet Canaan first, if that's okay?" He takes my hands and pulls me to my feet. "Your dad's not home?"

"Na. He's working."

A grin stretches his face like taffy, and I smile with him. It's impossible not to.

"What are you smiling at?"

He releases my hands and starts down the porch stairs. "Come on," he says, pushing through the trees toward his house. I follow him, the smell of wet pine and damp grass everywhere.

"You're awful at answering questions."

"It's a sickness. I'm working on it."

"You do that." Eleven steps later I ask, "So where have you been? I mean, I know you like to cut class, but three days?"

"Canaan got called away for work. Didn't want to leave me behind."

"Wow, he *is* overprotective."

"You have no idea," he says.

"Dad's left me behind for years."

"By yourself?"

"When I was younger I stayed with Kaylee and her aunt, but that's just a whole lotta chaos. I'm sure Canaan will loosen up eventually."

"Doubtful. But it's okay. He hasn't yanked me out of school since Spain. He was due."

"You lived in Spain?" Surprise after surprise. Puzzle piece after puzzle piece. Will I ever capture the entire picture?

"And Vienna. London for a few months." He doesn't seem enamored by this information. In fact, it seems to bore him. "For the past two years or so, we've been back in the U.S. I prefer it that way."

"Do you? I've only been on the one European tour, but we were shuffled around so much we didn't get to do much sight-seeing. I saw the Eiffel Tower from a bus. How lame is that? I'd really like to go back."

"I'll take you, then. One day. I'm a great tour guide," he says easily. So easily I'm lost again in the comfort and warmth of everything about him.

"I have to warn you, though, I hate flying."

"Really? That's funny."

His lips curve in that mischievous way, and he laughs. I love it. Could never hear enough of it.

"Bet you'd feel different if you had wings," he says.

"Well, who wouldn't?"

We're just steps from his front door now, and the fact that I have no idea how to do this smacks me in the face.

I've never been introduced to a guy's parents in a formal way. We all just sort of know each other here in Stratus. And Austen is an all-girls prep school—a place most parents ship their kids to without making much of an appearance. Jake, on the other hand, has apparently moved quite a lot and lived in some pretty exotic places. Surely he could give me some advice. But he doesn't stop as we climb the stairs.

He opens the door and pulls me through like he's done it a thousand times before.

The room has changed. The weathered cherry-wood table is still in the same place, as is the monstrosity of an entertainment center, but that's about it. The boxes have been cleared, evidently unpacked. An oversized armchair, couch, and love seat are positioned around the table, pointed at the entertainment center. Nothing is new, but it all looks well cared for. Past the living room is the kitchen, open and bright, with a small table and four chairs. To the right of the kitchen is a hallway, which I can only speculate leads to the bedrooms.

"Wow. Unpacked already?"

"Yeah, Canaan can't stand a mess. He worked all morning," Jake says. "Speaking of Canaan." He nods at the back door, visible through the kitchen. A man enters—the same man I saw on Main Street last week. He's even taller than I remember, his arms laden with boxes. His silhouette takes up nearly every inch of the door frame, leaving the gray light of December's first week to fill in the meager gaps.

"Canaan," Jake says, tugging me into the kitchen by my sleeve, "this is Brielle."

Canaan sets the stack of boxes down, spreading them evenly across the kitchen table to prevent it from tipping. As he draws closer, his large hand extended, another piece of the puzzle slides into place.

Waves of heat roll off his arms and chest—hotter even than Jake's skin. Hotter than the cuff latched on to my wrist. With the increase in temperature comes that remarkable peace, and for a fleeting moment my legs feel weak. His mitt of a hand, larger than Dad's even, swallows mine whole, and I regain my strength. His silver hair matches his eyes precisely, offset by a vibrant tawny complexion. Without being feminine in the slightest, he is striking.

Once, in Portland, I was introduced to a Nobel Prize winner. He was small and mousy, stank of sauerkraut, and had sweat stains in the armpits of his dress shirt. Still, something intangible made me very aware I was in the presence of genius. I felt lucky, special. Surely not many could claim they'd had the honor.

I have that same feeling now, minus the gag reflex.

"Brielle," Canaan says. "So happy to meet you. Jake can't stop talking about you. I hear you're quite the dancer."

My face warms, and I elbow Jake in the ribs.

"Thank you," I say. "It's great to meet you too."

Jake chuckles and pulls out a kitchen chair for me. I sit. He takes the chair next to mine as Canaan crosses to the sink to rinse his hands.

"I hope you're available for dinner," Canaan says. "Lasagna and baked apples."

Homemade dinner with Jake? Beats string cheese and a cup of yogurt any day.

"I'd like that. Thank you."

"Jake tells me you teach dance as well?"

Payback.

"Mm-hmm. Jake's asked for lessons," I say.

Canaan dries his hands. "Is that so?"

"Yeah. As soon as he has a tutu, we'll begin."

"Those are skirts, yes? Lace and, umm . . ."

"Tulle. Jake said he'd like an orange one."

Canaan's brow creases. "Well, his birthday's in January. I think something can be arranged."

Jake drums his fingers on the table and snorts.

"What?" I say, all innocence.

"Just trying to picture Canaan shopping for a tutu."

Canaan laughs, loud and free.

"Come on," Jake says. "I'll show you the rest of the house." He punches Canaan in the shoulder as we pass, which only serves to embolden Canaan's laughter.

There is something so attractive about a man who is able to laugh shamelessly. Both Jake and Canaan have it turned into an art form.

"This is the study," Jake says, waving his hand into a room with two large desks at opposite ends. A large bookcase covers the far wall.

Quiet awe slips from my mouth as I stop in the doorway. "Read much?" I say, stepping into the room. I turn in a slow circle. Shelves line all four walls, giving way only for the desks. Book spines stare back at us from nearly every empty space.

"This? This is nothing. We have boxes and boxes in the basement."

"Why?"

"Canaan and I like to read." He shrugs.

I walk to the nearest bookcase and pull out the first book I see. *"The Doorman and His Whiskers of Wonder?"* I raise my eyebrows at Jake.

His nose wrinkles, and he takes the book from my hands. "Yeah, some of them we really should throw away." He dumps it into the wastepaper basket by the door. "There's a reason you can get that book for ninety-nine cents on Amazon."

I follow him out the door and down the hall.

"This is where Canaan sleeps," he says, gesturing to a room on the right.

Feeling incredibly nosy, I stick my head inside and glance around. His room is so simple. An open window casts more gray light onto a large bed. With its black wrought-iron frame twisting floor to ceiling and dressed in a feathery down comforter—white as snow—it is, by far, the largest bed I've ever seen. A glossy nightstand, lacquered white, sits to the left of the bed, with a black alarm clock and lamp adorning it. At the foot of the bed is a hefty black chest. A closet has been carved out of the far wall, and above the bed hangs a framed photo of a white dove, wings spread against a velvety black sky.

"What a great shot!"

"You and Grace aren't the only dedicated photographers in Stratus," Jake says, placing a hand on my back and leading me into the room. It's a small, innocent gesture, but the heat sends a shiver up my spine, and goose bumps appear on my arms. It's a response I've never had to heat, and I rub my arms to rid them of the spontaneous prickles. Jake doesn't seem to notice.

"Canaan took that?" I ask, stopping at the foot of the bed.

The photograph is quite impressive. It's like the dove paused midflight, and the lighting is immaculate. Every detail on the dove is visible, down to the individual feather barbs. Though the shot was obviously taken at night, there's no awkward flash discoloration, which is hard to accomplish.

"I took it," Jake says. "In London. I had a lot of free time. We lived there during the summer, and Canaan was insanely busy with work. He liked this shot so much I blew it up and framed it for him. It seemed to fit."

"It defines the room, Jake. Really, it's flawless."

"Thank you," he says. He leans toward me, his hand moving toward my face. My stomach clenches as I breathe in the warmth of his skin, and I swear my chest purrs. He touches my cheek briefly, and when he pulls his hand away there's an eyelash resting on his fingertip. "Come on. One more room."

I silently chasten the purring butterflies and follow him out. He leads me past a bathroom to the end of the hallway and opens a door on the left-hand side.

"This is my room."

"I was hoping you had one," I say, a little nervous.

I'm all worked up after the eyelash, and not that I have any preconceived notions about Jake's bedroom, but it takes me off guard.

It's scandalous.

A disaster.

A complete and utter mess.

There are four or five boxes still packed. His bed isn't made. Books, newspapers, and magazines are scattered everywhere. Jeans and T-shirts hang from the lamp, the doorknob, and the handles of the dresser. After giving him superhero status, this blatant display of his humanity makes me giggle.

"Should I ask which of you is the neat freak?"

"Canaan. Definitely Canaan." He collapses onto the bed, wincing as he lands on the corner of a very large book. "I have to beg him on hands and knees to leave my room alone. Especially on days like today when he's unpacking and speed cleaning all at the same time."

"And making lasagna."

"The best lasagna ever," Jake says, tossing things off his bed. "Normally I'm a much bigger help, but I had an errand to run. I barely beat you home."

There's something about the way he says it . . .

"Were you *trying* to beat me home?"

Jake shoves a newspaper to the floor and pats the spot next to him.

I narrow my eyes.

"You're welcome to the desk chair, if you'd prefer."

I wouldn't. I wouldn't prefer.

I do my best to look unaffected as I climb up next to him. I cross my legs, careful to keep my muddy boots off the bed, and lean against the wall.

"You comfortable?" he asks, his smile like a tiny crescent moon.

"Perfectly. Go ahead."

His finger brushes my wrist as he hooks it through the cuff and pulls it off. "I thought you'd like an explanation maybe. About this, and maybe a few other things."

I sit up straighter. I would definitely like an explanation. Or two.

"Like how you fixed my ankle, and why you're so hot?"

My hands fly to my mouth.

Really? Did I just do it again?

"Yes, those things should be explained." His lips betray a hint of amusement, but the grin resting there is subtle. "You know," he says, "I've been told before that I have warm hands, but my 'hotness' has never been remarked upon."

"Did you just use air quotes?" I ask.

"Sorry. I have government with your friend Kaylee. I'm kind of 'addicted.'"

"Oh. My. Goodness."

"Anyway . . ." He places the cuff on the bed between us and takes a deep breath. "*This* is supernatural, Elle. *This* is how I healed your ankle."

My mouth is dry, probably because it's hanging open. I lick my lips and swallow slowly.

"And how does that work exactly?"

"I can't tell you the mechanics of it. And not because I don't want to. I don't understand everything about it myself."

"But you understand *some* things?"

"Yes, some things. It has a few physically obvious attributes. For example, it can take more than one form." Even as we watch, the cuff begins to thin and expand, reforming itself into the large ring. "And then there's the warmth . . ."

"Heat," I correct, as my pant leg grows feverish. Even inches away, the ring affects me.

"Okay, heat," he says. "More than anything, it seems to make things right. To restore them to their created purpose."

Created purpose? For some reason that phrase makes me uneasy.

"What does that mean, exactly?"

"It means we may each respond to it differently, making it even harder to understand. Although some things seem fairly consistent. When Canaan first gave it to me—"

"Canaan?"

"It's his," Jake says. "I found it one morning while rummaging through his room for a baseball mitt. I was eight and had been with Canaan for nearly two years. As screwed up as my parents were, I still missed them."

"Of course. You were a kid."

"Right. So to me, this became security," he explains, running his knuckles over the ring. "Its heat brought an unshakable sense of faith in Canaan and an awareness of complete sanctuary. In all his years, Canaan's never taken another child into his care. Just me. For a long time I wore this thing everywhere. Some kids have teddy bears, some kids have security blankets. I had this. It was my safe haven, and when I was parted from it, anxiety consumed me."

"And now?"

Who gives up that kind of peace for someone they've known a week?

"I haven't worn it in years," he says. "It became difficult to hide as I got older. It's not all that easy for a guy to get away with wearing something like this."

I run my finger around the edge of it, feeling open, vulnerable, and being okay with it. I like talking to him like this. It's quiet. Comfortable. It feels safe.

"I almost didn't put it on," I tell him. "But I was so cold. And being close to it was like . . . being close to you. It was like having your hands wrapped around my ankle again. Only, hotter maybe."

He leans his head against the wall.

"Hotter than me?" He's teasing, his eyes burning back at me. I would never, ever tell him this, but right now I can't imagine anything hotter than he is.

Canaan sticks his head in. "Hey, there."

Blood rushes to my face. We're not doing anything wrong. But I'm on a bed, with a boy. A first for me.

"You guys all right back here? High school seniors are not supposed to be this quiet."

"We're good," Jake says, running a hand through his hair. "Thanks, Canaan."

"All right, then. Dinner in about an hour." His eyes linger on the ring, and then his head disappears. He leaves the door wide open.

He's such a dad.

"Sorry," Jake says.

"Are you kidding? He's great. My dad would have already shown you his rifle collection. Up close."

Jake's eyes widen. "Good to know."

I turn my eyes back to the ring. There's still so much I don't understand. "If you don't wear it anymore, what about my ankle? How did you, you know, do that?"

"It's become such a fundamental part of my makeup that the source of its power is extended to me even when I'm not wearing it."

Source of its power?

"When Canaan asked me to accompany him on Sunday, I knew the only way I'd feel comfortable leaving Stratus was if you felt as safe and secure as this had always made me. I didn't realize, however, that you responded to me in the exact same way."

I avert my eyes, looking for courage in the corner of the room, but there's none to be found. Books, clothes, discarded CD cases, but no courage. I give up and turn back to him.

"Well, not *exactly.*"

"No?"

"Well, no. I mean . . ."

His face is so innocent, so curious.

"This thing is pretty and all, but I doubt Mr. Burns would let it vote on critique Tuesdays."

"Ah. And that changes things?"

I'm quiet now, embarrassed. But I continue.

"I could give this back to you right now with very little pain. I may not be able to sleep, and I'd have to wear gloves from time to time. I'd probably fall to pieces daily, but I'm confident now I'd eventually resemble something of my former self. For the past few weeks I've managed. Poorly, but I've managed." I blink away the tears. "But I can't imagine . . . A lot of people have disappeared on me, you know? Ali. My mom. I just . . . I'd hate to get all—and then have you . . ."

"I'm not leaving, Brielle," he says, resting a hand on my knee. My eyes close as a surge of heat shoots down my leg.

"But you could," I say, pulling my knee from his grip.

"Of course I *could*. But that doesn't mean—"

"But you could," I say with finality.

We're quiet for a minute—twenty-three of Jake's blinks, to be accurate—and then I remember something he said that doesn't make any sense.

"You said something before."

"I said a lot of things."

"Something about the source of its power?"

His cheek lifts slightly, and a small smile emerges. He lifts the ring from the bed and holds it at eye level. "What does this look like to you?"

"A ring. Not big enough for circus animals to jump through, of course," I say, trying to break the tension. "But way too big to wear on your finger."

He bites his lower lip and narrows his eyes. "Where *would* you wear it?"

My phone rings.

I curse under my breath at the interruption and fish my cell phone from my back pocket. I intend to silence it, but when I see the number my tummy does this sick little flip thing and I know I have to answer it.

"Jake, I'm so sorry. Do you mind? It's Ali's mom."

"Not at all. Answer. Please."

"Serena?" I say. "Everything okay?"

"No," she says. "No, it's not. Marco's out, Brielle. And I think he's headed to Stratus."

16

Canaan

*I*t's back: The darkness. The fear.

Canaan doesn't hesitate. With a demon nearby, he can't afford to. He transfers to the Celestial and turns his eyes to the room at the end of the hall.

Jake sits on his bed, facing the girl. She's on the phone, her back stiff, the black tar of fear soaking through her shirt and pouring thickly onto the floor. A fog rises like steam from the muck and settles heavily around them. From under her blond hair, the clingy substance oozes, running the length of her body. Her hands shake, desperate to be rid of it.

She isn't alone in her distress. It's leaking from Jake as well— his pants saturated. Fear is pooled on the floor of his room, but is not content with only two victims. Like a heat-seeking missile, it runs into the hall looking for someone, anyone to attach itself to.

If human beings could only see the manifestation of such a weapon, they would understand how it paralyzes, literally holding them captive with the glue of it.

Like every being of light, Canaan hates fear. It has little effect on him, but humans can't make such a claim. Only Celestial eyes can see it for what it is. Black and thick. Like tar, but icy and alive. It clings and oozes. It weighs down its victims until they are either frozen in a trench of indecision or worse—they make the first possible move, no matter how unwise, simply to rid themselves of it.

It's the deadliest weapon the Fallen possess. They can inflict it, to be sure, but the tragedy of fear is that since the Fall, humans have held it inside their very being and can unleash it, even unwittingly, on themselves and on others.

The girl's body is shaking more violently now. Canaan rises into the sky and examines the little town again. Patches of darkness spread here and there—fear and doubt, sadness and corruption, but no sign of Damien. Nothing to indicate an attack is imminent.

He slows his wings and allows himself to sink through the roof and into the kitchen. As soon as his feet touch the floor he forces himself into the Terrestrial, the earthly realm, just in time to see Brielle stumble out of Jake's room. She runs past him and out the front door.

Jake is behind her, moving slowly, unsure.

"What's happened?"

"I don't know," Jake says, his face ashen. "She got a phone call, and then it was like she couldn't stand to be near me."

He's in pain. Her rejection is what he fears most, and Canaan's been concerned for some time now that it could hinder the mission. It also hurts Canaan that this girl could cause Jake anguish. His time on this planet has not made him immune to the complexities of human relationships, and he is continually amazed at how much despair they cause one another. He steps toward his charge and places one hand on each shoulder.

"You can't let fear keep you from her," Canaan tells him. "I don't fully understand our role in the life of Brielle Matthews, but I know everything you and I have done together, everyone we've helped, has led us to this girl. Lives hang in the balance, Jake."

"I know. I just . . ."

Canaan can see his young charge struggling against something. He'd bet it's the same *something* that's been bothering Jake for days. Finally, he is able to put it into words.

"I can't force myself on her, Canaan."

Ah. That's the crux of it.

"The choice is hers, Jake," Canaan says. "It always has been and always will be."

"Is it?" Jake asks. "If we know even part of the outcome, how do we know she really has a choice?"

"Just because she hasn't made them yet, doesn't mean the decisions aren't hers to make." They've had similar discussions before. "Do you feel you've been robbed of choice?"

He lifts his chin. "Of course not."

"Then go," Canaan says.

Jake doesn't hesitate, but it's impossible to know whether it's Canaan's words or his own heart that pulls him after her.

17

Brielle

I run for the door, tripping more than once over books and shoes and my own feet. My shoulder scrapes the wall as I crash down the hallway and past Canaan. He's working over the stove, his face shrouded in steam. I throw the front door open and stumble down the porch steps. Turning right and breaking into an all-out sprint, I don't slow as my Uggs pound onto the road.

I'm on automatic now.

I hear Jake behind me, running and shouting my name. I can't stop. The fear is so real it almost has a face. There is only one place in this town that can erase all emotion from my being, and I head there.

I run until my legs ache and my lungs burn with the winter chill. Finally I reach a chain-link fence with a rusty gate. The roses that grow intertwined in this fence during the spring have withered and died, leaving behind nothing but dead wood.

How fitting.

The Stratus cemetery has been here for ages and has that

historic feel about it. Stone angels and gothic crosses protect the dead and gone. Here and there, pint-sized American flags mark the graves of brave soldiers.

There is such beauty here in the spring, when flowers with short life spans litter the lawn. Just another reminder—to those who don't need reminding—that life doesn't last forever.

Now, in the depths of autumn, there are no flowers to be seen. In their place rotting leaves and sticky mud jam into the thick tread of my boots as I pull open the gate and step onto the cobbled path that leads to my mother's grave.

Dad laid her to rest under a large weeping willow on the northernmost boundary of the cemetery. Beneath the tree's canopy sits a stone bench. I've sat here many times trying to remember what she was like, trying to remember her voice or her arms around me, and always, I feel nothing. I sink to the freezing cement and succumb to the fear, trusting this place to swallow it whole.

Within moments Jake's hands come to rest on my shoulders. The heat melts through my sweater. I stop trembling, and my mind begins to clear.

"I'm sorry," I say.

"What's happened, Brielle?"

I think of Serena. Of all she speculated on the phone. But it's the first sentence that matters.

"Marco's escaped," I say, repeating her words.

"Escaped?"

"Yes, escaped."

Jake circles the bench and sits next to me. He takes my shoulders in his hands and turns me to face him. "They'll catch him. You know that, right? Someone will."

It's something Dad would say—anything to make me feel better. I ignore it.

"They don't really have a lot of details, and what they do know doesn't make much sense."

"Tell me anyway."

A breeze blows through, cooling the tears that have warmed on my cheeks. I swipe at them and pass Serena's information along to Jake. When I'm done, I ball my hands into fists and cram them into my pockets to stop the trembling.

"Serena thinks he's on his way here."

"Why would she think that?"

I close my eyes, and another round of tears slips from beneath my lashes. "In custody, Marco made two requests. The first was to speak to Ali's parents, the second to speak to me. Ali's father's a judge. They have constant surveillance. So Serena figures I'm much easier to get to." I watch the drooping fingers of the willow tree scratch at the ground. "She's right, isn't she?"

Jake doesn't say anything. He doesn't need to. I'm very traceable. Everyone I've danced with or had classes with knows exactly where to find me. Not to mention that Dad's in the book, and Stratus is a ridiculously small town. If Marco makes it here, it's only a matter of time before he finds me.

"The authorities have already phoned the Stratus sheriff's department, and someone's supposed to be getting in contact with me."

"When did this happen? Yesterday? Today?"

"I don't know. I don't think she said."

We sit in silence, Jake like a furnace, his warmth a stark contrast to the frozen bench.

"Why? What purpose could finding you possibly serve?" Jake asks.

I shrink at the thought of the sickening task still before me.

"I was her best friend. The only one who knew how much time she spent with Marco."

"Ah," Jake groans. "You're testifying."

"I'm testifying," I confirm. "I saw the bruising and the change in her behavior. I should have done something. This is the only way I can help now."

"But I thought he confessed?"

"I guess he changed his mind."

Jake puts his arm around my shoulders and squeezes. Fire floods my senses and harmony washes over me.

"We'll figure it out, Brielle."

"Okay," I say, soaking up every ounce of him I can. It's stupid, I know, but I'm close to that heat-induced euphoric trance his proximity brings on, and though I'm conscious of the danger heading my way, I'm no longer afraid.

I stare at the stone angel weeping over my mother's grave. Considering Dad's aversion to religion, I've always thought it strange he chose an angel. Granite wings arch high above a bowed head. I wonder if Dad thought she looked like Mom—if that's why he chose her.

It's an absurd thought. The angel's face is completely obstructed, buried in her hands. It's really only the hair that makes me think of Mom: smooth under her halo with a bounty of curls right at the shoulder.

Wendy, John, and Michael!

Something is sliding into place—another piece of the puzzle has been handed to me. I stand up and take six steps, crossing my mother's grave until I stand before the stone angel. I reach out and trace her halo with my index finger.

Laced with adrenaline, I turn to Jake. He's smiling at me. It's tender, apprehensive.

"You asked me a question earlier, just before Serena called."

Jake stands very slowly and slides his hands into his pockets. "I did."

"Ask me again," I beg, electricity coursing through my veins.

He is quiet and still, but his fiery eyes are active, searching my face.

"The ring," he says. "Where would you wear it?"

I reach out my hand and place it on the solid stone crown of the weeping angel.

"On my head," I answer. "Like her."

Jake swallows, his eyes on mine.

"Yes. That's where Canaan wore it too."

18

Brielle

I'm kneeling on my mother's grave, the weeping angel behind me, Jake on his knees in front of me.

"Canaan's an angel." My voice quivers with revelation.

"Yes, Canaan's an angel."

"And you're . . ."

"Not," he says, shaking his head. *"I'm* not an angel, Elle. Just Canaan."

"But my ankle?"

"I was honest with you about that," Jake says, moving to sit. "Canaan had no way of knowing how I'd respond to the halo. There aren't many examples. It's not common for a Shield to share his halo with a human charge."

"A shield?"

"I'm sorry, an angel. Are you all right? It's a lot, I know."

"Why did you call Canaan a shield?" I ask, ignoring his concern for me.

"Angels have a hierarchy," he says. "Canaan is assigned here." Jake places his hands flat on the moist grass and mud. "He stands guard over certain individuals. He's a Shield. That's his rank."

"His rank."

"Yes," Jake answers, his eyes boring into mine. "Really, I will tell you anything you want to know, but please. Are you all right? Tell me what you're thinking."

What *am* I thinking?

"I don't . . . I don't know." I'm coming unraveled. I can feel it. My voice trembles. "My dad, he doesn't believe in this stuff."

Jake waits, expecting me to continue maybe. But I don't. I want to know what he thinks about my dad's disbelief. What he'd think about mine.

"A lot of people don't believe," he says.

His response isn't adequate, and I dig my fingers into the mud. "He says God's cruel. That He doesn't exist."

Jake's voice is steady. Quiet and calm. "He can't be both, Elle. He can't be cruel and nonexistent."

I'm shivering, the weight of his words too heavy for a girl made of ice. And the questions are piling up. The ice cracking.

"What about Ali?" I say, my voice shrill. "Murdered at eighteen. And my mom, dead before I knew her. A horrible, horrible death, Jake. Cancer at twenty-four." A tremor runs the length of my body. "There are angels? Angels who *protect* humans?"

"I know it's hard—"

"Hard? It's laughable."

But I'm not laughing, I'm shaking. The only thing tethering me to reality is Jake, and even he doesn't seem real. I draw my knees up and curl in on myself, ducking my head, shutting him out.

"But how can I not believe you?" I whisper, trying to will away the doubt. "After my ankle. After the . . . halo."

He places a blazing hot hand on mine. He offers comfort.

Friendship. My lungs beat against my ribs at the gesture, and I want to twist my fingers into his.

Instead, I pull my hand away. I want to forget all he's said and go back to the comfortable ignorance of before. I don't want to know these things. I don't want to know any of it.

"Why tell me?" I ask, frustrated at the knowledge he's given me.

The softness of his face hardens. It turns into something I don't recognize. His eyes bore into mine, their deep brown flame even brighter under the filtered light of the willow tree. He says nothing. His silence angers me.

Another ten seconds pass, and I ask again.

"Why tell me, Jake?"

It's another seventeen erratic heartbeats before his face shifts into resolution and he speaks. "I couldn't keep it from you, Elle. When I realized that, I knew I'd have to tell you."

"After my ankle?"

"No," he says. "Before."

"Before what?"

"We decided to tell you the Saturday before you returned to Stratus."

"What? That's impossible."

"Nothing's impossible," he whispers.

"But that was my last day in the city, and you—you were . . ."

"Still in Chicago," he says, watching my expression. "I know."

I roll back into a sitting position, and we stare at one another. There are just so many questions now. Which one do I ask first?

It's like I've been given the top of the puzzle box—a picture of Jake's world—only to find out it isn't a standard jigsaw puzzle. It's a three-dimensional globe, the kind I never could figure out. Here in front of me is a world so foreign, so alien I may never piece it all together. And even if I do, is it a world I can exist in? A world I'd *want* to exist in? A world with angels who let girls die? Who watch young mothers succumb to cancer?

I stand. "I don't want to know any more."

He looks up at me, his face expressionless, and blinks once, twice, three times.

"It's too much, Jake."

He nods, almost to himself.

"I understand," he says.

Is he relieved?

My heart breaks at his easy acceptance, and I turn my face to the sky, willing the tears to stay put. And then he's on his feet, stepping closer.

"It's okay," he says. "Really."

Overhead, the naked limbs of the willow moan and creak. It's a sad sound. Painful, even.

Like knowing.

Like walking away.

Where are the easy choices? The ones that don't hurt?

"It's just this, all of it: Marco and Ali, and *angels*." I can't even make myself say *God* again. "It's too much, you know?"

"It's a lot," he says. "I know that. I won't tell you anything you don't want to know. Most people are never aware their Shield is near. Canaan can still do his job, Elle. You don't have to do anything."

Why couldn't the stupid ring have been magic? Magic is easy.

"I'm a job?"

He cocks his head. "Does that offend you?"

"No. Yes. I don't know. Am I?"

He laughs lightly. "We think so."

"Because of Marco?"

"We honestly don't know."

I turn away, toward the stone angel. She continues to weep. I wish she'd lift her head and tell me what to do. But even I can't ignore the irony of that thought. Apparently, there's a real angel available to answer questions.

"You said you'd tell me anything I want to know."

"Anything," he says.

"Anything's not enough anymore, Jake. I want to know everything."

Enough with puzzles. This one piece at a time thing is ridiculous. I need the whole picture, and right now the world doesn't seem too much to ask for.

"You just said you didn't want to know any more, Elle."

"That was before you called me a job."

He stares at me a moment longer and then lifts the sleeve of his shirt. The halo is there, and I watch as he removes it.

"This is yours. Regardless of what you decide, I want you to have it."

Even here, in the dying light of day, the halo grabs hold of what light it can and sends it back brighter, more golden than seems possible. "But it's Canaan's. He—"

"Would do the same thing." Jake lifts my hand and sets the halo into it. He's barely pulled his own hand away when it moves against my palm. We watch as the cuff begins to remold and unravel, and once again it's the crown-like ring. It spins down my arm and settles in the crook of my elbow.

Strange.

"Put it on your head," Jake says. A tremor runs through his voice, but there's a challenge there, I think.

Do I dare?

I think I do.

My eyes on Jake, I take the halo in both hands and place it on my head. The effect is instantaneous. Warmth trails down my body, just like the nights with the halo tucked under my pillow. My toes nestle into my shearling boots, my shoulders sag, and my eyes flutter.

"Eyes open, sleepyhead."

I force my eyes open and shudder. The nearest limb of the willow tree, the one hanging just inches from my face, is now orange. At first I think it's a trick of the light—that the evening clouds have parted for a glimpse of the yellow sun—but then, it isn't just the tree limb.

Before me, Jake's face, his chest, his shoulders and arms—in front of my very eyes, Jake's appearance begins to change. It's like his flesh—his clothing even—is glowing. Oranges and yellows, violets and reds. Every surface hue rolling and spinning. It's a dance. A dance of color and light.

And his eyes.

His hazel eyes are gone, replaced by white flames—twin blazes stirring within glassy orbs. Both frightening and beautiful.

And then the fence and the grass are giving off rays of light as well. The stars, too, are brilliant, shining like tiny suns against the expanse of an ever-lightening sky. The darkness of evening begins to fade, and soon the sky is gold and red.

The temperature increases, and my lungs begin to burn. I reach my hands out, steadying myself against Jake's chest. But the movement jostles the halo, and it tumbles from my brow. A deafening bang assaults my ears, and the light vanishes, leaving me standing once again in a twilit cemetery. My eyes blink again and again.

Jake takes my face in his hands. "You okay?"

I scoop the halo from the ground and take one, two deep breaths before placing it back on my head. Instantly the fatigue is back, and I have to strain to keep my eyes open. But the light and heat return. I raise a hand before my eyes and watch as gradually my palm begins to swirl with color. Light flickers from my fingertips. Beyond Jake, the trunk of the willow churns— a kaleidoscope of earth tones. Raindrop prisms fall from its branches as the great tree drips away the recent downpour.

The whirling colors are in a constant state of movement, and I can't keep my eyes open for longer than a few seconds before they start to water. I close them, and the vibrant hues continue to swirl on my eyelids, absent any shape, just like my dreams.

I open them, and there's Jake. And his white eyes.

"What is all this?" I breathe.

"It's the Celestial," he says, his voice thick. "A realm seen only by angels and their kind."

"Why can I see it?"

"Why can I heal?"

In the corner of his eye, a drop of color forms. A crystal gem magnifying the luminescence of his face. It trails down his cheek, and he leans close, his breath sweet on my lips. He slides a warm hand across my cheek, then another. With my chin sitting lightly in his hands, he pulls me toward him, and with the weeping angel as our only witness, Jake kisses me.

He really kisses me.

My skin hasn't adjusted to the increase in temperature, and his mouth is hot against mine. I gasp and he pulls back, his white eyes questioning. Stepping forward, I place both hands on his chest. The color spins around my fingers like the liquid crystals of a mood ring, and I kiss him back. My lips are chapped, but his are soft against them, like balm, like healing balm.

Again the halo tumbles to the ground, and the noise causes me to jerk away.

Jake stoops to the ground, and before he's fully upright, the halo has taken the shape of a cuff. He slides it onto my wrist. And now my hands are back in his and the halo's doing its thing and I can't imagine living the rest of my life not understanding what I've seen.

The light and the color. The heat and the peace.

But knowing frightens me, and I force myself to step back. I push my hands into my pockets, hating the words I'm about to say.

"I need some time." The simple sentence scratches at my throat in protest, but I can't think with him here.

"You know where to find me," he says. There's something in his tone, hidden in the creases of his brow.

Apprehension?

He turns away, stepping onto the cobbled path. Twenty-three steps later he disappears behind the mausoleum. I sink back to the ground and lay back, my hair splayed against the thin grass. The ground is cold and moist, but with my haloed hand lying across my stomach, I feel it little. I stare at the stone arms above, at the chiseled curls, the wings arched high. This is the closest I've been to my mother in a very long time.

What would she say about Jake? About the halo?

What would she do?

I want to stay here, close to my mother, close to clarity, but I force myself to think about tangible things. Things that I know to be real.

First and foremost, and as much as I wish it wasn't true, Marco's out. I need to check in with the sheriff's department, and it'd probably be good to fill my dad in on the whole thing.

But my phone is at Jake's.

I throw my arms over my face and close my eyes.

My resolve doesn't stand a chance if I head back now.

19

Damien

Damien storms from the room. He transfers to the Celestial and erupts in a mass of anger.

He should have the boy by now.

There is little time to waste.

The release of flight is exhilarating, but he allows himself only moments of revelry. A Shield is nearby, and he can't afford to be detected. He scans the motel below. Three of his men sleep off a late night. He'd wake them, but until he has an assignment for them, their idiocy is best masked by nightmares.

Damien turns toward Stratus and pulls up just outside its border. Canaan and the boy left days ago. Damien waited, refusing to be baited into a one-on-one confrontation. He assumed they'd return. But it's been longer than he expected.

He scans the sky, the ground. Stratus has no reigning force of darkness to consult, and no power of light has been instated either. Very little territory has been taken on either side. Unless Damien succeeds, Canaan and the boy will likely change that.

Without an ally here, Damien is hesitant to enter. In Canaan's absence that little speck of an angel has been patrolling the border, and while she's small, she's fast. His sensitivity to the light makes him a weaker fighter—a tentative fighter. And after the debacle in Dothan, after his easy detection the other night, the idea of facing a Shield alone does not appeal to him.

But tomorrow night, when the buyers arrive, they'll be flanked by their demonic escorts, Javan and Maka, the Twins. Fallen angels who've extended their influence through the corruption of their charges.

And while the trade is something he's focused on for decades, tomorrow it has an added benefit. It will serve as a way to gather his kin. And surrounded by his brothers, he won't hesitate to engage a Shield. Even one as prominent as Canaan.

Once they see!

Just a glimpse of the boy's healing ability, and his brothers will agree that Canaan's charge must be corrupted. They could kill him, sure, but what good would that do? His physical death would serve darkness little. But if they can twist that healing gift of his—pervert it and use it for evil—they'll have something exceptional, uncommon.

Evil.

Damien tumbles in midair—savoring the rush of the fall— and presses a little deeper into Stratus. He flies above the empty highway, following it into town. His eyes squint and blink as he tries to process all he sees.

And there.

What is that?

A strange light. Familiar but foreign. Even for the Celestial it's bright. It's the exact shade of gold inlaid in the Creator's throne. His curiosity grows, getting the better of him, and he flies lower. Closer.

And then he laughs. Howling into the expansive Celestial sky.

There below him lies the girl. Brielle. Unattended. Like a juicy apple hanging on the tree. Amidst a collection of crumbling tombstones she lies, her wrist a blur of gold. He twists his head, angry like a bird of prey.

Where has he seen that ornament before?

As if in answer, Brielle removes the strange light from her wrist, and as he watches it transform, confusion rattles him.

It's a halo. An angelic crown. Given only to those angels who stayed committed to the Creator. As a reward. A thank-you for refusing the Prince. For rejecting the rebellion.

But why does the girl have it?

His hands find the trunk of a pine, and he settles down in its branches. He's to the left of the girl, watching her in profile.

She lifts the halo in her hands and spins it, forcing Damien to close his eyes. The movement of such a bright light pains him far more than it should. When he opens them again, she's placed the halo on her head. She stands and runs her fingers over the stone angel before her.

What has her so captivated?

A small leap, and he's standing on the chain-link fence. Through the arching wings of the statue, he faces the girl.

Her head jerks. Abruptly. She steadies the halo with her hands, and her eyes meet his.

But that's impossible!

And yet, she trembles. Mouthwatering fear leaks from her chest. Like a gunshot wound, a deep black hole soaks through the brightness of all she is and shakes her body.

And then it comes. The bloodcurdling scream of a terrified girl.

She can see him!

Like the boy in Dothan. Like Elisha's servant.

Is it the halo that lets them see?

Maybe. Canaan was there in Dothan, and he is here in Stratus.

Is the gift of sight hers by right, or will the halo allow any human to see? In any case, a human with Celestial sight can mean nothing good for darkness.

The jewel-toned sky bounces off his talons as he dives for the girl.

20

Brielle

Screaming and cursing, I stumble back. Something hits the back of my legs, and I topple over it. The halo falls from my head, and the Celestial realm implodes, drowning my cries.

The earth is cold, my back pressed into it, my legs sprawled over the stone bench. But I don't stop. Just because I can't see that thing anymore doesn't mean it's gone. I scramble backward, my hand falling on the halo. It's re-formed into a cuff, but I don't slide it on my wrist. I jam it into my pocket.

The thing terrifies me.

I jump to my feet and run down the cobbled path. The fence hangs open, and I press through it onto the paved road leading away from the cemetery.

I'm running and trying not to think and fighting to keep the image of that monster from my mind.

I don't hear the car until it's too late.

It pulls in front of me, and my hip rams the front quarter panel as I pull to a stop. Mud and rock fly from beneath its tires, and I throw my hands up, but debris peppers my face. Between my splayed fingers, I see a yellow convertible blocking my way.

I see the driver.

And I scream.

Serena was right.

Marco James is here.

In Stratus.

"Get in," he says.

I don't know what to do. I don't know what to say. I shake and shake and shake.

"Brielle, get in."

My feet want to backpedal, but I won't let them. There's something in that graveyard that just might be worse than Marco James. He slams his hand against the steering wheel and climbs out of the car. I can do nothing but tremble as he pushes me into the passenger seat and slams the door. And then we're flying down the road, back toward the cemetery. Back toward the monster, and I can't even find the strength to scream.

21

Canaan

It's the second time in a week Canaan's seen Damien reaching his gnarled hands toward Brielle. He understands the demon's interest in Jake, but what does he want with Brielle?

Canaan wraps his wings—all four of them—tight to his form, falling into a dive. He throws himself between Damien and the girl, taking a swipe of the demon's talons across his shoulder. He feels an outer wing tear but unfurls it and unsheathes his sword anyway.

Damien's scimitar is drawn, steaming as he swings it high and then low. Canaan blocks his advances, his fiery sword sliding on the icy blade of Damien's.

Mind to mind, he speaks to his fallen brother.

"What are you after, Damien? Why here?"

Damien doesn't answer, but he swings his sword more ferociously. Canaan can't help but notice the squint of his foe's eyes.

"Your eyes trouble you, brother?"

"I am *not* your brother," comes the reply.

Canaan pushes against Damien's sword, and they hover

several yards apart. Glaring at one another. Each seeking to understand.

"But you were once. My brother. My confidante."

"You should have come with me, Canaan. Should have taken hold of freedom while it was within your reach."

Canaan doesn't laugh. The loss of his brother—of so many brethren—is a sad one. "You're not so deceived, are you? Rebellion did not bring you freedom."

Canaan's words spark something in Damien, and he strikes, hard and without ceasing. Canaan is pushed back, his injured wing costing him, sapping energy, skewing his focus with pain. Damien plants one foot on Canaan's shoulder and the other on his thigh and swipes downward with his weapon. Both of Canaan's left wings are sliced through, and the Shield spirals to the ground. He lands on his feet, but all he can do is watch as Damien takes off into the sky, his four wings propelling him forward.

After the yellow car. After Brielle.

Canaan sees him drop low, into the car, and when Damien rises only two of his four wings move up and down.

When the car pitches off the side of the road and tumbles into an empty field, Canaan knows it's empty.

22

Brielle

It's stupid the things you think when you're yanked from a moving car.

And I am yanked. The collar of my shirt tightens, and then I'm lifted and slammed hard against something frozen.

But for the briefest of seconds, I'm just grateful Marco kyped a convertible.

And then I can't breathe. I can't see. Everything is dark. I'm screaming. I'm sure I am. So it takes a second for me to register that I'm not alone. I peel my eyes open to find myself crammed against Marco. He's a swirl of color and black goo. Our knees are smashed against one another's, our faces separated by just inches. His white eyes stare into mine, and together we tremble.

In my peripheral vision, through some sort of immovable, sheer barrier, I see the world pass by in a conglomeration of light and color. I don't understand how I'm seeing the Celestial. The halo's in my pocket, digging into my hip, but I figure a bright, shiny world is the least of my worries right now.

The cemetery, the empty farmland—it all passes below me.

I'm being carried. By something. Someone. And without know-ing *how* I know, I realize it's that monster in the graveyard. The one I could only see with the halo on my head.

My stomach lifts and falls, and I'm going to be sick. But I can't move even to hurl. I'm pinned, uncomfortably pinned, against something dark and frozen.

We're jostled left and right. Up and down. Up and down. Marco's yelling something, but I don't understand. And then my stomach flips. My ears ring as the Celestial disappears and dark-ness surrounds me.

We're falling.

Through the night sky.

Heavy raindrops fall with us, racing to the ground below.

Marco flails beneath me as I swing my arms and try to get my bearings.

The rushing wind fills my ears, so I don't hear a thing when Marco crashes into the roof of the barn. The only warning I have is the delayed realization that he's stopped. That I'm still mov-ing. And then I land on him, knees first. I pitch forward, and my forehead collides with his cheek. I feel bones crack, and the air empties from my lungs.

I gasp and gasp, but I don't move. I can't. Everything hurts, and nothing cooperates.

Nails squeak against rotting wood. The creaking of crumbling boards grows louder, more insistent, and I realize our combined weight is too much for the old roof. With a yelp of pain, I heave myself off Marco. But once I'm off I can't slow my momentum. I roll and slide, grasping at the roof. My fingers collect peeling paint and drenched wood slivers, nothing more. I've lost a shoe, and my sock collects rain water as I slide.

My feet swing over the ledge and into nothingness. My legs and hips next. My stomach scrapes against the lip of the roof.

But I don't fall.

My head snaps up and there, his face visible over the ledge of the roof, his hand wrapped around my wrist, is Marco.

He's panting. Rain or sweat or blood drips from his hair, his face a featureless shadow against the cloudy moonlit sky.

"I've got you," he says.

His breath comes in halting puffs. I'm pretty sure I broke his ribs when I landed on him.

Good.

He deserves pain. Lots of it. He killed Ali. A girl who loved him. My best friend.

And yet here he is, holding me, saving me from at least another round of injury.

Why?

I slip. It's just an inch or two, but I realize how slick our hands are, how badly Marco is trembling.

He can't hold me much longer. I look down now, assessing the distance. With my feet hanging, I'm only eight or nine feet off the ground.

"Let go," I tell him. "I can make the drop."

"You sure?" His voice is . . . I don't know . . . compassionate? Hypocrite.

"Let me go, Marco."

And then I'm falling again. My feet hit first, and a tremor ripples through my body. I can't hold myself upright, and I crumble. I'm on all fours when Marco lands next to me. His heels hit first and then his rear end.

I'm not in immediate danger, not from him at least. He looks worse off than I do—so miserable I turn my eyes away.

I'm not going to feel sorry for this guy. I'm not.

The highway here is sprinkled with the odd streetlamp, but we're a good distance from it now, surrounded by frozen mud and spindly trees. The light is sparse. Moonlit shadows close in on us, menacing and silent. Plinks of rain drop, crinkling leaves, splashing in puddles.

I can't stop flinching.

Marco forces himself to his feet and presses his back to the wall of the barn. His face is deathly pale. His teeth are clenched, and his brow is drenched in sweat. He has a wound somewhere on his head, and blood runs down his neck and shoulders, slick and purple in the moonlight. I try to stifle my concern, but the wound beneath that hand on his thigh could be deadly.

"Elle," he says, his voice strained.

"What's wrong with your leg?"

He's going to talk about Ali. I can see it in his eyes, and I don't want to hear it. Not from him. I'd rather he succumb to his injuries, flop around like a dying fish. *That*, I can handle. Mallet to the head, right? That's what Dad says.

"I didn't kill her," he says.

Right.

I close my eyes. "What's wrong with your leg?"

"I need you to believe me," he says, his voice ragged.

"Your leg, Marco."

He's silent.

Too silent.

I open my eyes, and he's still there. Staring back at me. Green eyes full of agony. Something there reminds me of myself. Of what I see when I look in the mirror these days. But after all, he's an actor. A good one. And I'll not be played.

I crawl forward, reaching for his leg.

"It's fine," he says, attempting to stand. His leg won't hold the weight, though, and he falls back against the barn. "We need to get out of here."

My fingers aren't gentle as they pull his hand away.

"It's not that bad," he says. "Really."

Blood runs thick and black from the inside of his thigh and down his leg. It puddles in his hideous loafers.

"It *is* that bad, Marco. How are you still conscious?"

And then he isn't. His tall, thin body slides down the side of the barn, peeling away curls of paint and leaving blood in its place. I drop to my knees and stare at him, no idea what to do.

In this moment, I don't hate him. I want to, but creeping up on me is an irresistible urge to rescue him. To fix whatever's broken. Though I don't believe a thing he just said and I'd really like to hit him with a mallet, I'd never recover if someone else died on me.

But I can't do what Jake can do.

I dig my fingers into the seam that attaches my sleeve to my sweatshirt and yank until it comes loose. I've never really been squeamish, but I'm not sure I've got Jake's bedside manner either. So I proceed carefully, sliding the sleeve under his thigh and knotting it on top.

That done, I stand and take inventory of my own wounds. Most of the blood covering my body appears to be Marco's. My eye is swelling, and I have a gash just above it. I press my remaining sleeve against my forehead to staunch the blood flow. It's tender. Beneath the wound a lump is forming.

I really should be falling apart. My best friend's killer is lying in front of me, and someone or something just wrenched me from a moving vehicle and then dropped me from—well, from really high.

But I'm not falling apart. I'm sure I will later, but now, now I just want to understand.

Jake says Canaan's an angel. So he has wings, right? Could he have done that? Pulled me from a moving vehicle? Would he have? I think again of the beast in the graveyard and shake my head.

There's no way Canaan looks like that in the Celestial.

I pull the halo from my pocket. The cuff twists and turns in my hand, reforming itself. It hangs from my index finger for an entire minute before I can decide what to do. I'm terrified of what I'll see if I put it back on, but I don't want to be attacked by an invisible creature either. In the end, it's the creepy crawly noises that decide it for me.

I can't stand being blind.

With two hands, I place the halo on my head. My body feels like it's been hit by a freight train, but I fight it, shoving aside the need for sleep. It's harder this time, harder to refuse the dreams that ebb and flow just behind closed eyelids, but after the darkness of this night, I crave the light and life I saw less than an hour ago. That's what keeps my eyes open.

And then it's here, the barn and the grass transformed— the night sky as bright as noonday. Even Marco adds light to the atmosphere. Blood-red flames consume his body, flickering with a drum-like rhythm and then dissolving into the sherbet sky. I tilt my head. Something about it doesn't seem normal.

"Brielle."

I spin around, my muscles screaming in protest. The halo falls from my head, and I catch it against my chest. My throat makes a funny noise.

It's Canaan.

I'm relieved and slightly disappointed, to be honest. He's

wearing the same clothes as before: slacks and a red polo. No wings. No white robe. And I'm holding his halo.

"Jake told me," I say.

His face is calm, knowing. "It was time."

Marco moans in his sleep and I want to kick him, but I'd rather he be awake to feel that.

"Um . . . you have wings or something, right?"

"Four, actually."

I lean sideways, trying to find them in the darkness. "Four?"

"And we'd be wise to use them."

"Okay. Um, yes."

Canaan peers around me, and I step sideways to give him a better look.

"He needs help," I say.

"Quickly, then."

Canaan steps to Marco's side and scoops him into his arms. It's a bit comical, to say the least. He's holding Marco the way one holds a toddler. His forearm is under Marco's rear, and Marco's head lolls onto the angel's shoulder.

When Canaan turns around, his eyes fall on the halo clenched in my hands. "You've seen the Celestial, then?"

My thumb rubs the hot, slick metal, and I nod.

"You can put it back on your wrist. My wings will give you Celestial eyes tonight."

Celestial eyes?

At Canaan's word, the halo transforms. With it back on my wrist, I turn my attention to him, nervous.

"What do I do now?"

"Nothing," he says.

Canaan steps toward me, and I lose sight of everything.

"I'd open my eyes if I were you."

Before I can obey, a gush of wind fills my nose and mouth. I'm drowning, I'm sure of it. And then a surge of light blinds me, and a loud snap causes me to flinch. I gasp, finally able to inhale. The air is hot and burns my lungs when I breathe it in. The change is stark and sudden, not gradual like the halo's effect. My face and neck are on fire. I kick and twist against Canaan, but he's immovable.

"It's okay, it's okay. Open your eyes."

I obey, hoping that somehow the action will fill my lungs with cool, fresh air. It takes my eyes a second to adjust, but when they do I am dumbfounded. My heart rate slows as my lungs adjust to the temperature of the air. We haven't moved. We're still standing in the field outside the barn. The halo's on my wrist, but the night sky is bright again.

"Hold on," Canaan says.

The sound of a thousand birds taking flight assaults my ears. I try to duck and cover my head, but Canaan holds me fast. Somehow he's holding both Marco and me to his chest, though I'm facing out. The backs of our heads bump, and my tender scalp stings at the touch.

In my peripheral vision I see two massive wings moving up and down. Canaan crouches, and then we're airborne. My stomach jumps into my throat and I scream, pinching my eyes shut against the nausea of motion sickness.

"It's okay, Brielle. It's okay."

His voice is calm, and he holds me secure. I stop screaming but refuse to open my eyes. His wings press against the air, reverberating in my ears. It's frightening at first, and then, like the bass of Jake's stereo and the beat of the metronome, their consistency steadies me.

Canaan's movement slows and I chance it, opening my eyes carefully. I'm viewing the world through a thin, sheer barrier. Like the veins on a leaf, it's sinewy, almost reptilian. I press my forehead against it. It's hard, harder than it looks. And hot.

It's the heat that convinces me. It wasn't Canaan who ripped us from the car.

So who was it? What was it?

We're hovering about fifty feet above the ground, bobbing in midair as his wings hold us in place. Beyond the barrier, I see Jake. He sits on the steps of the old Miller place, the hues of his clothes swirling and changing. We're home. Shiny raindrops like diamonds fall past us, soaking him. Unlike Jake, I'm not touched by the rain or the cold, and can only assume Marco and Canaan are free of it as well.

Unreal.

Every surface glows as if reflecting, in different degrees, the light of the sun. My car and Jake's, the gnarled oak out front, the gravel drive, the porch and the swing—everything.

And Jake is no exception. Against the still dazzling but muted light radiating from the trees and houses, Jake glows fiercely, easily the brightest thing in sight.

"Does he know we're here?" I ask Canaan.

"No," Canaan says, "but he will."

And then with a flash of white his wings propel us forward, and a shallow dive plunges us through the roof and into the living room of the old Miller place.

I'm still screaming when our feet touch the ground. Jake walks through the front door, glowing and dripping rainbows of water everywhere. With the deafening sound of a ball being fired from a cannon, the world of light is stripped away, leaving the mundane, but very welcome, atmosphere I'm accustomed to. Jake is still in front of me, soaking wet and as engaging as ever, but like the rest of the room, he is no longer glowing.

"Brielle?" he asks from the doorway. "Are you all right?"

Craving the safety of his embrace, I take a step toward him. But my legs have the vitality of Jell-O, and I drop to my knees.

"I really don't like flying," I whisper.

Jake rushes forward, but Canaan is closer, and having already placed Marco on the couch, he lifts me carefully and lays me on the love seat. My eyes flicker with the release of it all, and I allow them to close.

"I assume this is Marco," Jake says.

"That would be a good guess. The wound on his head needs mending."

"I'll do it," Jake says.

"The first-aid kit is in the closet, yes?" Canaan says. "We should stitch his thigh."

I try to sit up, but exhaustion wins and I succeed only in opening my eyes. Jake sits on the couch, his hands cradling Marco's head.

"Jake?" I say.

"You okay?" he asks.

His smile is there, honest and soft. And mischievous, even now. Marco's bled on him too. Jake's hands and clothes are covered with the life that seems desperate to abandon the tragic actor.

"There was a monster," I say.

Jake's eyes snap to Canaan, who's just returned with a blue duffel bag, the red cross on its side indicating it contains medical supplies.

"Damien," Canaan says. "Helene's following him."

Helene? Where have I heard that name before?

Jake's face is pale. Paler than I've ever seen it. "I'm sorry, Elle. I shouldn't have left you."

But my eyes are on Canaan. He rifles through the duffel bag, pulling out gauze, thread, scissors, a needle, and a bottle of fluid.

"I don't understand," I say. "Why can't you do that thing? That healing thing?"

"We could," Canaan says, cutting Marco's pants away. "But then we'd have a lot of explaining to do. We have no choice with his head wound, but this, this I can stitch."

I have questions. So many questions, but my body's shutting down and I can't fight it anymore. Again my eyes shut. I drift into that fuzzy place between sleep and awake. I hear their quiet conversation and vaguely want to participate, but am rendered still by the overwhelming weight of tranquility that has settled on my mind.

"Have you checked the chest?" Jake asks.

"There's nothing new, Jake. Not since the copy of *Hamlet*."

Hamlet?

"Helene and I are going to redouble our efforts. We'll take shifts searching the warehouses and circling Stratus. You'll need to stay prayerful. I can't promise you'll be attended at all times."

"We'll be okay, Canaan. Do what you have to do."

"This is done."

I hear the snip of scissors and the zip of a bag. Soft footsteps pass by my head and fade away. The room is warm and quiet, and the ache has left my head.

And then I hear words. Soft with the rattle of tears.

"Dear God, please," Jake says. "Please."

That's it. That's all he says, but there's fervency buried in the words. The couch squeaks, and another set of footsteps drifts by. I hear water running and smell soap—sandalwood, I think—but I'm still, lost in the Neverlands, without wings, without any desire to go.

"I'm off," Canaan says. His voice is far—so far away. "I'll call when I can."

"What do we do about Marco?"

I count to twelve before an answer comes, and to my weary ears it's not sufficient.

"We need to tell Brielle. I don't think we'll get any more direction until that's done."

Tell me what?

"Would you like me to do it?" Canaan asks.

"No," Jake says. "I'd like to. It should be me."

But whatever Jake says, it doesn't sound as though he'd *like* to tell me anything. I strain my ears, hoping for a clue, but the conversation is over and a hot, damp hand comes to rest on my forehead.

Jake.

He sits next to me and lifts my head into his lap. In my mind, tendrils of steam linger between his fingers, and my attachment to consciousness begins to melt away. One final thought severs all ties.

Hamlet's debate is flawed.

Death can't end heartache.

But love?

Love just might.

23

Brielle

I had no idea I could be this cold."

It's Christmas Eve—my second Christmas here in the city—and the power in the dorms is out. No lights. No heat. Ali and I are huddled in a mass on her bed, trying to keep warm.

"I have another pair of toe socks, if you want them," she offers.

"You have tiny little munchkin feet. How will that help me?"

"My flashlight's dying," she says. "Can you hand me a couple batteries?"

"You want me to move?"

"No," she says, closing the leather-bound book in her lap and tucking the pen behind her ear. "Not if it will make you any grumpier than you already are. Let's do Shakespeare again."

"I thought you were documenting our demise in that journal of yours."

"Your entertainment is more important. And clearly, you're bored."

"I'm not bored. I'm cold."

"You get grumpy when you're bored."

"I get grumpy when I'm cold," I insist.

"Same difference. Shakespeare?"

"Sure."

She thinks for a second and then delivers a quote. "'We are such stuff as dreams are made on.'"

Easy peazy.

"Prospero, The Tempest."

"Ding, ding, ding. One point, Elle. A harder one this time," she says, leaning back against the wall. She adopts a lilting ghostly accent. "'Thy crown does sear mine eyeballs.'"

"It's Macbeth from Macbeth."

I don't recognize the quote, but she always uses eerie voices when she does Macbeth.

"Two points! And now, a favorite of mine: 'There is special providence in the fall of a sparrow.'"

"Also a favorite of mine. It's Hamlet," I say. "If I die first, put it on my tombstone, will you?"

"Ooo, good idea. I'd like it on mine as well. So return the favor, please, if the situation is reversed."

"Deal. Now try harder this time. I'm winning three–zip."

Her fingers drum against the book in her lap, making a series of soft, dull thuds. "'Light, seeking light, doth light of light beguile.'"

"You made that one up," I say.

"I'm flattered, but no. The credit belongs entirely with William Shakespeare, or whoever it was who wrote his plays."

"What does it mean?"

"You're stalling. In which work can it be found?"

I honestly don't know, but I'm saved by a strange grinding sound and the sudden sputtering of lights. Our desk lamps spark to life, and the clock radio on my bedside table blinks back at us.

"Oh, thank goodness," I cry.

Ali and I leap off the bed and dive at the metal grate on the *floor. I slide my fingers into the vent as warm air slowly seeps through the opening. My fingers ache as the numbness fades. Ali's striped toes wriggle next to my hands, and I eye her ludicrous socks.*

"Thought you said those things kept your feet warm."

She shivers and pulls the comforter off the bed. "I lied. They're more for decoration. Okay, next one."

"You didn't tell me which play the last quote was from," *I say.*

"Correction: You didn't tell me. But it's Love's Labour's Lost. Act I, Scene i."

"How do you remember all this stuff?" *I ask, reaching for my mug that's sitting on the windowsill. The coffee in it is cold now, but still I sip.*

"I write it down," *she says.*

"Everything? In your journal?"

"Sure. Quotes I like. Books I want to read. All my top-secret research."

"You're doing top-secret research?"

"Of course."

"And I thought you spent your nights scratching dreamy thoughts about Marco into that thing."

"I do that too. But you're stalling again. Ready for the last one?"

I take another sip of coffee. "Just waiting on you."

With the room lit, I see an impish expression cross her face, and then she says the most ridiculous thing I've ever heard.

"'I will smite his noddles.'"

I snort, and cold coffee shoots out my nose. "His noddles?" *It burns, and I snort again. More coffee dribbles out, but I can't stop laughing. And now Ali's laughing too. At me, I'm sure.* "There's no way that's from Shakespeare!"

"It most certainly is. Sir Hugh Evans," *she says.* "The Merry Wives of Windsor."

This just makes me laugh harder. And then, with the sound of a starting gun, the power goes out again. No sputtering, no flickering. Just on and then—bang!—off.

Ali groans, but I can't stop laughing.

"I will smite your noddles," I shout at the darkness.

Now it's Ali who snorts. But she's so small and dainty, it comes out all squeaky, and I'm sent back into a hysterical fit. My stomach aches with laughter, with the happy pain of it all.

And then, out of nowhere, my hand feels like it weighs a ton. I try to lift it, but something holds it down, pinning it against my stomach. I turn my eyes to Ali, but she's gone. Replaced by the creature from the graveyard. Black wings and a charred, melted face. Long scraggly nails that reach for me. I pedal backward, but he keeps coming.

"Brielle? Brielle, wake up."

I'm trying. Trying, trying.

"Open your eyes, Elle."

The saying of my name settles me, makes the monster fade, and at last my eyes spring open. Jake stares down at me, concerned.

"Hey there," he says.

I exhale, unaware I've been holding my breath. The wildly alive Ali, it seems, was just a memory.

After a long moment, I will myself to sit up.

"You seemed to be enjoying yourself there for a while," Jake says.

Yeah, until the monster . . .

I lean back against him and tug the halo from my wrist. "It's so heavy, you know. Makes it impossible to sleep."

"All evidence to the contrary," he says.

Filmy sunlight slips through the sheer window coverings

and it's easy to pretend the monster was a nightmare. Here in this warm, safe house. Here with Jake.

"Can we skip school today?" I ask, stifling a yawn.

"Thought you'd never ask," he says, looking far too elated for a guy who's been gone all week.

"What time is it?"

He checks his phone. "Eight oh two. You want a doughnut?"

A pink cardboard box sits on the coffee table. He flips open the lid. Chocolate éclairs and cherry crullers. Dad's favorite.

"You have an addiction, you know that?"

"Deputy Wimby dropped them by," he says, eating half an éclair in one bite.

"Who's Deputy Wimby?"

Jake stands, and I topple into the gap left by his body. I wonder if I can burrow into it and forget everything else. Just for a bit.

"*That's* Deputy Wimby," Jake says, pulling the curtain aside.

Parked on the street between Jake's house and mine is a cop car. I stand and cross to Jake's side. Pressing my fingers to the cold glass, I see a portly officer leaning against his driver's side door, a cup of joe in one hand and a radio in the other. He catches sight of us at the window and waves, coffee splashing from his cup and onto his shoes. He tucks the radio under his arm as he stoops to wipe it off. The movement of his body jostles the radio and it slips free, falling to the gravel just in time for a steaming Jelly's to-go cup to land on top of it.

"He's here to protect you," Jake says.

"That's unfortunate."

"He arrived while we were at the cemetery yesterday. Said he couldn't get through to your dad's cell."

"Yeah, he'll be hard to reach for the next few days."

"Canaan let him know you'd be staying here while your father's away. I hope that's okay."

"I don't really have to, do I?"

"Angels can see through walls. If you need to go home, that's fine."

I rub my neck, pretending that statement doesn't make me uncomfortable. "And Marco?" I say, looking to the empty couch, scrubbed clean by the smell of it.

"Moved him to my room. He's okay. He's sleeping. You want to talk to him?"

"No," I say, turning to him. "Not yet."

Jake's eyes are disarming, his lips parted slightly as if he has something to say. I've never wanted to read someone's mind so much in all my life.

"You said you'd tell me . . ."

"Everything," Jake finishes.

"It seems we have time."

He lets the curtain fall from his fingers. Wimby disappears, and we're alone.

"There's a lot to tell. Where should I start?"

I want to ask him about the monster. I want to know why Canaan needs two sets of wings. I want to know what we're going to do about Marco and why Canaan hasn't just turned the guy over to Deputy Wimby out there. But the thing holding my attention is Jake's trembling hands.

"I want to know what you're afraid of," I say.

I don't mean the words to sound so biting, but I can't quite muster the energy to apologize.

"I'm sorry?"

"It's just, *my* paranoia makes sense, right? Invisible monsters, escaped murderers, Deputy Wimby, for crying out loud. But you seem just as scared as I am, and I want to know why."

Jake shifts his weight from one foot to the other. "Brielle . . ."

"I've gutted myself, Jake. Told you all the little things that terrify me. In the spirit of fairness . . ."

"Fairness, huh?"

He stares at me a minute longer and then hooks his finger into the pocket of my sweatshirt and tugs. "Okay," he says, his tone reluctant. "Come on."

He leads me through the kitchen and down the hall. I assume we're heading to his room, so I'm surprised when he turns into Canaan's. He drops to the floor at the foot of the bed. Confused, I do the same.

"I told you before, Canaan's a Shield. He's an angel, right, but more precisely, he's a Shield. His role here is specific to the charges he's given. Make sense?"

"I guess so."

Jake continues, his tone more resolute, his face staid. "For example, about twelve years ago Canaan was sent to an apartment building in Portland where he was to locate and recover a young boy who'd been abandoned: me. He says it's the easiest assignment he's ever been given. He entered our ratty apartment, and there I was, curled up on the end of the couch, syringes on the floor and cocaine on the kitchen table. He carried me from the building remaining entirely in this realm, but no one stopped him, no one questioned, and no one's seen my parents in years."

I fidget. "This realm?"

"Yes. The halo, Canaan's wings—both let you see into the Celestial realm. This realm, the realm where angels breathe air and eat food—the realm you and I see daily—we call the Terrestrial. Anyway, Canaan took me home with him and raised me as best he could. He cared for me and taught me, and until last week he'd received no further assignment regarding me."

"Okay, you say *assignment* like it's homework or something." My question frightens me a little, but it has to be asked. "Who makes these assignments?"

"The Father," he says softly. So honest, so straightforward. "The Creator. El Shaddai. The Almighty. He has many names."

I shift my gaze and pick at my fingernails. Dad would so be dragging me from the room about now. "So, God, then."

Jake chews his lip. "Yes, God. The assignments come from his Throne Room."

"His Throne Room?"

"Yes. The Shield are just one group of angels, one rank. Canaan carries a sword, he's prepared to fight—to protect humanity. That job falls to the Shield."

I want to ask who he's prepared to fight, but the possible answers terrify me.

Jake continues, "But he hasn't always been a Shield. He spent over a thousand years as a Throne."

I demanded he tell me all this, but the endless string of details is overwhelming. Maybe I was right before. Maybe it's all just too much.

But would not knowing make it all go away?

"A Throne?"

"Yes. I know you envision an ornate chair, but it's also a Celestial rank," Jake explains. "Thrones are angelic beings assigned to the Throne Room of the Father. They're responsible for dispensing His instructions to angels positioned throughout the earth. He requires all Celestial beings to spend time in His presence before entrusting the task of guardianship to any one of them."

Jake's gaze slides away from my eyes and rests near my collarbone.

"That's how much He loves humankind. He'll only give the very best the rank of Shield because with it comes the responsibility of keeping watch over His children. Of course, the Father's omniscience allows Him to complete any task Himself, but like a good father, He *includes* His creation, *uses* His creation to accomplish His will." Jake pauses, and his eyes drift back to mine. "Questions?"

My face must have betrayed my discomfort. "The halo?"

"The halo." Jake takes a deep breath. "What do you know about the fall of Lucifer?"

I shift. "He was an angel, right? And then he got thrown out of heaven."

"Right. He rebelled. He thought he could be like God, and he convinced a third of the angels he was right. And when Lucifer fell, those angels followed."

"Demons." And I know, without having to ask, what that thing in the graveyard was. I know who Canaan is prepared to fight.

Jake nods. "The Fallen, yes. But the angels who remained— those who refused Lucifer and his lies—were rewarded. To honor their loyalty, the Creator gave them crowns. Halos."

"Wow. And Canaan can just . . . give it away? His crown?"

"The Father gives without regret."

I'm antsy. I want to look away, but his magnetic eyes are locked on mine. I don't know what to do with this information— information I knew was coming. It means Dad is wrong about

God being a fairy tale, and it means he's right about God being cruel. It means God really exists, and it means He allowed my mother to die. He allowed Ali to die.

"So what's the deal with the chest, then? This is it, right? The one you asked Canaan about earlier." I run my hand across the top of it. It seems to be fashioned from some sort of marble or granite. Onyx, maybe? But it's not natural. Not entirely. Its stone surface has the same liquid look to it as the halo, the blackness eddying like shifting steam.

"It is." He places his hand next to mine, our fingers inches apart. "This is how the Throne Room communicates with Canaan."

I clear my throat. "The chest?"

"Yes," Jake says. "Occasionally items are placed inside by the Throne Room—things to indicate our next move: deeds to land, rental agreements, adoption papers, keys, employment offers, pictures. There's a reason angels are required to spend time in the Throne Room before assuming the rank of Shield. Their time there helps them understand and interpret. More time in His presence means more insight into His ways. Less time, less insight."

"I still don't understand."

"Okay. What exactly?"

"Why you are terrifed . . ."

"I'm getting there," he says. "You'll know all my deep dark secrets soon."

"I don't need all of them."

"In the spirit of fairness, right? Anyway, I told you we lived in Chicago. Canaan managed an inner-city orphanage there. It had been months since he'd received any new direction, and then an employment application appeared in the chest. Understanding his instructions, he arranged an interview. By the time it was over he knew that the woman, a Mary Borst, was fully qualified to take control of the orphanage. He'd found his replacement. That evening, a page from the classified section of the Stratus *Herald* appeared in the chest. Most of the page had been smudged, but one ad was legible—a For Rent ad with this address listed. Within the week he had hired Mrs. Borst to run the orphanage and we'd signed the Millers' rental agreement."

He's talking faster now, and keeping up is difficult. Still, he looks at me like I'm supposed to respond.

"Wow. That's . . . just . . . I . . . that's amazing."

I watch as he slides the lid off the chest and props it against the bed. A woodsy, earthy smell is released. Jake reaches inside and pulls out a silver jewelry box. There's something engraved on the top, but I'm captivated by his hand.

Which is trembling.

Again.

"The Saturday before we arrived in Stratus," he says, "this appeared in the chest."

He releases a pearl clasp, and there, shining back at me, is a diamond wedding ring.

I'm bewildered. "It's beautiful, Jake. Whose is it?"

"It's yours," he says. "I think."

There's a hint of the wildness I'd seen in the graveyard burning in his eyes, but it's controlled.

He's serious.

"I'm sorry, what?"

"Read the engraving."

I take the platinum ring from his blistering hand and hold it up to the light. The perfectly round diamond sparkles as I tilt the ring and read the eight tiny words etched into the band.

From hands that heal to eyes that see.

I squint at it, confused. Conflicted.

"Say something," Jake says. A glance at him and I realize I'm not the only one conflicted.

"It's just . . . I'm not seeing it, Jake. I mean, *Hands that heal*, I get that. But *eyes that see*? Really, that could be anyone."

Jake is shaking his head. "The halo, Elle. It doesn't let me see into the Celestial. It never has. The only way I can see into that realm is from the safety of an angel's wings."

"But . . ."

"Canaan's halo gave me healing hands. It's given you eyes to see. My guess is you won't always need the halo either. One day you'll see the Celestial without it."

My heart hammers against my windpipe, and my throat makes strange squeaky noises. It's just ridiculous. A chest. A ring. And a halo.

It's a fairy tale, right? Dress-up and make-believe.

"So this means . . ."

"It means you have a choice," Jake says quietly. "It means one day when I offer you this ring, you can decide if you want to accept it or not." He is adamant, intense—emphasizing each word like it belongs in its own universe. "It just means one day *I'll* want to marry you. That's it, Brielle. That's all it means."

"But that's . . . that's stupid. You've barely known me a week. What if you change your mind?" I'm beginning to understand the fear he struggles to bury. "Don't *you* have a choice? If, and I mean *if* you and I . . . and if you ask that . . . question, I want . . . any girl would want . . . you to do it because you *want* to, not because some box thought you should!"

I'm escalating quickly, but I can't seem to find the off switch. Jake places his hands on my shoulders, sending a firestorm surging through my body. I relax, and my breathing returns to normal.

With a shaky hand I give the ring back. He takes it and tucks it into a small velvet pillow, and then he closes the jewelry box. There, engraved on the lid, in elegant gothic script, are my initials: GM.

He sets the box on the bottom of the chest and slides the top in place. I like it better that way. Closed. The future hidden. Unknown.

My hands are cold again. I want to bury them in Jake's, but I'm afraid of the message that'll send. So I lock them together and shove them between my knees.

"I don't have to believe you," I say.

"No," he says. "No, you don't."

"Will it change anything? If I choose not to believe?"

Jake's hands are taut against his jeans, white with the strain of whatever he's thinking.

"I don't know."

We stare at the chest for a long time—its blackness curving gracefully this way and that, snaking onto itself over and over again.

"What were you doing out in the storm?" I ask.

He looks at me, confused.

"The night you healed my ankle. You had a flashlight. What were you looking for?"

"Ah." He stands and walks to Canaan's side table, pulling out one of the drawers. "I was looking for you."

He removes a stack of papers and hands the top one to me.

It's a page torn from the Stratus *Herald*. I look at the date on the top. The paper is nearly a year old.

"What is this?"

"It took me awhile too," he admits. "See the article at the bottom?"

Jake crouches and indicates a square of text taking up the bottom quarter of the page. A title sprawls above the article in big bold letters: BRIAR CREEK DAM CONSTRUCTION POSTPONED. The article is short, and I read it quickly. It indicates that the dam will not be built, due to conflicting environmental reports, and that further development is postponed indefinitely. There are a few quotes from local citizens on either side of the issue. Of note is an angry farmer claiming that each year the flooding creek causes a considerable amount of damage to his crops, and therefore to his family's livelihood. I finish reading and look up at Jake.

"Okay," I say, ready for the rest of the explanation.

"This page appeared in the chest along with the For Rent ad," he explains, handing me the page from the classified section—a page we've already discussed. Above the Millers' address it reads:

> For Rent
> Three-bedroom farmhouse
> Right off the highway
> Horse property / Briar Creek view

"So you learned your new home had a creek running through its property, and that same creek flooded every year."

"Yes, and that led us to the Internet," he says, "where we checked the forecast here in Stratus. The first storm of the season was expected to hit that week, the week after our arrival."

"And that made you think what, exactly?"

"It made me think I should watch the creek! I didn't know *what* to expect, really, but that first day, in calculus, I realized that the creek ran through your property as well. I realized we were neighbors."

"How?"

"Your, um, mailbox has your last name written on it."

"Oh, sheesh. My 'mailbox.'"

"Anyway, after noticing your . . . fragile state, and knowing the creek has a tendency to flood . . ."

"So the night I broke my ankle, you were what? Waiting for me?"

The thought is overwhelming. He was looking out for me because of some random newspaper article? Because of some crazy supernatural chest?

He shrugs. "I didn't really know *what* I was waiting for, but yeah, last week I spent my nights walking up and down the creek between your property and ours."

I don't know what to say. He's done so much on my behalf. And he'd done much of it before we ever met. My heart's a lost cause, so I press my hands into the carpet, hoping to steady them.

"You're not going to kneel down when you propose, are you?"

He laughs. "Not a fan?"

"It's overdone, is all."

I let my eyes wander. They find the white dove on the wall—the one surrounded by all that darkness.

"What happens, Jake, if I choose not to believe any of this?"

"I don't know. But after what you've seen, is that possible?"

In spite of all my misgivings, and a shaky hand to my chest, I can't stop my heart from thrumming.

"You said it yourself, Jake. Anything's possible."

24

Brielle

You need a maid, kid." Marco sticks his head into Canaan's room and slides down the door frame. "Nearly killed myself trying to get outta bed."

The mood in the room changes. Jake's words have left me unsettled and confused, but Marco unleashes a whole new brand of frustration.

The sight of him here, walking around, in Jake's house, in a place that's warm and safe, is like an invasion of something sacred. It's pain. It's an ache that starts in my chest and spreads to every other part of me.

I remind myself of the detective's words. Of the bruises on Ali's body.

He doesn't belong here.

"What are you doing in Stratus, Marco? How did you get out of jail?"

"Elle . . . ," Jake says, with a hand to my knee.

I shove it off and stand.

Marco looks like he has something to say, but whatever it is, he's not fast enough.

"Speak, Marco. How did you get out of jail?"

"I don't know, okay? I don't know how I got out of jail." He runs both hands through his hair. "Yesterday I was in the psych ward trying to convince some crazy shrink that I'm innocent. The next minute, he's passed out cold and the door's standing wide open."

"You're joking, right? That's your story?"

"Then you explain it," Marco demands. "Tell me, Elle. How'd I get out of jail?"

"Serena said you incapacitated the guards somehow. Said they couldn't figure it out. They were still investigating."

It's weak. Even I know that.

He gives me a half smile. "They were asleep. All of them."

I want to smack him. "Do you honestly expect me to believe—"

Jake interrupts. "It wouldn't be the first time, Elle."

I round on Jake. "You believe him?"

"I'd like to hear him out."

Jake helps Marco to the couch where he can sit more comfortably, and then he starts a pot of coffee. I sit across from Marco in an armchair and scowl.

"I know you hate me, Elle. I hate me too, but I didn't kill her. And the guy who did is still out there."

I say nothing. Spoons and cups clang about in the kitchen, and Marco's twitchy. His leg shifts, and the pillow beneath it nearly falls from the coffee table. I reach out to catch it—instinct, really—but the gesture is almost too much for him.

"You don't have to do that," Marco says. "And you really

don't have to make coffee," he shouts toward the kitchen, holding his ribs and wincing. "We need to talk."

"Start," I tell him. "I'm listening."

Marco gives me a look of mingled exasperation and discomfort.

"I need . . . Jake, man, could you just leave the coffee? I really need you *both* to just sit and listen for a minute."

Jake obliges and sits on the arm of my chair, his long legs dangling to the floor.

"Thank you," Marco huffs. But after his passionate insistence that we listen, he doesn't say a thing. It's infuriating.

He scratches his knee fourteen times, and then he finally opens his mouth. "I would never, ever hurt Ali. She was my life."

I need more than a nostalgic declaration and well-timed tears from this actor, but as much as he seems to have something to say, Marco is painfully quiet.

"What about the bruises, Marco?" For Jake's sake I work to keep the sting of accusation out of my voice but am only moderately successful. "When I returned from Europe—"

"Ali has—had—anemia," Marco interrupts, avoiding my stare. The next words are hushed. Like the brush of silk, like a lullaby, they are precious and delicate. "She was having a baby. My baby. The pregnancy made her severely anemic. So she bruised. A lot."

In a world of possibilities, this one had not occurred to me.

"She . . . Ali would have told me if she was pregnant," I stutter.

"She was planning to tell you. She wanted to wait, but she knew the bruises were freaking you out." Marco pauses, giving me time to digest this new scenario.

"But the detective, or her mom—someone would have told me."

"No one else knows, Brielle. And Jimmy Krantz wouldn't have told you anything anyway," Marco says bitterly.

"Why? Why wouldn't he tell me? Detective Krantz was nothing but helpful. For weeks he called me daily to follow up. He told me about your fingerprints on the gun and your confession—"

"Did he tell you they couldn't find any gunshot residue on my hands or arms? Did he tell you I'd also been attacked?"

His words throw me back in the chair. "No," I say. "No, he didn't."

For the first time I wonder if I've been wrong. If what seemed true was nothing but a clever lie. I have no idea what to believe anymore.

"Will you tell us what *did* happen, Marco?" Jake asks, taking my hand.

Marco's face wrinkles, the memory aging him, but a tremulous smile breaks through the folds. "That's the reason I'm here. The reason I came to Stratus."

I don't know if I'm strong enough to hear this. Strong enough to live this nightmare again. And through the eyes of the man accused of Ali's murder. But not knowing won't make it go away.

"I met Ali at her dorm," Marco begins, "interrupting your study session, Brielle, to give her the news. The film was done, the editing complete, and Horacio was going to be in town that night to view it. Well, he was going to be in town, at least. I planned on surprising him with the finished copy."

I remember that day so well, but it seems Marco remembers it even better, and while it hurts to hear the details from his perspective, it seems to pain him more deeply to tell it.

"Horacio made my film a reality, and while hands-down, the guy was creepy, I felt I owed him. I couldn't wait to show him what his money had paid for. Ali's acting was superb. The story was fresh and thought provoking. And with my connections around the city, even the soundtrack turned out okay—always a concern with low-budget films."

His gaze settles on a spot above my head, and again he's the consummate actor—telling a story, drawing us in.

"Jake, man, when I first met Horacio, he was throwing down thousands for a rookie piece of art. I thought perhaps he'd be willing to invest in an innovative, albeit green, filmmaker as well. I'd never imagined it could be this easy. I mean, *he* approached *me*. See, my dad owned a chain of warehouses—rented them out to small businesses or whatever—but when the economy went belly-up, most of his renters did too. A couple years ago he ran off, left my mom. I didn't think a thing about his warehouses, right, until my mom called. Her name was on the mortgage, and if she couldn't get rid of the warehouses, and fast, she was going to lose the house. Something about the way they were purchased, I don't know. And then, out of the blue, there's this guy Horacio, and he's got tons of money and he wants the warehouses. He agreed to finance my film—the whole thing—if I'd transfer ownership of the warehouses to him and keep the deal quiet. Anyway, I jumped at it."

Marco shrinks into the couch cushions. Reduced somehow. Ashamed even.

"We'd just found out Ali was pregnant, and we were planning to get married. I needed the money. Needed the opportunity. He even lent me one of the warehouses for filming. The whole thing seemed perfect. I look back on it, and I know it was a little too perfect.

"You didn't want Ali to leave that day, Elle. I wish she'd stayed. You have no idea how badly I wish that. But in true Ali fashion, she rolled her eyes at your concern, and I was happy to have won her time. I heard what she whispered to you before we left. She said, 'You're wrong. He's good for me.'"

"I remember," I say. "That's the last thing she ever said to me."

It's a minute before Marco continues. "We walked to the subway and rode toward the docks, toward the warehouse we'd been using. I'd shot several scenes there, and it housed our production and editing equipment. Horacio kept a small office there too.

"Ali and I talked about the film and about the baby. She figured her parents would withdraw their support when they found out, and she couldn't stand that you hated me too. She made up her mind that day to tell you, Elle. She wanted you on her side."

"I'll always be on her side," I say, my chest knotted.

"I know." Marco runs a hand through his hair and lets it rest behind his head. "Have you ever been to the industrial district, Jake?"

"No, I don't think so."

"The downside of working there is that it's rarely ever quiet and always smells of diesel fuel. As soon as the smell hit us, Ali got sick. Right there on the street. I ran to the mini-mart on the corner for crackers and soda, and Ali took my keys so she could let herself into the warehouse. She just wanted to lie down."

He swipes both hands across his face, but the effort is a waste. The tears he pushes aside are instantly replaced with a fresh batch.

"I watched her walk away, swinging my keys and singing a show tune."

Jake hands him a box of tissues, but Marco just holds it, his thin fingers denting the cardboard.

"When I arrived at the warehouse, I could see the bumper of Horacio's car in the narrow gap next to the building. The engine was running, but I couldn't tell if he'd just arrived or was heading out, so I hurried, anxious to catch him, hoping he'd stay to watch the film."

The tears run fast and furious down his face now, but he leaves them and continues on.

"When I reached my hand out to the door, I was knocked to the ground. Three sobbing children tumbled out of the warehouse and landed on top of me. Children. In the industrial district. It didn't make sense.

"And then this voice was yelling from inside the warehouse, telling them to shut up. To stop crying. It was unreal. It wasn't until I reached out a hand to help one of the girls to her feet that I noticed the cuffs."

"The cuffs?"

I cross my arms across my cramping stomach.

"The children—all three of them—were handcuffed together. They were dirty and scared. It was . . . awful. And then Horacio stepped into the light.

"I asked him what was going on, what the children were doing there. He was too busy smiling to answer, enjoying their pain. When he shoved past me, I saw the blood. His hands and arms were freckled with it, and his boots left red footprints on the pavement.

"Until that moment I'd just been confused, you know, but when I saw the blood . . . I'll never forget that moment. And then he said, 'Today was a bad day to bring your girlfriend down here.'

"And I just lost it. I swung at him, tried to get between him and the kids. Tried to find Ali in the darkness. Yelled for her over the cries of the children. Eventually he pulled a gun from his belt and pointed it at my face."

Marco is sobbing. His chest heaving. I can hardly stand it, this story. This reality. But I have to know. "What happened next, Marco?"

"Another man stepped in then. Big. Really, really big. It was like he materialized out of the air. For the first time I saw Horacio balk. He asked the man for instructions. Said, 'What do you want to do with him?' I'd never seen Horacio defer to anyone, ask anyone else for advice."

"Who was he, Marco?" Jake asks.

"Horacio called him Damien. Scary, right? I'd never seen him before."

Damien. Isn't that what Canaan called the monster? The fallen angel?

I turn to Jake, my eyes pleading, but he shakes off my silent question. "Go ahead, Marco."

Marco's head falls to the side then, like he's tired, like he's done.

"After that, the world went black. When I came to, my head was pounding. Worst headache I'd ever had, but there was Ali, her face angelic, her eyes closed. It looked like she was praying, you know? I was lucky—I remember thinking that—how lucky I was.

"And then I saw the blood. And then the gun. Horacio's gun was in my hand."

He weeps openly, unashamed.

I'm physically ill, sickened by this man Horacio, mortified that Ali died at his hand. And for what?

"An hour before, I'd had my own little family, and now . . . nothing, no one. It was my fault, Brielle. I know that. I brought Horacio into her life. But I swear, I didn't kill her."

If it hadn't been for the halo on my wrist and Jake's proximity, panic would have swallowed me. Even now it threatens to overtake.

Jake's face is stoic, and he stands quickly. "I'll be right back."

"Jake?" I'm shaking again. The halo is on my wrist, and still I shake.

"I'll be right back," he repeats, leaving the room.

"Brielle," Marco says, blanching as he adjusts his leg again. "Horacio isn't going to let me live very long, and the shrink knew I wanted to speak to you. Horacio will find out. You and Jake have got to get out of here. Go somewhere and hide. Call the authorities, not Detective Krantz. Elle—Krantz is on Horacio's payroll. Find someone who can keep you safe, and don't leave until Horacio and his men are dead or behind bars."

I don't know what to say. My fragile snow globe of a world has been shaken, and instead of the snow swirling, it's me. I'm upside down and sideways, seeing things from a terrifying new perspective.

There's a knock at the door.

I throw a blanket over Marco in a panic and dash to the peephole.

Wimby.

Shoot.

I open the door, careful to block his line of sight with my body. "Everything okay, officer?"

"Well, Miss Matthews, looks like I'm outta here." The pudgy man extends his hand.

"Oh?"

"Yup. Precinct got a call from that Detective Krantz fella."

"Detective Krantz?"

"Looks like they got this Marco character back in custody."

I choke, then try to cover it as a sneeze. "Excuse me. Um. Wow, that's . . . that's great, Officer. Thank you."

He tips his hat. "Been my pleasure, miss. You tell your pa I said hello."

"I will. Absolutely. Thank you, Officer Wimby."

He trips down the stairs and back to his cruiser. I close the door and turn my back on it.

Marco lowers the blanket covering his face, and I lean back against the door, my mind spinning.

"Detective Krantz will do anything for a few twenties," Marco says.

Jake's cell phone vibrates on the table between Marco and me, drawing our attention. I rush the table and scoop it up. Canaan's name flashes on the screen. I'd gotten so lost in Marco's story I'd forgotten all about him.

"Jake!"

I run through the kitchen and down the hall. I find him in Canaan's room, kneeling in front of the chest, holding a beeping cell phone. I pull up, embarrassed and out of breath.

He's praying.

"I'm sorry. I didn't mean to interrupt."

"It's okay," he says, opening his eyes and holding the beeping phone out. "This appeared in the chest."

"Whose is it?"

"Screensaver says it's Horacio's."

Why would the Throne Room send Horacio's phone to Jake?

"Who's on that one?"

"It's Canaan," I say.

He stands and trades me the phone in his hand for the phone in mine.

"Canaan?"

I hear only Jake's side of the conversation—a lot of yeses and okays. At one point Jake grabs a pen off Canaan's side table and scribbles something on his palm. But I'm not really paying attention to their conversation. My focus is arrested by the phone in my hands.

I fiddle with it, trying to silence the alarm, but succeed only in opening the calendar. A reminder pops up. BUYERS TONIGHT. ELEVEN O'CLOCK.

The words blink back at me, but I can't make sense of them.

Buyers tonight? What does that mean?

My heart does a swan dive.

"Jake," I hiss, turning the phone toward him. "Look!"

His face drains of color.

"We're on our way, Canaan," he says, "but listen."

He retells Marco's story, focusing only on the highlights. And then he tells Canaan about the phone, Horacio's phone.

"We should go," Jake says, tugging me toward the door.

I stop in the doorway of Canaan's room, pulling on Jake's hand. "Talk to me, Jake," I plead. "Are we going to be okay?"

Jake stops, his body close. "Sometimes it's not about us," he says, pushing the hair away from my face. "Sometimes we aren't the main characters in the story. Sometimes we get to be the hero."

The words aren't reassuring, but his peace with it unnerves me.

"Sometimes the hero doesn't make it," I say.

"But sometimes he does," Jake says tenderly.

I want to crawl into the confidence he exudes. I want to wear it like a sweater, like a shield.

Behind me something falls to the ground. I hear it hit the floor with a muffled echo.

"What's that?"

"The chest," Jake says, releasing my face. "There's something else." We rush to the trunk and slide off the lid in a unified motion. At the bottom of the chest, next to the jewelry box, is a journal. A leather-bound journal. My heart jumps as I reach for it.

"You know this?" Jake says.

"I do," I whisper. "It's Ali's."

Ali wrote in this journal every night. Every single night. And every night, since the Christmas we became roommates, she tucked it beneath her mattress as if her thoughts were the most valuable thing in the world. Not once had I considered violating her privacy, and even now, as I hold the journal in my hands, it feels wrong. There's a part of me that longs to see her handwriting, craves to hear her thoughts again. But I can't open this book. It isn't mine to read.

"But why would the Throne Room send you Ali's journal?"

"I'm pretty sure it's not for me," Jake says.

"Then why? Is the Throne Room always so cryptic?" I ask.

"The ring was pretty straightforward."

My face flushes with heat. "Right."

"It's important to keep as much from Marco as possible, at least for now. I meant to tell you before, but he thinks his injuries are from the car accident. I told him his car was totaled, and he filled in the rest himself. He attributes most of last night's memories to a nightmare. He's been having nightmares for weeks, so he has no reason to think this one is more than imagination."

"I understand." And I do. I understand nightmares.

"Marco doesn't need to know about Horacio's phone, okay, but we're going to have to figure out a way to get him that journal. The Throne Room meant him to have it. Of that, I'm absolutely certain."

"I'll take care of it," I say, happy to have a task.

"There's one more thing you need to know," Jake says. "About Damien."

He has that look of gravity about him, his eyes smoking behind thick sooty lashes, his jaw set and his gaze focused on mine.

"Okay."

"Damien's a fallen angel, Brielle."

It's terrifying to hear him say it aloud, but I'm not surprised. "I, um, put that together myself."

He nods. "Canaan knows him, personally. He's worse than most because he suffers."

"Suffers?"

"He's been assigned to earth, like Canaan. But unlike the Shield, the Fallen cannot tolerate the light of the Celestial for extended periods of time. The rush they get from flight is addictive, and while his time in the light slowly destroys him, he doesn't have the self-control to keep himself from it. His master could recall him from the front lines with just a word and give him time to mend, but some failure on Damien's behalf has kept him here, out of favor. Canaan thinks his eyes are damaged."

"His master?" I'm exasperated.

"We talked about Lucifer, remember?"

"Yes, but, you know, some things are . . . figurative."

Jake's half smile returns. "You can't believe in heaven and not hell, sweetheart. That's just denial."

Did he just call me sweetheart?

"I don't know what to do with this information, Jake."

"I understand," he says, "but you need to know. You and Marco need to stay as far away from Damien as possible, and when we get to Canaan, I want you to stay with him at all times."

"And you?"

"If there's any way possible, my hand will never leave yours, but you're safer with Canaan."

"We're both safer with Canaan."

"No argument there. But knowing Damien, he'll try to split us up and use us against each other. He'd be wise to do so."

"Why?"

"He saw me heal your ankle, Elle. He knows what my hands can do."

The thought makes me light-headed.

How long has Damien been here? Been watching us?

"He'll target me if he can, but he'll use you—I have no doubt he'll use you to get to me. You've seen what he can do. Look at Marco's injuries, Elle. It could have been a lot worse. Stay with Canaan. Your capture could be fatal for both of us."

I'm confused and terrified, but Jake just said *us*. And something about the word, about the idea of it, makes me brave. I reach my fingers out and brush them along his cheek. He hasn't shaved today, and I wonder if his face would be uncomfortable against my skin.

"What?" Jake says, his eyes searching my face.

I shake my head, but I don't drop my hand. "You haven't shaved."

Jake licks his lips. "Is that a problem?"

"I don't know," I say, leaning into him.

Slowly, carefully, I press my lips against his. My eyes close, and I turn my face right and left, feeling the stubble brush against my chin. The smell of his skin is intoxicating, and like a drug-seeking addict, I press closer. And then his mouth is moving against mine and I'm lost. Jake twists his hands into my hair and pulls me tight against him.

Us, I think.

When at last our lips separate, I stare into Jake's breathless face and find a new kind of courage.

It's a courage to fight. And an audacity to believe in a God who may or may not protect us. All this talk about choosing to believe—but if I choose to ignore this world of angels and demons, my disbelief could literally kill me. Kill us. If I don't acknowledge Damien's existence, both Jake and I are as good as dead. We have to fight. Evil leaves us no choice.

"So?" he says, his breath coming fast.

I blush again, and again. "The stubble's not a problem."

I run home and change. I toss my mud-splattered, bloodstained clothes in the trash can out back. No time for a shower, but I run a brush through my hair and gargle some mouthwash before dashing out the door. I'm not particularly clean, but I feel human again in my favorite skinny jeans and a black hoodie. The halo is tucked under my sleeve.

When I skid to a stop in Jake's driveway, he's cramming Marco into the Karmann Ghia, ignoring his questions and promising some sort of explanation once we're on the road. I still have no idea where we're going, but I trust Jake, and he trusts God. Like standing on the shoulders of someone stronger, I'll depend on his faith to hold me up. Until I can be sure of my own, his will have to suffice.

"Would somebody please tell me what's going on?" Marco moans as we pull onto the road. "Who was on the phone?"

I look to Jake, as curious as Marco.

"The phone call was from Canaan, my guardian," Jake answers.

"And . . ."

"He's familiar with Damien."

"He's familiar with him?"

"Yes. And Canaan's been doing some research. He has someone following Damien as we speak."

"Following him? Does he have any idea how dangerous that man is?" Marco asks, trying to sit up, groping painfully at his ribs and gasping for air.

"He knows."

"That still doesn't tell me where we're going." Marco settles carefully back onto the pillow I'd crammed behind him.

"These warehouses of yours—"

"Not mine. Not anymore."

"Canaan's been checking them out."

"Have there been . . . were there . . ."

"He hasn't found anything yet, Marco. But there were signs. Evidence that maltreatment had taken place. He . . . he's under the impression that something is happening tonight. Something that needs to be stopped. He's got a handful of warehouses still to check, and there's one just a few hours away, in Portland. He said he'll meet us there."

"In the industrial district?" Marco asks, his voice dripping with anxiety. I don't imagine he wants to return there.

"No," Jake answers. He glances at his hand and reads Marco an address. "Do you know it?"

"I've never been there, but it belonged to my dad. It's Horacio's now. It's near the river, under the Maelstrom Bridge."

"You should rest," Jake tells him. "We have a long drive."

Jake turns left and takes the road through town. We're past both Jelly's and the high school before the silence is broken.

"Why are we going to the warehouse, Jake?" Marco asks.

"You have somewhere more important to be?" Jake answers, glancing at Marco in his broken rearview mirror.

Marco huffs.

"Because I trust Canaan," Jake says. "And he's asked me to check it out. Okay?"

"Okay."

"Now, sleep. You're no good to us exhausted."

Marco rambles on, detailing the horrific things he'd like to do to Horacio, but within minutes he's snoring in the backseat. We drive in silence, my mind working feverishly, struggling to make pieces of the story fit.

"Do you mind?" Jake pulls his hand from mine and reaches into the backseat. He places it ever so lightly on Marco's rib cage. Marco moans but does not wake. "If I had known his ribs were broken, I'd have taken care of that while he slept this morning. Firsthand experience has taught me how painful that can be."

My phone beeps, and I pull it from my hoodie. It's a missed call from Dad. I return it, but he doesn't answer, so I leave a message. I tell him about Marco escaping and then quickly tell him what Deputy Wimby said about their catching him. I feel a little guilty, but it's not a lie, right? Not a big one anyway. The deputy did say they'd apprehended him.

I tell him I'm fine and ask him to pick up more Cocoa

Pebbles before he comes home tomorrow. I try to sound chipper and snarky, but I'm not sure I pulled it off. I hang up and send Kaylee a text. This has to be an acceptable excuse for cancelling our movie plans.

That done, I stare past the spiderweb cracks spreading from one corner of Jake's windshield to the other, and I wonder.

"What do you think we'll find there, Jake? At the warehouse?"

"God willing," he says, slamming his foot down hard on the accelerator, "we'll find life."

25

Damien

*K*nock knock.

Someone's been knocking at his motel room door for a good thirty seconds now, but Damien doesn't answer. Instead, he sends the knife in his hand spinning toward the wall.

Knock . . . Knock . . . Knock. Knock.

Damien cracks each knuckle intentionally, listening for the snap. He focuses on the sound, attempting to dispel the anxiety consuming him, and then crosses to the wall to reclaim his knife. His self-control is slipping, and he knows it.

It took nearly every tool in his arsenal to wake his men—his brainless, hungover men. In the end, Damien inhaled a mouthful of Celestial air and let it rot in his diseased mouth. When it settled grainy and toxic against his teeth, he spewed it into the atmosphere, where it spiraled invisibly to the nostrils of those slumbering. And then he transferred to the Terrestrial, towering over them as they woke, slobbering, mucous running down their faces.

Stupid, stupid humans.

Threatening dismemberment, he sent them into Stratus. Demanded they locate and apprehend Jake and Brielle. But it's been hours, and his phone remains silent. They could be anywhere, and Damien is out of time.

The buyers will be arriving tonight. Tonight! And with them, the Fallen. Gathering four such influential brothers again will be difficult. This may be the very last chance he has to impress the Prince.

"Um, sir?" From outside the motel room door, a whiny voice makes its way inside. "We've had complaints about the noise."

With a flick of his wrist, Damien sends the knife tumbling across the room again. It lands with a thud in the wall beyond. He crosses the room to retrieve it.

"Yes, sir," the whine continues. "That's just the noise I'm talking about. The lady who shares that wall with you—well, she won't stop calling the front desk, and—"

Damien stalks to the door and yanks it open. Before him is a pimply-faced boy with a passion for all things Vulcan, by the looks of his shirt. The boy blanches, his mouth gapes. Damien pulls back his fist and slams it into the kid's jaw. The kid collapses—all knees and elbows—but Damien finds little delight in the pain he's inflicted.

Pain is not nearly as satisfying as fear.

He turns and aims his knife once more at the wall behind him. End over end it flies, shooting with ease through the wall in question. The resulting shriek of his peace-loving neighbor whets his appetite, and he closes his eyes, imagining how satisfying it will be to hear Jake Shield scream like that.

A moment is all he allows himself, and then he advances on the wall. It's a small room, and three strides is all it takes. Eyeing the puncture wound he's just given it, he abandons himself to rage and smashes first his left fist and then his right through the wall. They cut through with ease, and he repeats the action again and again, until at last the opening is large enough to permit his powerful build to pass through.

He ignores his neighbor's quaking, squealing form. She huddles against the queen-sized headboard as he stomps through her room, Sheetrock dust marking each step. Damien pulls his knife from the wall, where it's sunk to the hilt, pinning the polyester drape to the door frame.

He flings open the door, now on the far side of the motel, opposite the parking lot, and slides the Green Beret tactical knife into a sheath strapped to his thigh. He took it years ago from a captive, and soon thereafter assassinated, soldier.

Human weapons are of limited value to the Fallen, useful only in the Terrestrial. But this one he has kept. It reminds him of the violence people inflict upon themselves, of their sheer depravity. It reminds him that sometimes terror triumphs, and even knights on white horses can be defeated.

Today of all days, he needs these reassurances.

Because Canaan's right. Damien's not free. Not really. Mortal, immortal—all serve one master or the other. He's free *to not worship* the Creator, that's true. The Creator won't accept halfhearted worship anyway and seemed more than willing to release the malcontent to follow the Deceiver. But that freedom came with a price. It chained them to utter darkness and caused their spirit selves to atrophy.

It forced them to cling to the Deceiver.

To the Prince of Darkness.

Originally they were enamored by him—his beauty, his

charisma, his courageous challenge of the only power in the universe. But their preference for the Deceiver soon grew into downright hatred of the Creator and His world of light. Eventually the light itself turned on them and began to eat away at their senses. Darkness and its Prince were their only refuge. The Fallen serve him now because they have no choice, and it's nothing less than a battle to secure positions away from the light.

Damien shakes his head clear of recollection. If he's going to get Jake and Brielle to the warehouse in time, he has to act now. If he doesn't have something of value to show his brothers when they arrive, they will likely turn on him.

He doesn't want to risk another one-on-one with Canaan. Or Helene, for that matter—wretched little angel made him drop the girl last night—but he's out of options. He throws a rigid glance over each shoulder and then transfers with a groan of release into the Celestial. As he does, his phone vibrates.

With some exertion he pulls himself back to the Terrestrial and snaps the phone to his ear. "Juan, tell me you've found them."

"They're in the city."

This news takes him by surprise, and his pulse quickens.

"Where?"

Juan's voice wavers. "We don't . . . know exactly."

"What *do you* know?" Damien shouts, spit flying.

"There's a girl here . . ."

"Brielle Matthews?"

"No, a friend of hers."

The idiot launches into a story. An excuse. Damien's chest rumbles with impatience.

"We got here, to the house, but it was empty. We went door to door for a while, flashing Jake's picture, pretending to be the

Feds, but the only thing the neighbors could tell us was that the kid was new in town. We decided to check the house again and found this sweet little thing sitting on the porch waiting for us."

Damien hears muffled cries in the background.

"She heard we were asking around and wanted to make sure her friend was all right. It seems they had plans and Brielle cancelled. Meeting her boyfriend's dad in the city, she said. The text message says it's some sort of an emergency." Juan doesn't continue.

Is he pausing for effect?

Wrong audience.

"Is that it?!" Damien roars into the phone.

"Yes, yes. That's it. That's all she knows."

Fury tightens Damien's muscled body. They're on their way to Canaan. It's possible, likely even, they've already met up. Hours and hours of futile patience, and his prey have driven right by. A cold chill climbs up his spine as he considers the words he's just heard: some sort of an emergency.

What kind of emergency?

Do they know about the trade?

About tonight?

The consequences of his own mistakes are piling up, and if Damien doesn't act quickly they're sure to crush him.

"Yo, D. You there?"

Damien grinds his teeth, forces his temper into submission.

"Get to the warehouse, Juan. You're handling the buyers tonight."

"Where's Horacio?"

This is exactly why he needs a right hand—all these details, minutiae he despises.

"The warehouse. Be there."

"Sure, Boss, whatever you say. What do you want me to do with the girl?"

"Bring her with you," Damien says.

"No prob. Eddie will like that."

Damien wads the phone up, like a mistake, the first draft of a saga he means to rewrite, and he drops the plastic remnants to the floor.

He couldn't care less what Eddie will like.

He transfers to the Celestial and launches into the sky. The sickness in his chest—the panic spreading like wildfire—fuels him. He flies hard and fast away from the motel, away from the taunting little town of Stratus, toward the warehouse by the river.

Has his nasty little secret been unearthed?

26

Brielle

The warehouse is positioned at an angle under the Maelstrom Bridge. Its crooked position seems accidental, a haphazard mistake. Behind it, the dirty river reflects the city lights. I peer out my window, looking for the moon, but she's not showing herself tonight. Instead I see heavy black clouds. They close in slowly, bringing the very storm we've been hoping to avoid. The silhouettes of several other warehouses line the water, and the whistle of a train sounds overhead. Dust and rubble sprinkle the air as the train pulls in.

Next to the warehouse is a gravel lot surrounded by a tarnished chain-link fence. A van, ghostly white against the night sky, is parked there. Jake pulls the car into an abandoned gas station across the street, and I glare out my window at a rusted tin sign squeaking back and forth in the wind.

There's an old garage bay next to a boarded-up mini-mart. Jake jumps out and tries the rolling door. With a little effort it slides open. The bay is empty, so Jake backs the car into it. The shadows swallow the Karmann Ghia, though I doubt anyone would think twice if it were seen. Jake's car looks as old and abandoned as the gas station.

I slide into my green Chucks and stare out the windshield.

What could be hiding in the depths of that aluminum building? Two light fixtures hang precariously over the front sliding doors. Like the torches framing the gateway to Kong's Skull Island, they flicker erratically. A line I memorized in acting class comes to mind.

Screw your courage to the sticking-place and we'll not fail, Lady Macbeth told her husband. Of course, she was advocating murder.

I shake off the thought. Her counsel, beneficial though it is, brings visions of violence and bloodstained hands to mind—visions that contradict the apparent wisdom of her words.

Next to me, Jake sits rigid in the driver's seat.

"Are you okay?" I ask.

"I've just never done this without Canaan."

"Should we try his cell?"

It's been hours since our last contact with Canaan, and though Jake assures me my concerns for his guardian are ridiculous, I'm worried about him.

"No. As soon as he's able to talk, he'll call. We could interrupt or give away his position."

"What about Marco? Should we wake him?"

Behind us, Marco snores lightly, Ali's journal clutched to his chest, the halo sitting lightly on his knee. Jake's eyes drift to the backseat and scrutinize the peaceful form quizzically, as though Marco is a calculus problem he can't solve.

"I don't think so. If this turns into anything, he's really not up for it."

I just nod. I want to ask what this could possibly "turn into"—what he expects that I do not—but I'm too chicken to ask.

As promised, I delivered the journal to Marco. At the half-way point, we stopped at a service station so Jake could refill his battered car with gas. I waited until Jake went inside to pay before I slipped the journal out of my bag and passed it to Marco.

"What's this?"

"Ali's journal," I said softly.

A muffled sob escaped Marco's lips. "Did you . . ."

"I haven't read it," I told him. "I couldn't. It isn't mine to read."

He picked up the leather book and turned it in his hands.

"I shouldn't," he said. "Maybe her mom or . . ."

"Ali'd want you to have it," I said as generously as I could. "If you want to share it with her mom that's up to you, but it's yours. She gave you everything she had to give, Marco—her heart, her body. She wouldn't want anyone else to possess her mind."

Glistening tears magnified Marco's emerald eyes, and he ran a hand through his black hair—a move he seems to have trade-marked. He nodded and opened the journal. Slowly his fingers moved over the words written on the first page. Her pixie-like hand penned each and every thought there. I blinked against the tears stinging my eyes and turned my face away. He deserved time alone with her. Time to say good-bye. Time that had been stolen by a psycho with a gun.

Over the next few hours Marco was quietly immersed in Ali's memories. Several times a suppressed laugh or cry would betray his silence, but mostly he spent the drive alone with Ali. Jake and I did our best to honor his vigil and spoke quietly, if at all, listening to music on whatever radio signals we happened to catch. Finally Marco fell into a restless sleep, and in a move I considered genius, I slid the halo off my wrist and laid it softly on his knee. Within moments his body stilled. I smiled up at Jake, and he winked back at me, though his face showed some concern.

Now, with Marco snoring in the backseat, Jake's face again shows apprehension.

"You should stay with him," he says.

I should have known he'd try to be noble.

"Not a chance," I say. "Maybe *I* wanna be the hero this time."

In truth, I can't imagine sending Jake in there alone. Knowing what Marco looked like after a run-in with Damien, knowing that somewhere that beast is searching for Jake—I want to protect him, to be his shield. And I want to destroy Damien, whatever he is. I have no idea how to do these things, but I can't do any of them from the car.

"Sometimes the hero doesn't make it," Jake says, repeating my earlier caution.

"Sometimes she does."

We stare at each other for a minute or two, our fingers knotted together, the rumbling train overhead. At last he pulls the halo from Marco's knee.

"If we can't have Canaan, at least we have his eyes."

We climb out, meeting again at the Karmann Ghia's dented hood, still shrouded by the dark garage. Jake steps toward me, the halo in his outstretched hands.

"Angel eyes," he offers.

"You proposing that as a nickname?"

He smirks, that crescent moon of a smile returning. He places the halo on my head and drops his hands to my shoulders. The familiar sensation of heat and quietude washes over me, and though Jake stands before me as beautiful as ever, it's with Terrestrial eyes that I view him.

"Nothing," I say.

"Patience."

My muscles begin to relax, and my eyes flutter. I stifle a yawn and force my eyes open. His face shines bright, golden like the noonday sun. His eyes are white with light, and his skin and clothing swirl with color. Unable, or perhaps unwilling, to stop myself, I lean forward and kiss him lightly. His lips are cooler now. Cooler than the flaming air I breathe. Cooler than the heat now bathing my face. But warmer still than they have any right to be.

He clears his throat and turns me toward the warehouse. "What do you see?"

I turn and examine the scene before me, but it takes a minute for everything to make sense. Color churns on every surface, reflecting light just as it had before. The warehouse is still visible, of course, but the longer I stare at it, the thinner its walls appear. Soon they are thinner than rice paper, and I see straight through them.

"Oh, Jake."

"What is it?"

"Children. Everywhere."

"Okay," Jake says softly, rubbing my shoulders. "I expected that. Don't panic. We're here to help them. What else do you see?"

I take another lungful of flaming air and focus again on the building. There are at least a couple dozen children sitting in groups on the floor, their ages impossible to determine from this distance. Thick, black tar undulates across the floor of the warehouse, gooey and clumpy, leaking from every nook and cranny.

Red flames seep through the walls, like angry fingers reaching to the sky.

All this I relay to Jake.

"The red flames—are they still?" Jake asks, his voice rushed.

"Still?" I question, looking around. "No, they're flickering—spastic-like."

"All the flames are moving? None of them are still?"

I scan the room again. "No, they're all moving. Is that bad?"

"No, that's good." He sighs, pulling me back against him. "That's very, very good. Can you tell if anyone's guarding the children? Are they alone?"

My eyes pick through the warehouse slowly, carefully. It seems the building is split in two, with the largest portion to the left, where the children are. To the right of the divide is a smaller room. An office maybe? I focus hard on this area. Red flames block much of my view here, and though they are transparent, their rapid movement makes it hard to keep anything in view for more than a moment. Finally a figure, dark and hunched, becomes visible. It's larger than the children, and absent the tar attached to each of them.

"Just the one guy?" Jake asks when I tell him about the man.

"Yes," I answer. "I'm pretty sure there's just one. He seems to be in an office or something." I tilt my head, trying to focus on a plethora of chaotic light in the corner. "He's watching television."

"Okay." Jake takes a huge breath. "I think we can handle this."

"What do you mean, 'handle this'? Shouldn't we call the police?"

"With Marco in the car?"

I look through the windshield at Marco's sleeping form.

"Right."

"We wait for Canaan. We don't do anything unless we have to. I'm not putting you or Marco in danger if we can monitor the children from here."

"Okay. So, what now?"

"Well, first off, we need to cover that up," Jake says, indicating the halo. "Just in case."

He climbs inside the passenger seat and rummages through the glove compartment. He returns with a fuzzy black beanie, and I pull it on over the halo. It's a little uncomfortable, considering the heat I'm already exposed to, but it keeps the halo strapped to my head.

And it's worth it. We need to see what's going on inside that building.

"Are you still tired?" Jake asks.

"No," I answer. "It's funny. As soon as the Celestial comes into view, the warm, cozy feeling is replaced by serious heat. I can't imagine sleeping now."

I climb up next to him and continue my watch. Nothing has changed, and I wonder if the children are asleep. The light and color merge together, making movement hard to distinguish from this distance. The little man is still sitting hunched in his office, the TV flashing away.

"Jake?"

"Yeah?"

"Back at the house you said Damien might try to split us up, use us against each other. That he'd be wise to do so," I recall, as matter-of-factly as I can manage. "What did you mean by that?"

Jake slides off the hood. "The man in the office, how much can you see of his face?"

"Nothing," I say. "He's facing the far corner where the TV is. I just see the back of his head."

He grabs my hand and starts across the street, pulling me after him.

"I'd wait and show you with Marco, but that won't work either."

"Where are we going?" I ask.

"Don't worry," Jake says, placing my hand between both of his. Even with the halo on my head, his hands bring a different kind of warmth, and I relax. Kinda. "I just want to show you something."

We cross the jagged street. Potholes and chunks of broken blacktop litter the road. We step carefully over the debris and move quietly around a rancid-smelling Dumpster. Eventually we stand in front of the east-facing wall, the river running a hundred yards to our right. The slimy little man is just ten feet from us, lounging on a tattered plaid couch, his dirty boots propped on a wooden crate. A bowl of potato chips is balanced on his stomach.

From this distance I notice things I hadn't seen from afar. The light that surrounds him is odd. It's like his very skin absorbs it—and unlike Jake's skin or mine, it does not reflect back into the atmosphere. This man is a shadow, his features visible, but barely. Neither his clothes nor skin swirl with color like every other surface. Instead they vibrate slightly with a flat, lifeless charcoal tint. Color and light disappear inside him, leaving a stain of darkness on the canvas of illumination.

"He's disgusting," I whisper.

"That bad, huh?" Jake asks. "He may not be a good example either, but we'll try."

"Try?"

"Look at his eyes," Jake says. "What color are they?"

I crouch a little, trying to see under his droopy lids. When I finally achieve the correct position, I'm actually surprised to find color there. "They're yellow—a dirty, grimy yellow. Nothing like the light surrounding him."

"And mine," Jake says. "What color are mine?"

"White." I don't need to look at Jake's eyes again to know their shade. The minute I saw his eyes in the Celestial, I knew I'd never forget them. "Pure white."

"My eyes aren't always white though."

"Of course not. In the Terrestrial—"

"Even in the Celestial," Jake interrupts. I try to think back, to remember a time in this realm when I've seen a different color in his eyes. Granted, I haven't had much time with him here, but still, nothing comes to mind. "Watch."

Jake pulls his eyes from mine and turns them to the shadow of a man lying on the couch. I know Jake can't see through the wall, can't see the man lounging there, but all the same, the white light that has consumed his eyes fades until his perfect hazel eyes remain. Like the inviting fireplace I envisioned the first time I looked into them, they glow bright, reflecting every bit of light touching them. Still incredible, but very different than the white I'd seen just moments ago.

"Wow," I whisper. "What makes them change?"

Jake grins and turns again to face me. Rays of white light slowly break through his russet-green eyes until it's all I can see there.

"You've heard the ancient proverb that says the eyes are the window to the soul? It's not untrue, but it would be more precisely accurate to say *the eyes are the window to the will.*"

"You're going to have to explain that."

"Come on," he says softly. "Let's get out of here."

We make our way back toward the car, staying in the Terrestrial shadows thrown by the city lights. Once we're away from the warehouse, Jake explains.

"You know all those love songs, the ones where lovers claim they'd swim oceans and cross deserts to be with each other—acts that would, without a doubt, cost them their life?"

"Sure."

"Well, in the Celestial you wouldn't be able to lie about something like that."

I don't even try to hide my confusion.

"In the Celestial, when someone's eyes are glowing white it means they've made a decision about the person they're focused on."

"What kind of decision?"

Jake pauses ever so slightly and then dives in. "Jesus said the greatest expression of love is laying down your life for someone else. The white light you see when I look at you means that either consciously or subconsciously, I've decided I would lay my life down for you if the occasion called for it."

I'm flabbergasted.

"Literally?" I manage to choke out.

"Literally. It means that if necessary, I'd die in your place. I'd sacrifice myself so you could live."

There aren't words. At any other time such a declaration would make me feel adored, cherished, and, if I'm honest, uncomfortable. But now, knowing we face real evil, the idea of Jake sacrificing himself for me—or for anyone for that matter—is terrifying.

I close my eyes against the white fire in his and will it to disappear. Colors dance on my eyelids as I try to unknow what he's just made plain.

"Promise not to do anything stupid, Jake," I say. "Even if Damien tries to use me against you. Let Canaan handle it, let Damien hurt me and fix it later, but please, *please* ... ." I can't finish the thought. It's just too awful.

"I can't promise that, Brielle. Can you?"

I know the answer as well as he does, and the truth of it sits like a rock in the pit of my stomach.

I'm heated through, tucked away in the Celestial, but Jake's hands are uncharacteristically cold. I break the uncomfortable silence by suggesting we keep an eye on the children from inside the car. He agrees, and after another silent moment we join a snoring Marco in the cramped little Karmann Ghia. We don't speak.

There aren't words important enough to fill this silence.

I watch the light bounce off the children in the warehouse and count them as best I can. Forty-two, I think.

Forty-two.

There are forty-two children across the street from where I sit. Forty-two children who are not reading bedtime stories. Not brushing up before lights out. There are forty-two children who didn't get a kiss good night, who didn't practice their numbers or letters today. Across the street from where I sit are forty-two children who deserve to be protected.

I try to focus on their individual faces, but that amount of concentration makes my eyes water. Instead, I lean back against the headrest and observe the scene as though it were a tragic piece of art.

"I recognize Marco," Jake says.

"What do you mean? From where?"

"I don't know. I feel like I should know him, like we've met before, but I can't quite place him."

I consider his words. "It doesn't really seem possible, does it? I mean, you grew up mostly abroad, and Marco's never lived anywhere but the city."

"You're right," he says, running a hand down his face. "It's weird though. There's just something . . . familiar . . ."

Out of nowhere, the calm resting on the car is broken. Jake's eyes swivel back and forth, like they're searching frantically for something to latch on to. Finally he turns, settling his radiant white eyes on Marco. "Oh man, Brielle."

"What is it, Jake? Do you remember?"

"No, I just—"

But Jake doesn't get a chance to finish his sentence. The sound of tires crunching over gravel startles us to attention, and we watch, transfixed, as a glossy black car pulls into the small lot next to the warehouse.

"What do we do?"

"Look at me," Jake says. "We cannot panic. We don't have time."

"Okay," I say, closing my eyes. I concentrate on the heat of the halo and the feel of Jake's hands, refusing to acknowledge the anxiety bubbling like ragout in my stomach. "I'm all right now."

"Good," Jake says, turning back to the warehouse. "What do you see?"

Again I focus my eyes on the building. A little more effort causes the walls to thin away. And now I know what it looks like when forty-two children move. Similar to a time-lapsed photo, smears of light and color meld together in long, arching movements, making it difficult to keep my eyes on any single child. If I were closer perhaps I could focus, but from here . . .

"The children seem to be moving around now, like they've heard the car," I tell him. "The scumbag in the office hasn't moved. He must be asleep."

Two men step out of the car. The driver is tall and dark with a long ponytail and severe features. The other is short and dumpy.

With dimples.

"I know him!"

"Who is he?" Jake asks.

"He works at the Auto Body. In Stratus. He's supposed to be on a date tonight with—"

Dimples has opened the trunk, and a pair of sequined army boots emerges, bound but kicking.

Kaylee!

I squeal and start forward, but Jake's arm is already across my waist.

"We'll get her, Elle," he says. "But not now."

I watch in horror as the tall man lifts her from the car. He's not gentle, but he stands her upright, and I can see she's able to stand on her own. Red flames surround her body, her hands and feet bound, a bag over her head. The tall man throws her over his shoulder, and Dimples leads him toward the sliding front doors. His head turns slowly this way and that, and after a minute he slides his key into the lock.

Despite the terror I have for Kay, the hands of the men enthrall me. They're stained red, and I think again of Lady Macbeth.

Dimples unlocks the chain barring the doors, and they enter.

"Okay, Brielle," Jake says, "tell me."

"They're talking," I say. "I can't hear them, but I can see they're talking." Because the light of the Celestial overrides any other light source, it takes me a moment to figure out what they're doing. "The tall guy is waving something around the room. I can't quite . . . Oh, he has a flashlight. He's waving it around. Oh man, Jake, he's pointing at certain ones, and Dimples is untying the kids he's singled out. Three girls, my age maybe."

The rest of the kids are hardly moving now, and I get a clear view of the girls as they cling to one another and trip after the tall guy. With Dimples's gun pointed at their little bubble, the girls stumble ahead of him.

"He's taking them into the office. The three girls and Kaylee."

"We can't wait any longer, Brielle," Jake says, but I'm already reaching for the door handle, my eyes arrested by what's happening in the little office. The tall guy's gun is outstretched, menace written in the feverish colors of his face.

And then it happens. So fast. Two sharp blasts into the night air.

Pop! Pop!

Jake's body tenses beside mine. I grip the door handle, unable to move, even to open it. I watch as the glass bowl shatters, sending potato chips flying like shrapnel. Involuntarily, it seems, the man's right arm flies into the air as he twists in pain. Another loud *pop*, and the three girls behind Marco drop to the floor. They cover their ears as blood-red flames erupt around the man lounging on the couch. Erratically the inferno throbs into the light of the Celestial, until moments later the flames still and his thin, shadowy arm falls dead to the floor. The crimson flames are motionless now, but their brutal color stains the entire room, and at once I understand their significance.

"Who?" Jake asks quietly. He reaches slowly behind himself and places a hand on Marco's stirring frame. Immediately Marco's breathing returns to normal and the snoring resumes.

"The man," I stutter, as hot tears spring to my eyes. "The slimy little man in the office. He was sleeping. The tall guy shot him."

I've never seen a person's life end before. I've been touched by tragedy more than any one person ever should be, but I've never seen it. I've never watched a person twist, and wheeze, and try desperately to find another heartbeat, only to come up empty. I think of my mom. I think of . . .

"Do you think it was like that for Ali?" I ask.

"Let's not think about that right now," Jake says.

He's at my door, holding it open. I look into his face, alive with purpose, and I stumble upon courage. They cannot be allowed to harm any of those children. They won't end another life. Not while I'm here. Not while I can see what they're doing. What they're really, really doing.

I take Jake's hand, and we race across the ravaged street until we stand in front of the sliding warehouse doors. The chain hangs from the left door's handle, dragging in the dirt. The door is closed, but with a quick tug of Jake's hand it slides open several inches, bumping the chain with a soft metallic echo—still too loud for my comfort.

He pushes the door open a bit farther, just enough for the two of us to squeeze in. I follow and turn to pull the door shut behind us.

Jake's hand stops me.

"Leave it," he whispers, twisting his fingers into mine. "I won't be able to see much if you close it."

Around us, whimpers prickle like static electricity. Now that we're closer, I notice that the black substance coating the floor seems to be oozing from the children—from their very skin.

"What is it, Jake?"

"What is what?" he murmurs, pulling me along.

"The black tar. It's stuck to everything." I want to scrub the hateful mud from each of their faces.

"Fear," Jake answers. "Now you know why it's so hard to shake."

Seeing it like this is crushing. How do you eliminate something that multiplies? Something so prolific?

"It's everywhere."

"Yes," Jake says softly. "Fear does that."

The children are whispering now. They've seen us. I let Jake lead me to the center of the room where they're gathered. They're tied in groups of four or five around metal poles.

"We're here to help you," Jake says quietly. We drop to our knees, and I feel the tar soak through my jeans and slide up my thighs. Lukewarm and soupy at first, its temperature begins to drop, and my body is caught in a battle of climate: the heat radiating from the halo verses the icy fear wrapping me tight. Tears sting my eyes as I look around.

The children are so young—most of them too young to fight back, some of them closer to my age. Here and there they bear the marks of violence, a busted lip, a black eye. Transparent red flames consume these, and although Jake's voice is kind, they shrink away from us, as far as their ropes will allow.

With both hands I pull the beanie tight to my head, craving the halo's warmth. I shudder with relief as courage itself seems to creep from under the cap, chasing the chill of fear from my body.

From somewhere comes the sound of a door creaking open and slamming hard against metal. We look around, but even my Celestial eyes can't find the source.

"Through there," a boy says, pointing toward the office door, now closed. His eyes are wide in his hollow face, and though he's far too thin, he's most likely the oldest of the captives. "There's a door that opens to the outside. That's where they hose you off before they sell you."

"Sell you?" I ask, spitting the bitter words from my mouth.

Large, sad eyes stare back at me, but no one answers.

"No one's getting sold tonight," Jake says. "I promise." He looks around, squinting. "You might not see us for a bit, but we'll be back."

Something grabs my free hand, and I jump. I turn to see a girl, no more than ten, clutching at me. Her dirty brown hair has been braided recently.

"I want my mom," she says.

My jaw trembles. "Me too."

"Let go, Ali," an older girl whispers, pulling the child away. The two halves of my broken heart clank and bump together until my chest rises and falls.

"It's okay," I tell the older girl, and she loosens her grasp on the child. "Your name is Ali?" The little girl nods at me, and I can't contain the tears now running down my face. "That's a beautiful name."

Child after child inches toward us. I feel another hand on my back. Little fingers close around my ankle. I have never in my life felt so utterly helpless and so absolutely necessary at the same time.

"Feel her hand," I hear a small voice say.

"His too," comes another voice.

The child Ali runs an icy finger down my forearm. "You're warm like the sunshine," she says. I pull her tiny frame against mine and squeeze with all my might, wishing the heat of the Celestial could warm each and every one of them.

More noise. Heavy thuds echo through the warehouse.

We freeze in our hunched positions as the sound of running water pounds the side of the aluminum building. I stand, knowing I'm the only one able to see through the darkness. I turn my eyes toward the office and focus hard.

I see the vile man dead on the floor and focus on the far wall beyond him. It, too, thins out, and I see all three girls lined up against the building. Dimples directs a garden hose at each of them, and they turn this way and that according to his command. The tall man stands close, his hand wrapped around Kaylee's bicep. She's next to him, still bound, still blind, her entire body soaked in fear.

I swallow. "They're hosing the girls off out back."

Another car, maybe two, can be heard pulling into the gravel lot outside. And then voices, many different voices, fill the night, heated and arguing.

"We'll be back," Jake says, his voice heavy with emotion. "I promise."

As he says these binding words, the golden light of the Celestial breaks through a smear of tar on Ali's forehead. The fear glued there dissolves like sugar in water.

I am shaken by this reality—that how we feel, what we do, is all connected inextricably to this realm. It seems the choices we make start here somehow.

The Celestial is every bit as real as the world we walk around in every day, and as I stare around this room of horrors, it occurs to me that the Celestial holds more truth than I'll ever fully comprehend. The Terrestrial is a facade, a place where we can control how we're viewed, how our friends and neighbors see us. Here, though, in this heavenly realm, nothing can be covered, nothing hidden. Fear is *literally* painted on the faces of the afflicted.

I turn and look at Jake. His eyes glow white with compassion as he takes in the sea of hopelessness that surrounds us. I, too, would die before I let anything else happen to these children.

"We need to hide," he says.

Like me, Jake is wrapped up in little arms, all straining against their bonds to reach us. We gently pull ourselves away and scamper to the darkest corner of the warehouse, ducking behind a pile of garbage. As we hunker there I realize we have absolutely no plan. The more I think about it, the more foolish it seems to have come all this way empty-handed. Although what I'd do with a gun, I have no idea. So instead of gripping the lifeless steel of a handgun, my hand blazes hot inside of Jake's, and I feel brave. Whatever it takes, we'll get these children out of here.

Still I wonder: Will help come?

Where are the angels when so many lives hang in the balance?

27

Canaan

Two Shields cut through the air, Helene taking the lead, Canaan just behind. He's never encountered an angel as fast as she is, and keeping up with her swift movements is exhilarating. A wind, warm against his Celestial skin but frosty cold in the Terrestrial, has picked up, sweeping the storm along with them toward the city. Through flashes of clouds and shimmering raindrops falling anxiously to the ground, they fly.

Canaan opens his mouth and allows the praises of the Almighty to flood his lips. The swell of his tenor is joined by Helene's melodic alto, vibrantly rich and full for such a tiny being. Together they sing, on and on, until before them, like the surge of a perfect storm, the clouds gather heavy and full. In the distance shocks of lightning fall, and the rumble of thunder shakes the sky. Canaan pulls up, arriving at Helene's side.

Her mind speaks. "There's more than one."

Canaan follows her line of sight until he locates the warehouse nestled at the base of a massive bridge. It's hardly visible through the haze.

How he hates fear!

Its thick sludge shamelessly glues men to their anxiety, but even worse is the sense of dread it brings as it settles around them like fog. So heavy, so thick is *this* concentration of terror that the two angels can see it easily from a distance.

Atop the warehouse, like the grotesque gargoyles haunting the gothic cathedral of Notre Dame, three demons crouch vigilant. Their forms have deteriorated over the centuries, the light taking its toll. Their strength, however, is not to be underestimated.

"Damien is not among them," Canaan notes.

"I have no doubt he will join his brothers before long." Helene is tensed for battle, her hand already resting on the hilt of her blade.

"We must move carefully."

Helene's hand eases off her sword, and she drops her head in prayer. A moment later her white eyes find Canaan's.

"Forgive my impatience. I have worked alone for far too long. I did not expect my attachment to the Father's beloved to be such. Their sorrow, their fear, is heavy upon me, and your caution is well received. I do not wish to be rash."

"Victory is secured for the little ones," Canaan assures her. "Of that I am certain. But there are other lives at stake. We must act decisively."

She turns her face to the warehouse. "I will follow your lead."

28

Brielle

Through the garbage heap in the far corner of the warehouse, my eyes focus on the gaggle of strangers who have entered. They stand in clusters near the entrance. I've lost track of the number of cars I heard pull into the gravel lot outside, but for now at least, all the visitors seem to be indoors.

The group closest to the door consists of a very old man and his bodyguard. In the Celestial, the old man is nearly as shadowy as the dead man in the office. His bald head shakes on his shoulders with what I recognize as Parkinson's disease, but his yellow eyes are alert and greedy as he scans the children. His bodyguard pounds a switch on the wall with his fist. Overhead, industrial lights brighten the warehouse—something I only notice when Jake points it out to me. He sighs in relief, and I understand how much he hates being blind.

It seems these two have been here before. The bodyguard grows impatient and begins to wander to and fro through the sea of children, causing me to nearly crawl out of my skin with anxiety. He strolls through the captives, shoving at the children with the toe of his boot like he's examining the sturdiness of

furniture at a rummage sale. As I focus on him, his figure transforms before my eyes.

He's not human.

Like a holographic trading card, parts of his true self come
into view as he turns this way and that. He makes his way toward
us, angling his head to take in the cherubic face of a towheaded
girl. With a sharp intake of air, I nearly give away our position.

"What is it?" Jake peers through a gap in the pile, straining
as he takes in the large blond man.

"He's not right," I answer. "Not normal."

"What do you mean?"

"The left side of his face," I say, my voice hushed. "I could
have sworn it—" But I don't finish. The man tilts his head upright
again, and the anomaly disappears. There he stands, seemingly
human. The Marlboro man personified.

"What, Elle?" Jake says. "What did you see?"

"His face . . . it was almost skeletal. His skin was black,
scorched, and it hung from his face like it had been nearly
melted away."

The light around Jake flashes bright and then fades back to
its normal shine. His face takes on a sickened glaze.

"What does it mean?"

"A demon, Elle. He's a demon."

"Another one?"

I turn my eyes back to the Marlboro man. He takes the
child's face in one of his oversized hands. As he raises her chin,
his fleshy human hand transforms into a black claw—a black
claw only I can see. Sharp talons, invisible to the child, pierce
her smooth skin. She stifles a gulp, and silent tears slide down
her cheeks. The old man leans forward on his cane and laughs

maliciously as he watches his accomplice terrorize the girl. The demon smiles at her response and stands, releasing the child's face with a careless flick. The black mud of fear pours liberally from each of the four holes he's cut into her skin—three from the piercings along her cheek and one from a larger hole his opposing talon has punctured in her chin. I squeeze Jake's hand because I don't know what else to do.

"She'll be all right," he assures me, though his face is painfully stoic. "It's just fear. We'll take care of that, okay?"

Jake can't see the holes cut into her face, but he can see her fear.

We can all see her fear.

Another group stands talking among themselves. Farthest from the old man is an attractive but harsh-looking woman. She is voluptuously squeezed into her bodice, and her round chest heaves up and down beneath a faux leather jacket. She puffs on a cigarette and casually waves it about as she speaks. The trail of metallic fire it leaves in the Celestial reminds me of the sparklers Dad and I used to wave about on Independence Day.

A pang of angst strikes me as I think of Dad, entirely unaware of this world of light and darkness and the danger I'm now in. This reality, dangerous or not, has the capacity to devastate him. I shake off the feeling. I don't have time to be distracted.

Again I take in the provocative woman. She is flanked by a feminine-looking man dressed in a fitted purple suit and a girl, probably my age, her face covered with thick makeup. The girl stands, arms folded across her chest, in skinny jeans and a heavy down jacket. Expensive designer boots are laced to her knees. She seems to respond appropriately to whatever the other two are saying, but fear seeps through her clothing, and a murky liquid streams down her face. She struggles to keep her watery eyes from the children.

Between this group and the old man stands a lone wolf. He fiddles with his cell phone, utterly bored and unmoved by the despair before him.

The light surrounding these six individuals varies. The old man alone has a shadowy appearance, but the atmosphere around the others is hardly reassuring. A fuzzy gray light bounces dully from most of them.

The Marlboro man, of course, is different. Mostly, the light responds to him in the same manner as the others, but whenever I catch a glimpse of his demonic appearance the light pulls away, leaving an empty blackness between his form and the brightness of the Celestial.

I jump as the office door bangs open. The guy with the ponytail strides into the room, his hands stained red with murder.

"Sorry to keep you all waiting," he says with a roguish grin. "First things first, if you don't mind. This is a gun-free zone, ladies and gentlemen."

Dimples stomps up from behind Ponytail and pats down each of them, pulling a few guns from the lot before retreating into the office. By far, the lone wolf is the most reluctant to hand over his handgun, but the voluptuous woman is none too pleased herself.

"What is this, Juan? Where's Horacio?" she demands, one hand on her hip.

Juan steps up to the trio, taking the woman's hand and kissing it. "Cleo! You look ravishing."

She bats her lashes and drops her cigarette to the dirt, where she grinds it out under the heel of her ridiculously inappropriate stiletto. He turns his eyes on the younger girl at her side.

"Horacio didn't tell me Michelle would be accompanying you!" His gaze makes the girl blush. He pulls her to his chest and kisses her cheek. He is suave, but even I can see he's insincere. "It's been a long time, Michelle." He slaps her on the behind and briskly moves away, offering his arm to Cleo.

"Really, Juan," she complains. "You've kept us waiting, you strip us of our weapons, and still, where is Horacio? He assured me he would be here."

"I cannot tell you, my lady, where Mr. Santilla is. All I know is he's asked me to stand in for him. Tell me, Cleo, wouldn't you rather look at me?" He winks at her and leads her toward the man in black, smirking at the others.

"Jules," Juan says, extending his hand. "We haven't met, but Horacio speaks highly of you."

"Well," the man says with a sneer, "Santilla's always been a fool."

Juan chuckles and continues past him to the old man and his escort.

"Henry," Juan says, bowing elegantly. "Nice to see you again. I've pulled a few of the girls I thought may fit each of your needs, but of course you're welcome to take your pick of the lot." He gestures grandly to the rows of children now doing their best to disappear behind their binds. "Eddie!"

Dimples pushes and prods the four older girls into the room, Kaylee bringing up the rear. With the exception of Kaylee, the girls stand dripping with hose water—their clothes pasted to their wet bodies. Kaylee's face is uncovered now. Her hands and mouth remain taped.

All business now, Cleo struts toward the girls, her two comrades joining her. Seeing they're in the market for a similar purchase, Jules moves quickly as well.

Henry stays put. "Did Horacio tell you—I requested a blonde. Several, actually."

Juan answers him, but his voice is drowned by the heated discussion Cleo and Jules are having. They're arguing over a red-head—fifteen, sixteen years old, maybe. She stands drenched so heavily in fear I can no longer make out her facial expression. Her thin frame rattles side to side, and she cries out as they each yank on one of her arms in a sadistic game of tug-of-war.

"I do not think so, madam." Jules's voice rises to a feverish pitch. "You seemed perfectly content with the brunette until I showed interest in this one."

"I was here first, you crazy little man, and that means I get first pick!" Cleo screams back.

"First pick, my—"

A shot rings out into the night air and everyone freezes, their eyes trained on Juan's .45.

"What happened to your no-gun policy?" Jules says. Both Cleo and Henry also look put out.

"No guns for the *customers*, Jules," Juan says with a smirk. "I'm sure you understand."

"No, I don't understand," Jules hisses back. "You are just as likely to turn on us. How do I know you even work for Horacio?"

"You'll just have to trust me," Juan answers. "Or not. It makes no difference to me."

Jules crosses his arms defiantly but is silent.

"This room is full of suitable merchandise, and you two are fighting over one worthless girl."

"Worthless to you, but this girl could make me a decent stack of cash," Cleo argues, tugging on the girl's arm again.

"I'll tell you what," Jules counters. "I'll drop her off on your street corner when I'm done with her."

"My street corner!" Cleo is furious. "My girls do not stand on street corners!"

Again Juan fires his gun into the air, silencing both Jules and Cleo. The children duck and cover their ears. Their cries pierce the air, and the older children try to quiet the younger ones. Henry clucks at the chaos.

Dimples steps up.

"Here," he says, grabbing Kaylee.

I have to clamp a hand over my mouth to stifle the cry building up inside.

"She's fresh, pretty. You'll have to keep her muzzled—got quite a mouth on her—but I'm sure she'll bring either of you exactly what you're looking for."

Kaylee releases a string of unintelligible angry words and swings her long arms toward Dimples. Her elbow connects with his temple, and he drops. He tries to stand, but before he gets a chance she kicks out with those sequined cowboy boots. His head snaps sideways, and he flops back, unconscious.

"Wow," Jake breathes.

Cleo shakes her head. "I have enough attitude as it is."

Jules, though, is obviously intrigued. "There is something very spirited about her, isn't there?" He blocks Kaylee's arms with a single hand and takes her chin in the other. "What do you think, darling? Would you like to be a movie star?"

"Noooooooooo!!!!!!"

From behind a stack of empty pallets, Marco dives at Juan

and knocks the gun away. It skids across the concrete and disappears into the mass of children. With a resounding clatter and several moments of echoing clamor, the pallets, unsettled by Marco's movement, totter and fall—one after the other—to the ground.

Jules takes advantage of the distraction and heaves Kaylee over his shoulder. She swings and kicks, but Jules continues on, making for the door.

Surprise had been on Marco's side, and now he sits straddling Juan's chest. He throws punch after punch at him, but Juan's much larger and his forearms seem to be taking the brunt of it. I fear Marco isn't doing much damage.

"We have to help him!"

"No, we don't," Jake says. "We have to help her."

I follow his gaze to the door. Kaylee has grasped the steel door frame with her bound hands, but she's hopeless against Jules. He throws his shoulder into her stomach, forcing her hands free, and she screams.

Jake releases my hand and sprints from behind the garbage heap.

"Jake!"

But he doesn't respond. He's too far away already, running fast toward the door. Through the wall I watch as Jules turns right, toward the gravel lot. Kaylee swings her bound arms and kicks her legs, fighting hard against her captor. Jake's close, but Jules reaches his vehicle, a dark SUV. He opens the front passenger door and shoves Kaylee inside.

A wounded yelp draws my attention, and with my lack of focus the wall rematerializes, blinding me to the action in the parking lot. I look around for the source of the distraction.

It seems the tables have turned for Marco, and now Juan sits astride his torso, bringing practiced elbow after practiced elbow down on Marco's face. Flames of violence erupt around the two men, keeping time with their accelerating heart rates.

My eyes move desperately around the warehouse, but there's nothing there to inspire faith. No savior come to rescue us. What I *do* see causes chilling beads of sweat to race down my warm spine.

Cleo, following Jules's lead, is dragging the screaming redhead toward the door by her long, wet hair. Michelle and the man in the purple suit scurry behind.

They pass the old man, Henry. His gnarled hands grip his cane, and he guffaws at the spectacle before him, his demon-friend gone.

An unnatural movement draws my attention, and I turn my face toward the aluminum ceiling.

There he is.

The demon hovers above us, invisible to everyone but me. I know it's him, and yet his appearance is so frightfully different than it had been. The scorched skin, skeletal masses protruding here and there—it's all exaggerated now, almost unbelievably so. Black talons, dangerous talons, grow out of his chalky gray hands.

I crouch behind the garbage heap, too scared to move. Despite the halo's warmth, my hands are shaking, flinging black tar into the air. My feet are gummed to the cement floor with the stuff, and I realize, painfully, that I'm paralyzed. My lips barely move as I utter the first words that come to mind.

"Please, God. Help."

And then he's gone.

The demon shoots through the roof and into the sky, leaving

a trail of smoke behind. The gut-wrenching realization that only I can see him—that there are forces here the others are unaware of—reminds me that something, somewhere is hunting Jake. Damien, the author of this nightmare, could arrive at any time.

I scan the room again. Violent flames blackened by fear and sadness stain the creamy orange expanse of the Celestial. We have to get these children out of here, and we have to do it now.

I wrench my eyes toward Marco and cringe as he narrowly avoids an overhand arching punch thrown by Juan. He's doing everything he can. Outside, Jake is doing the same.

Now it's my turn. I can't just stand here and shake.

Swallowing the fear I have for Jake and Marco, and without a plan of any sort, I duck out from my hiding place and run pell-mell for the door, arriving just as Cleo and gang exit the warehouse. At top speed I follow them outside, catching my hip on the chain that's kept so many children locked inside this netherworld. I ignore the welt I know is forming and force myself forward. I'm quite possibly the redhead's only hope.

Michelle is at the back of the cluster, her high-heeled boots slowing her down. I grab a yank of her hair and pull. Together we tumble to the ground, and she screams out. Cleo stops at the noise and turns back, pulling the redhead with her.

"If you want this girl back, you'll have to trade me!" I shout over Michelle's screams. I have her pinned to the ground, my knees pressing into her lower back, my long arms jamming hers to her sides.

"Get the car, Sam," Cleo says irritably. The purple-suited man scampers off, his expression dim. "Who are you, princess?" Cleo asks, her painted eyes narrowed.

"Just give me the girl and you can have this one back."

Beneath me, Michelle whimpers. "I don't want to go back," she sobs.

My head drops. I've just lost my bargaining chip. I could never force this girl to return to such a life. For all I know, her story is no different than that of the dozens of children tied up inside.

Cleo laughs. "Well, that changes things, doesn't it?"

I sit up and lean back, releasing Michelle's arms. My hand lands on cold, hard steel.

"I guess it does," I answer. Cleo turns to go, and with a swift prayer that my aim has improved since a misguided attempt at archery years ago, I swing the heavy chain over my head. It narrowly misses the redhead as it connects with Cleo's neck. Her head snaps forward with a crack, and she drops heavily to the ground and does not move. The two girls look at me, and my chest heaves as I consider the possibility that I've killed her.

Tires squeal, kicking up rocks and gravel. We dive out of the way as the driver pulls up inches from Cleo in a midnight-blue Monte Carlo. He sticks a ferrety face out the window and covers his mouth at the sight of the still form on the ground. With a quick glance at Michelle, he drives away, nearly colliding with the Dumpster that Jake and I skirted earlier tonight.

Michelle walks over to Cleo's body, turning her over with the toe of her boot.

"Did I . . . is she . . ."

There are no red flames. No marks of violence, but I can't even formulate the question.

"No," Michelle says, the sludge of fear evaporating from her legs. "She's not dead."

"Too bad." It's the redhead.

Michelle turns, and a quirky smile replaces the fear.

"You guys have to get out of here," I say, dropping the chain and pushing to my feet.

"What about you?" Michelle asks, stripping off her jacket and passing it to the dripping redhead.

"I've got work to do. Go and don't come back."

"We'll send help," the redhead promises.

"Help is already on its way," I say. It's a statement. It's a prayer. "Just get as far away from here as you can."

They stare at me, and I know—without knowing them at all—that these two girls are braver than I've ever had cause to be.

"Just go," I say. "Please."

"Come on," Michelle says, grabbing the other girl's hand and pulling her to her feet. "Let's go."

"Thank you," the redhead tells me, her face now entirely clear of the blackness. She and Michelle take off, running fast down the broken road.

Thunder rolls across the sky, followed by a flash of lightning. Heavy raindrops fall from the black clouds above. The storm has arrived.

I turn and run toward the parking lot, where I last saw Jules struggling with Kaylee. The rain pours down, soaking my face, my clothes. My eyes rake the lot, but there's no sign of Jake, and the SUV is gone.

If I hadn't hesitated, if I'd moved faster . . . maybe . . .

Again a squeal of tires causes me to jerk, and I turn to see Jules's SUV coming down the road toward me. I stand in the direct beam of his headlights, which look strange and milky in the light of the Celestial—but I'm frozen. Like a deer.

For the first time I understand the expression.

29

Damien

amien!"

His name rings silently across the night sky, perceptible to him and four others.

He knows he's late. But is he too late?

The demon stops abruptly. With his outer wings humming against the night, he stretches his inner wings wide, unfurling them against the blushing sky.

He must appear powerful. In control.

He opens his eyes as wide as possible, but they dry out and glaze over. He fights the discomfort and stares jealously at his fallen brothers as they advance from a distance.

They're still several hundred yards off, but their fitness is apparent. They approach with more daring than he's had in nearly a century. There's no doubt in Damien's mind they've either been shielded from the light for some time or been given ample opportunity to heal. They fly with abandon, their eyes barely registering the radiance that is his nemesis.

A hundred yards in front of the others, flying straight at Damien, is Maka. He is by far Damien's biggest risk. Rarely assigned to earth, he's spent most of his days in the direct company of the Prince. He's strong, influential among their kind, and has the ear of Lucifer himself. Exactly what Damien needs. Although if this goes wrong, Maka's involvement ensures that Damien's failures will be paraded before the very being he desires to impress. It's a gamble, but he's desperate, and opportunities like this do not come along often.

Flanking him are the Twins: Larat and Latham. At one time these two were comrades of Damien's. But, characteristic of their kind, the alliance lasted only as long as it was mutually beneficial. A breed entrenched in deception can hardly be expected to work well together for extended periods. And yet Larat and Latham have maintained a peace for centuries. The Prince himself dubbed them "the Twins" long ago. Very similar in build and appearance, the two have had consistent success that has continued to secure them common assignments.

This allows them to swap realms more often, to alternate between the scorching light of the Celestial and the comfortable but restricting realm of the Terrestrial. And, like Maka, they are favorites of those higher up the food chain than Damien—frequently recalled from the front lines.

Another twenty yards or so, beyond the Twins, gyrating in midair, is Javan. Over and over he flips, falling nearly to the earth before pumping his wings and launching himself into the sky again. Javan's been on assignment in the Terrestrial for many years and is the brother Damien runs into with the most frequency. For the past fifty years or so he's been attached to the same charge: Henry Madison. The nature of his job with Henry keeps him almost entirely in the Terrestrial.

Based on the amount of freedom Javan appears to be reveling

in, Damien can tell it's been some time since that brother has been able to escape into the Celestial. Javan has complained about this aspect of his job, but even Damien understands the benefits. Javan's eyes are not nearly as damaged.

For a long moment Damien rests his eyes, closing them firmly against the light, hoping to show as little weakness as possible when he and his brothers are finally face-to-face. It's a few seconds only before he feels Maka's breath upon his brow, and he opens them, dull and tainted.

"*You* orchestrated this?" Maka draws his scimitar and points it at Damien's throat.

Dozens of times Damien has considered the best way to play this—the best approach. They're all masters of deception, distrusting one another and the world around them. It doesn't matter what he says, what he does, Damien's brothers will assume the worst of his motives, and lying to them will not get him any closer to the Prince.

"Yes, I orchestrated this," Damien answers. "I need your eyes."

"Take care of your own, and you will not need to borrow mine!" Maka is angry, but not nearly as angry as Damien feared. His lips twist, betraying his curiosity, and it becomes apparent he'll hear his brother out.

Damien will wait for the others, though. He won't repeat himself. Not tonight.

Moments later Larat and Latham arrive, grinning maliciously as Maka's blade brushes against Damien's neck.

Larat shakes his head in disapproval, and his mind joins the conversation. "Surely you know better, Damien. What could be worth deceiving four superior beings?"

"Three superior beings, I think," Latham corrects, shoving the just-arrived Javan with a muscled arm.

Javan, for his part, continues to bounce on the Celestial currents, his tongue hanging beneath jagged teeth like an eager dog, breathless and beaming.

"Still," Larat continues, "this doesn't sit well." He, too, brandishes his scimitar. "There are reasons we don't gather often."

Maka drops his weapon to the side and approaches, his fangs just inches from Damien's.

"Exposing our charges to the power of a Shield is enough to merit my wrath, but to expose us—your brothers—without so much as a warning! Surely you've considered the consequences."

The power of a Shield. So Canaan is here.

"It's highly unlikely all of our charges will make it out alive," Latham agrees.

"Mine's about to croak anyway."

"Shut up, Javan. It's even more unlikely each of us will make it out unscathed. And I promise you this, Damien," Maka says, "you will be the first one we feed to the light."

Envy and resentment swell until Damien can take it no more. He moves forward, forcing Maka back. A growl escapes his lips. "Of course I have considered the consequences! What I have to show you is far more dangerous than anything I am exposing you or your charges to."

Rain falls past the demonic assembly, but in the distance slivers of light break through the fog, encasing the warehouse.

Cursing, Maka sheathes his weapon. "Speak, then, fool, and make it fast. We're already losing ground."

30

Brielle

*L*ike lightning from the sky, something falls fast and hard, landing on the hood of the moving SUV. A blood-curdling scream pierces the night air, and it's several moments before I realize it's coming from me. Finally my eyes focus on the source of the collision, and I clamp a hand to my mouth.

I can't believe what I'm seeing.

Canaan crouches—invisible to Jules—on the entirely demolished hood of the SUV. Jules is stunned, his car imploding before his very eyes. He sits there bleeding and staring absently. I squint at the silvery sheen of Canaan's extensive wingspan. His feet and arms are bare, but his torso and legs are wrapped in heavy threads of golden light. His silver hair flutters on waves of yellow heat.

Canaan drives a muscled arm through the windshield and grabs Jules by the shirt, pulling him roughly through the windshield. The violent gesture rocks Jules into hysteria, and he bawls like a baby. He kicks his feet madly, trying to find the ground. Canaan throws his own head forward, his Celestial skull connecting with Jules's forehead. It's such an unangelic thing to do, I laugh aloud.

Canaan turns and laughs with me, and the bizarre sight gets even stranger. I see Jake, tightly strapped to Canaan's chest like a tandem skydiver. Only what's holding them together seems to be a pair of sinewy wings—all but transparent. They cover Jake from head to toe, and while I know I'm viewing something sacred, I can't help but think the poor boy looks swathed in Cling Wrap. Like a satin scarf fluttering on the wind, the wings open, and Jake steps onto the hood of the car and jumps to the ground. Jules, Jake, and I get wetter and wetter with each passing second while Canaan remains completely dry—the raindrops nothing but sparkling diamonds falling from the heavens above and soaking into the ground.

"Jake said you'd come."

"And I did," Canaan answers.

It's strange. His lips don't move, but I hear his voice clearly. Like he's speaking into my ear. Like he's inside my head.

Jake has already retrieved Kaylee from the SUV. She's uninjured but catatonic. In shock, I'm sure. He wraps her tight against his chest, shielding her from the rain and whispering something softly in her ear.

The emotion that chokes me at this precious sight feels confused: I want to be like Jake. I want to protect my best friend. *This* best friend. But I, too, yearn to be protected—like Kaylee— held tight in loving arms. Guarded. Safe.

Again Canaan's voice sounds in my head. "Will you grab the woman?"

Cleo.

Aware that hefting her is not an option, I grab hold of each arm and drag. Her heels cut tracks in the mottled ground, and she looks almost kind in her sleep. It's amazing what changes when we dream.

Canaan lifts both Jules and Cleo into the backseat of the SUV, where they lie quieter and more civil to one another than they've been all evening.

An unfamiliar sound draws my gaze to the sky. Bat-like figures cut through the atmosphere high above, but I can't make out anything beyond their dark wings.

And then I hear Canaan's voice saying, "I have to go. Stay with Jake."

Before I can respond, Canaan leaves the ground, the whiteness of his wings glistening as they propel him upward.

"What is it?" Jake asks.

"Canaan. He had to go."

A maniacal cry makes its way outside.

"Marco," I say.

But Jake's already running, Kaylee curled tight against him. I follow, panic fighting against the halo for control of my emotions. "Please, please." I focus hard on the wall before me, and it disappears as we close in.

Celestially, the warehouse is a mess. Fear has multiplied, nearly drowning the mass of children. I can't imagine the weight they feel as it presses against them. Flames continue here and there, but none so ferocious as the blaze roaring around Marco and Juan. They continue to circle, both bruised and battered and hesitant to engage.

Suddenly Juan lunges at Marco, swatting at him like a bear. Marco slides to the side, and with a jab to Juan's ear sends him sprawling to the ground.

"We have to hurry!" I yell.

Jake crosses the threshold and sets Kaylee on her feet. His momentum keeps him moving forward. I grab her hand and continue to run, pulling her with me.

"Watch out!" I cry, but it's too late.

Juan is already in the air, diving straight for Marco's knees. He finds his target, and the two plummet into the mess of broken pallets. With a loud crack, Marco's head connects with the corner of one. He struggles to right himself, and his nemesis laughs.

"You'd think karma would be on your side," Juan snorts.

He crouches down, reaching for something at his feet and giving me a better view of Marco. A sickening realization attacks me. Marco's arm is pinned between two pallets, the weight of Juan's body holding him there.

"Karma and I have never seen eye to eye," Marco says, continuing to squirm. He moves his arm back and forth in a futile attempt to break free.

Juan pulls himself upright, and in his hand he holds a broken two-by-four dislodged from one of the pallets. Nails protrude hazardously from the end of the board. He raises it high above his head, and Marco ducks awkwardly.

Jake picks up speed as the children scream and wail. But he's not going to get there in time. There's no way.

And then, *pop!*

The hollow sound of a gunshot drives me to the ground. I fall on top of Kaylee as it echoes through the warehouse.

Where did it come from? I chance a look.

Jake is sprawled just feet from the dueling men, and a shock wave pummels my chest at the thought of him taking a bullet. But he, too, raises his head. Silence permeates the room as Juan turns toward us in surprise. The left shoulder of his shirt blossoms like a monstrous flower and in seconds is soaked through with blood.

Rage tears from his chest, raw and terrifying. Again he raises the board. Marco covers his head with his free arm.

"Shoot now!" I yell, looking frantically about for the shooter. "Shoot!"

From the center of the room someone fires. I flinch in response but keep my focus on Juan. The bullet finds its mark, and he drops instantly. Like a rag doll he flops from one pallet to the next until with a dull thud he sprawls to the ground. His putrid, sallow eyes fade into darkness, and the flames surrounding him still.

"Who?" I ask, looking around for the shooter.

Jake pushes to his knees and looks around the room. "There," he says. He stands and makes his way toward the children.

A girl, maybe fourteen, kneels near the middle of the group, still bound to those on her right and left. In her hand is Juan's gun—the only gun left in the building. She shakes, and tears stream down her dirty face. Jake runs to her, sinks to the ground at her side, and reaches a steady hand out for the gun.

"It's okay," Jake says. "You . . . did good."

"Daddy taught me to shoot," she says, her lip quivering. "Just birds though. Birds are different."

She drops the gun then, letting it fall into Jake's hand. He pulls the girl into his arms and lets her cry.

I leave Kaylee where she is, huddled on the floor, and move to help Marco. It takes me a minute, but when I'm done he's free of the pallets holding him hostage.

"Your skin." Marco stares incredulously at my hands. "It's so hot."

I release his arm and he steps back, wary.

I've been there. I understand.

He turns slowly away, his eyes on mine until the last possible second, and then he walks toward the children. He weaves through them, stopping between Jake and the shooter.

"Thank you," Marco says, dropping to his knees and pulling the girl into his arms.

"Can I go home now?" the girl asks.

Marco looks to Jake.

"Yes," Jake says. "Soon."

From somewhere near the door, clapping hands and laughter can be heard. In a room full of calamity, the noise is unhinging. The old man, Henry, shakes from head to toe, the hook of his cane draped over his arm as he cheers.

"Bravo, young lady," he exclaims. "I fear this evening's purchase will be postponed, but I do like a girl with spirit."

Marco stands and lunges toward the old man. Jake tries to stop him, but Marco breaks free, craze consuming his face.

And then Henry's gone.

The clapping and the laughter are silenced.

The old man has disappeared into thin air.

31

Canaan

*F*rom high above, Canaan watches. Four fallen angels far below maintain their distance from the warehouse. They take turns scanning the sky, presumably looking for a Shield. It's this alone that forces Canaan to conclude they've yet to spot him and Helene beyond the cloud bank.

"What are they doing?" her mind asks.

"Waiting for a diversion."

"Of their own making?"

The sound of foreign wings answers in Canaan's place. The two Shields flip their legs horizontal and watch as directly below them, flying erratically, another fallen creature soars toward the warehouse.

"Watch the others," Canaan commands. "If Damien gets his hands on Brielle, there's no knowing what Jake will do to get her back."

Canaan drops below the clouds, familiar with the demon flying below him. Over the centuries Javan has adapted so well to the Terrestrial he rarely leaves it. He isn't much of a warrior but has mastered the arts of human addiction and lust. His charges are usually so deeply entrenched in their obsessions and cravings that they allow Javan an unprecedented level of control in their lives. He thrives on it, and a sick sort of symbiotic relationship is formed, tying Javan to his charge for decades longer than most demons stay with theirs.

One moment Javan is dipping through the roof and the next he's exploding out if it. But this time he's not alone. His inner wings smash a human bundle to his chest as he pushes higher and higher into the sky. But his charge slows him, and with the use of all four wings Canaan easily outstrips the fallen angel. Rising above him and dropping down, he draws his sword and blocks Javan's path.

Somersaulting backward through the air, the fallen one evades attack, but only just. Canaan torpedoes forward and swipes with his sword, slicing at Javan's wings. He connects with the primary feathers on Javan's right side, turning them to ash.

Javan hisses and wraps his outer wings tight against his frame. He drops a hundred feet or more before unfurling them and shooting away.

Canaan follows.

32

Damien

amien lands on the roof of the warehouse. Seconds
later Maka and the twins do the same. The devasta-
tion below sets his companions growling—both their
charges lie unconscious in a demolished SUV—evidence that
Canaan has indeed been here. Where he is now, Damien has no
idea, but it can't be far.

Damien opens his mouth and howls with delight. The boy
with the divine gift, so valuable to the Prince and his world of darkness, sits below them, unguarded and defenseless. He's moving
from child to child, cutting them free. Marco is here too, dragging
the lifeless body of Juan away from the children and into the office.
Jake stands, absent his Shield and surrounded by children.

It's almost too easy.

"Which one is it?" Maka demands. He doesn't believe Damien,
but he's too careful a demon to leave without making sure.

"That one there. With the child in his arms."

"If what you say is true, surely he will extend his hand to
one of the many injured below," Latham interjects, watching the
enticing flames lick at the captives. "We can observe from here."

"He'll never expose himself in front of so many witnesses."

Latham huffs. "How do you know that?"

"Would *you*?"

His brother bristles, but does not answer.

Damien continues. "It's up to you, of course, but it would be easier if you transferred."

"With a Shield nearby?" It's Larat.

"If Jake is reluctant to comply, it may take all of us to persuade him. That will move faster if he can see you. As you said, there's a Shield nearby, and I'd prefer to get this over with as quickly as possible."

"Javan's an idiot, but he can keep the Shield occupied for a few minutes." With a wheeze of irritation, Maka transfers to the Terrestrial, taking on his human form. He glares at the sky and shakes off the rain drenching him. The other two follow suit.

Silent as a wraith, Damien drops through the roof, hovering just above Jake's head. The boy stiffens. Before Jake can release the child in his arms, Damien cloaks them both with his inner wings and rises back to the roof. The demon releases the boy and child roughly and transfers to the Terrestrial.

Jake stumbles onto the roof, slides on the rain-soaked aluminum, and drops to his knees, the child pale and trembling as her wide eyes move from one demon to the other.

"Damien," Jake says. "It's been awhile."

"Not for me," Damien answers, relishing the opportunity to explain.

He stoops so he and the boy are eye level. The girl shrinks away, whimpering.

"I saw you last week, with the girl. You put your hands on her broken ankle, and the bone obeyed the grace in your hands.

You healed her with a touch. Impressive." He leans closer to Jake. He wants to taste his fear. "And then I saw her. The girl. Brielle Matthews. I saw her with the halo. I saw her *see*."

Even on this moonless night, Damien watches the blood drain from Jake's face, and though the boy works hard to stifle emotion, it's there, concealed by the Terrestrial, but palpable all the same: the fear, the anxiety the Fallen crave. Damien sniffs at the air in delight. Maka, Larat, and Latham—his brothers sense it too. They look from one to the other, their eyes wild with incredulity. The presence of fear isn't a complete confirmation of all Damien's told them, but it's a start.

"Is it true, boy?" Maka growls. "Can you heal?"

Jake doesn't answer. Instead his eyes move madly over the horizon, searching, finding nothing. Finally they settle again on Damien's face.

"You don't have to answer." Damien laughs. "But how about a little show and tell?"

He rips the girl from Jake's hands and shoves her away from him, sliding on the slick surface.

"Ali!" Jake cries as the girl comes to a stop a foot from the ledge.

Damien stands and pulls the Green Beret tactical knife from its sheath. He flings it, spinning, toward the girl. It slices through her forearm and into the aluminum building. Her chest heaves, and she groans.

"Girl has a nasty cut on her arm," he says. "Fix it."

The Twins grin, but Maka keeps his eyes glued to Jake's face.

The girl tries to sit up, but the knife holds her arm pinned. She yanks at it and chokes on her tears as she begins to understand the pain. She looks at Jake, who remains on his knees, and then at the four massive forms behind him. Her breathing accelerates, and as fear envelops her, they smile back.

Finally her screams pierce the night.

"Ali," Jake says, inching closer and closer to the girl.

He controls his emotions better than most. The demons can all smell the fear, so thick it nearly gives off flavor, but he keeps his voice calm as he takes the girl's face in his hands.

"Listen to me."

But the girl is hysterical, sobbing, fighting Jake off and pulling at the knife. Finally, despite Jake's best efforts to stop her, she pulls the knife free. Blood flows down her arm, running over her knuckles and onto the aluminum. As the blood mixes with the water flooding the roof, it seems to multiply, and her hysteria grows. She cradles her arm against her body and backs away from Jake. With her other hand she swings the knife around, keeping him at a distance. She is just inches from the ledge now, and Jake lunges for her, taking a swipe of the blade across his shoulder. He ignores it, grabs her shoe, and pulls her toward him. The knife falls from her hand and over the ledge of the building into the darkness below.

The boy reaches out his hand and pulls the girl's wounded arm toward him. "Ali, stop! You have to calm down. Please. I'll take care of it."

This is it! The moment Damien's worked so hard for. He holds his breath, knowing all his mistakes are meaningless now.

33

Brielle

This time when I'm pulled beneath the wings of an angel, I'm better prepared. Still, to say I'm disoriented would be to put it mildly.

One moment I'm cutting a raven-headed girl free, and the next I'm lifted up and away. Hot wind and the pounding of wings fill my senses, and I scream, but only momentarily. A soft, quiet voice speaks to me, settling my racing heart. And I know it's not Canaan. It's Helene.

"Miss Macy's new teacher?" I ask, realizing now where I'd heard the name.

"Yes," she croons.

I'm taller than she is, but she's strong. She holds me upright, facing out. My head below her chin, my feet hanging past hers. Her transparent wings wrap me tight from the beanie on my head to the toes of my green Chucks.

We emerge from the side of the warehouse, flying fast. I have no control over where we go or what we do, and that's unnerving. But Helene's humming. Something fast and lively that trills against my neck. Reverberates in my chest. Makes me brave.

And then I see the demons.

And Jake.

And the child, Ali.

She's so close to the ledge of the warehouse, and she's bleeding.

But Jake's there.

He reaches out a hand . . .

34

Damien

The girl disappears.

There and then gone.

The six eyes of Damien's fallen brothers burn into him. Every hair on his human arms stands tall, and he curses under his breath.

Jake drops his hand, and his shoulders sag in relief.

"The Shield," Maka says bitterly.

Without hesitation the four demons transfer to the Celestial and unsheathe their weapons.

"Canaan," Damien snarls. Now that his brothers suspect his words of truth, they'll fight at his side. He squints against the light and looks around.

"There," Larat's mind screams. He dives into the sky, Latham at his heels. Like well-aimed arrows, they fly toward the roof of a building across the way where a Shield stands, her sword drawn, the girl Ali tucked close against her body.

"Helene."

"Another Shield?" Maka's thoughts are incredulous. "What have you committed us to?"

The child is not alone in the safety of Helene's embrace. Through her translucent inner wings, Damien identifies the form of Brielle Matthews. The angel carries two.

"There are five of us, and only two of them," Damien's mind fights back. "It's worth it."

"You'd better hope so."

35

Canaan

anaan knows Javan's a diversion, but he carries with him a human soul. A tortured, corrupted human soul, but valuable nonetheless. Still, the unpredictable pursuit takes Canaan farther and farther from the warehouse, and it's not long before the Shield chooses to turn back. Leaving Helene four demons to contend with would yield a greater loss.

Not only that, but he's left Jake and Brielle in danger for far too long. Determination speeds the angel's wings, and the warehouse comes into view.

Jake is there. And Damien. But they're not alone. Leaping from the building is an enormous demon, midnight black and menacing. Canaan recognizes him by description alone.

He is Maka. More rumor than anything else.

Maka's massive wings expand and catch a gust of wind. He uses it to propel himself after two smaller demons, still substantial but not quite as large.

Canaan doesn't recognize them, but they fly in uncommon unity, sharing the wind as they move this way and that.

The three demons fly at Helene, stationed not far away on

the top of a neighboring building. She is dwarfed by the muscled bodies and immense wingspans diving at her, but Canaan judges their speed and is certain she's faster. Her sword is drawn, and her hair flies about wildly. She turns to the north, over the river, and the demons follow.

She takes orders well and is providing a much needed distraction. While Damien is hardly the highest ranking demon present, Jake won't be safe until Damien is sent to the pit. He has to be Canaan's first priority. Damien's eyesight, though weakened, should pick up the Shield's approach any time. Canaan unsheathes his weapon and opens his mouth, releasing waves of praise. They reverberate across the heavens like a war cry.

Damien lifts his eyes, glancing from Jake to the angel's flying form before launching himself into the sky and cutting off Canaan's path. His stance is weak—he expects the Shield to slow.

But Canaan doesn't.

The Shield lifts his sword to a hanging guard with the hilt by his ear and the tip of his sword aimed directly at Damien's chest. The demon's face registers alarm, and he dives to the side, swinging his scimitar recklessly. It misses. Canaan's sword, however, catches the wrist joint of Damien's wing. It snaps, and the feathers sizzle as the white light of Canaan's sword singes through them. Damien spins as he grapples with the imbalance. He falls several hundred feet before finally digging his talons into the side of a telephone pole to slow his fall.

Canaan knows he isn't out of the battle, but he takes advantage of Damien's drop and hovers over the roof of the warehouse where Jake sits alone in the rain. His knees are drawn up, and his head is bowed between them in prayer. The battle rages around him unseen, and as Canaan slows his wings and sets down he can hear Jake fighting with the only weapon at the boy's disposal.

"For we do not wrestle against flesh and blood, but against principalities, against powers, against the rulers of the darkness of this age, against spiritual hosts of wickedness in the heavenly places . . ."

Canaan transfers to the Terrestrial and pulls Jake to his feet.

"That was you, then?" Jake asks, relief in his words, on his face.

"What was me?"

"You took the child," he says. "That was you."

"The child?"

Jake swipes at the rain running down his face and squares his shoulders. "Damien doesn't just know about me. He knows about Brielle. He knows about the halo . . ."

Canaan is chagrined that he didn't consider it before. "Of course," he says. "The cemetery." He places his hands on Jake's shoulders—shoulders weighted with such a hefty burden. "It's my fault, and I am so sorry."

They stand facing one another—the Shield and his charge. Words can't erase their mistakes, and they know it. Damien must be defeated. He must be sent to the pit. There's no other way.

"Where is Brielle?"

"Inside."

Canaan moves his powerful Celestial eyes over the rooms below. "She's not inside, Jake." He realizes, too late, he's spoken the worst words possible.

Jake blanches and sputters, "Then I don't . . . I don't . . ."

"Helene," Canaan says. "She must have Brielle. You said something about a child?"

"Yes, a little girl. Someone cloaked her, took her. If it wasn't you . . ."

"Then it has to be Helene." Canaan is certain, but as the realization sets in, he struggles to stay in his Terrestrial form. Helene has two charges tucked to her body, and she is being chased by three demons.

"We have to go," he says.

He wraps Jake tight to his frame and transfers to the Celestial.

36

Brielle

We dip toward the roof, and a gust of wind fills my mouth as Helene opens her wings and closes them. So fast, so deft. And then the child is next to me, trembling and bleeding.

Helene's voice sounds in my head. "Hold her tight, Brielle. She needs you."

We're crammed so close I can't move to hug Ali, but I squirm until I'm able to wrap my hand around hers. Her head is sideways against Helene's chest, her eyes on me. Tears and snot run down her face, but her eyes flutter, and the fear melts away. She's succumbing to the heat and the peace of Helene's embrace.

If she remembers anything of this night, I hope it's this. This moment and nothing more.

The city flies by in a haze of lights.

And then I hear the demons.

Hissing and spitting.

Something grabs my shoe, but Helene's grip is fast and she flies harder, pulling us away. Still, I feel air whip by now, on my shins and ankles, pressing against my pants. Have her wings been injured?

We fly in and among the buildings, dropping between skyscrapers, Helene's outer wings pressing hard through the air. I hear the effort she's expending, feel it in the shudder of her body.

And then something sharp rakes my leg. I drop at least a foot as Helene's grip on me loosens. The child slides lower and lower as we fly. I tighten my left hand in hers and wrap my right arm tight about Helene's waist. Her grip is loose, so loose.

I pinch my eyes shut and wish for ground. Dirt and grass. Rock. Mud. Anything but sky.

My feet hit something hard, and I open my eyes. Before me is the most hideous thing I've ever seen. Scarier than Damien in the graveyard. Scarier than the demon I saw earlier in the warehouse. This one is massive. Thick and muscled. His wings hold him before me, flapping in the Celestial. They whip up a wind that smells of death and decay.

Helene swings her sword at him. She's not doing much damage, but she's keeping him at bay. I tighten my grip on her waist, my grip on the child. I can do nothing but hold on.

And then two more demons show up. Still large, but thinner than the beast before me. They fly back and forth in a sort of dance, making stabbing attempts with their strange-looking weapons.

Helene's better with the sword and disarms both of them before they do much damage. But still they keep coming. With their ugly, gnarled hands. Sharp talons slice at us, at Helene's outer wings. They make strange noises, cruel and inhuman, but I can see the fear in their eyes. Of her sword. Of an angel not even half their size.

Still, Helene's not going to make it much longer. Her inner wings hang in ruined tatters, and snowy white feathers are hacked away in bunches. I chance a look down.

There's no way we'll survive this fall.

And then Canaan blasts through the wall next to us. His arms high over his head, Jake crushed to his chest. He brings his sword down hard on the nearest demon, slicing through his shoulder and chest in a diagonal movement. The demon screams as the two pieces of his flailing form linger in midair, burning like the smoldering remains of a campfire. The smell of sulfur burns my nostrils as the brilliant light of the Celestial swallows what's left of him.

There are still two more demons, but my eyes are on Jake. His hands are pressed against Canaan's inner wings, and his white eyes stare into mine. They are light and life and hope and . . .

Panic.

His eyes trail to the girl hanging from my arm. I realize now how tired I am, how much my arm aches, but I won't let go. I know that.

Canaan turns, lifting his sword.

"Back up." His voice is loud in my mind. So much louder than Helene's.

Is she still humming?

"I said back up." Canaan looks from one demon to the other.

The gigantic one raises his hands, his weapon held tightly. He moves back a pace, casting an authoritative glance at the demon on his left. He, too, retreats.

For a moment they all stare.

And then the big one lunges, swinging his crooked sword

at Canaan. There's a decisive clang, and Canaan beats his wings hard, shoving him back. And then his elbow comes up, and he smacks the demon in the face with the hilt of his sword.

The demon roars and swings his crooked sword again and again. He's larger, but Canaan's faster, and though the demon's sword could devastate, it never touches the Shield.

The other demon takes advantage of Canaan's entanglement and darts past. Black talons reach again for me, for Ali. They reach for Helene, clawing at her face and neck. She aims her sword and plunges vigorously, losing her grip on the ledge but sinking her weapon deep into the chest of the demon.

And then we fall.

Don't let go. Don't let go.

That's all I can think as we tumble, wing over broken wing, toward the ground. Wind beats my face, tearing my closed eyes open. The ground is dazzling as it closes in on us, all bright and shiny. But I don't want to die. Not now, not today.

And then I stop.

In midair.

Canaan's hands are beneath my arms, stopping my momentum. His wings hold us in place.

"You all right, Brielle?"

"Helene . . . ."

She hangs against me, unconscious, my hold on her waist the only thing keeping us together. The child dangles from my left hand. I can't see her face but hope with everything in me that she's also unconscious.

"She'll be all right." Canaan wraps all of us in his enormous wings and launches into the sky.

37

Brielle

I topple from Canaan's wings and slide to my knees on the slick corrugated roof.

"Brielle!" Jake cries, stumbling out behind me. "Are you hurt?"

"No," I say. "I'm not hurt."

Canaan kneels next to me in his human form. He cradles the child against his shoulder, and Helene lies next to me, still in her Celestial form. Her angelic flesh is torn, her wings shredded.

"You're sure, Brielle? You're okay?" Canaan asks.

Am I? I don't know.

It's a skin-deep question with an answer too buried to dig up right now. I keep my eyes on Helene. "She was . . . brilliant."

"She'll heal, Brielle. We angels aren't quite so fragile as you."

"Good," I say, rubbing my hands against my stomach, willing my clenched muscles to relax. "That's good."

"Then you're okay?" Jake says. "You're sure?"

"Yes, I'm all right, I just didn't expect—I mean, one minute I'm standing in a circle of kids, and the next . . ." I'm calming down, my breathing returning to normal. "Was that a light saber, Canaan?"

Canaan sputters. "No, it wasn't a light saber."

"Close enough, though," Jake says, squeezing me against him. "You're getting better at this fear stuff."

He's right. I am.

"The halo helps," I say.

"Keep it on," Canaan says, standing. "Maka didn't pursue us after Helene fell, but he won't have gone far. And there's still Damien to account for."

"Where are you going?" I ask.

"I'll be back shortly. These two need somewhere to mend. Somewhere safe. And this," he says, looking around, "doesn't qualify."

Canaan dives from the building, two bundles tucked in the safety of his wings. I watch him step into nothingness, banking to the right and circling the warehouse, his Celestial head moving to and fro. Eventually he shoots to the north, over the river, and disappears from sight.

There's no break in the downpour. Even the bridge hanging over the warehouse can't keep the storm from reaching us, and it beats down hard—glossy projectiles falling from the clouds above and soaking our very human forms. Jake and I sit facing one another on the rooftop. The rain falls angrily, and we pull our heads together in a tired attempt to keep it out.

Jake hasn't stopped moving. He fumbles with my hoodie, my hat. He scratches mud from my jeans and pulls something from my hair. I place my hands, celestially hot, on either side of his face. Finally, he breathes deeply and lets his hands rest on my knees.

"What are you thinking?" I say.

He hastily wipes the rain from his eyes. "I'm wishing I'd been more careful with your ankle. That I hadn't put everyone in danger."

I stare at his face, so full of regret, and I wonder aloud, "But do you think we'd have found this place otherwise? All these children, Jake. How long have they been here? Your little 'mistake' led us to them."

He nods, but there's regret there. I wonder if he'll be more discriminating with his gift. The thought makes me sad.

"And you," he says. "What are you thinking?"

"I don't know," I say. "Trying to make sense of everything, I guess, trying to make it all fit."

"How's that working out for you?"

"Not so well."

"Yeah," Jake says. "Angels and demons are hard to pencil in next to pointe class."

"You know what pointe class is?"

"I Googled you."

"You Googled me?"

"I was curious," he says, the Celestial colors of his face blending into a blush. "Do you miss teaching?"

"It was just the younger girls at Miss Macy's," I say with a nod. "Just kids, but yeah, I miss it."

"Like the kids down there," he says. The wind shifts, and the rain slides sideways and then vertical again, sounding like tribal drums on the aluminum roof. "Don't try to make all this fit into your world, okay? It won't. Once you've seen the world like this, once it takes hold of you, you can't ignore it and pretend it's not there. Even without the halo, Elle, you'll start to see fear and oppression. You'll begin to see them for what they really are."

"And what do I do with all of that?" I say, uncomfortable with the thought. "I have more than enough trouble managing my own emotions. How do I . . . cope . . . with everyone else's fear? With *this* reality?"

Conviction hardens his face. "You fight it. Have you noticed—darkness can't survive in a world of light? Eventually evil everywhere will burn, but until it does, the kingdom of light, God's kingdom, needs warriors."

I swallow against the turmoil sloshing around inside me. Jake tilts his head, waiting for me to speak.

"There's no doubt in my mind that Canaan is good. That you are good. That Damien is evil. And I can see that God cares—even loves you, loves people—enough to send angels like Canaan to protect them."

"Brielle, He's done so much more than that." Jake's face is full of passion and fervor.

"I believe you, and I want to understand," I say through a haze of tears. "It's ridiculous to feel this way, because it's so obvious I'm supposed to be here, that someone has been guiding this whole thing along, but . . . I just keep hitting a wall. I can't figure out why a God who would do all of this for me, for you, would allow Ali to die—would take my mom without anything, even the smallest memory to comfort me."

Jake doesn't speak.

"It just seems wrong, you know? For a righteous God to allow injustice. It just seems wrong." I wish I felt differently, but at least I have put words to the ache I've been stifling all day. "I'm sorry, Jake," I apologize, feeling miserable for being disappointed in the God he so willingly follows. "I just have a problem with blind faith."

Jake's eyes snap to mine. Prismatic raindrops run down his cheeks and lips, but his smile is warm.

"You know, second to me—and maybe the apostle John—you've seen more of the true world than just about anyone. God doesn't call us to blind faith, Brielle. Don't let anyone tell you that. He just asks us to believe Him, to believe that what He said about Himself is true. Even when it doesn't make sense. Even when it's hard. I would give anything to understand God and why He does what He does." Jake pulls my face closer to his. "But we're *His* creation, Brielle. Not the other way around. We can't make God into what we think He should be. With everything you've now seen, is it so hard to believe that *perhaps* the tragedy of your mother's death—of Ali's murder—that maybe these things were allowed to happen as part of some larger plan?"

The air seems too thin, and I can't breathe in enough of it. The thought of their lives being thrown away to accommodate some divine arrangement stabs like a thousand knives. I pull away, trying to find more air.

"Why should their deaths be necessary? With everything He could have done, all the angels He could have sent, why didn't they have a Shield? Wasn't my mom worth it? Wasn't Ali? Are you saying God wanted them to die?"

"Everyone dies," Jake says, releasing me.

"But He could have stopped it?"

The silence buzzes. Waspish. Like me.

"Yes. He could've stopped it."

The honesty of his words, the truth of it, tears at my heart, and I sob—the pain of loss worse than it's been in days. "So He didn't care, then? He just let them die!"

"Brielle, listen to me. It's possible God's greater plan includes the deaths of your mother and Ali, but that doesn't say anything about their worth to Him. You *have* to believe that.

"It's also possible their deaths were brought about by the very existence of evil. Look around you. We live in a world plagued by darkness. Every choice we make affects the balance of light here. You've seen how fear debilitates us. The only way bad things will stop happening to good people is for darkness to be completely eradicated, and that will only happen in God's timing. But you can trust that God will somehow use their deaths, and your loss, to one day eliminate evil forever."

"God's plan or not, Jake, I hate death."

"God does too."

Those three little words are unfathomable to me. I'm still reeling when Jake continues.

"But let me ask you this: when Canaan cloaked you with his wings and you disappeared from the Terrestrial realm, did you just . . . stop existing?"

"Of course not," I say, surprised by the question.

"It's the same thing, Elle. Ali and your mother have been cloaked by death. You can't see them, but they're not gone. Not really. Our spirits will outlive our physical bodies, so it's our spirits we have to take care of."

Jake grabs the collar of my sweatshirt, and I let him pull me to him, leaning my forehead against his. The halo's kept me warm, warmer even than Jake.

"Anybody ever told you how hot you are?" he asks.

My lips twitch. "You really want me to answer that question."

He laughs.

"Do you think I'll see them again, Jake? In heaven?"

"That's between them and God," he says, closing his eyes. Their white light is shut away, and still the Celestial shines. "And you and God. Belief is always a choice. And it's a choice no one else can make for you."

"It's not that I don't believe, Jake. I just want to understand."

Jake breathes a small, gentle laugh. "It's a journey, Elle. A process. There's a proverb that says, 'Trust in the Lord with all your heart, and lean not on your own understanding.'"

"Lean not on your own understanding." The words are melodic, fortune cookie-ish.

"In the past few days your eyes have been opened to an entirely different realm—one you didn't even know existed. God's creation is so vast it'd be crazy to think we could ever understand it all."

I think of Dad. I can't imagine explaining all this to him, but there's a part of me that aches to. He'd never believe me without seeing it himself.

"That's so hard for me," I say.

"I know. But it starts with trusting that you don't know everything. That God does. That His decisions are better than yours, even when they hurt. You do that for a while, and you realize that regardless of what He allows, God's our best hope. Our only hope."

Hope.

The word trills inside me. Like the lyrics of a song I knew once but had forgotten. And now it's here, suddenly. *Hope* on my tongue and in my heart. I cling to it, afraid of forgetting all over again.

Jake pulls the sopping beanie down tighter on my head, and the halo releases such a strong wave of heat my eyes quiver and almost close.

"And having seen the world through Celestial eyes, what do you think about the Terrestrial, about the world you've always known?"

I open my eyes wide and look around at the canvas of color, at the way things really are. I try to picture the world as I'd known it before, without the light and the rainbow hues shading everything, without the splotches of darkness.

"I think it's a facade—like a puppet show, you know? We can only see what's going on above the curtain. But with the halo on, it's like the curtains have been removed and there's a whole world of activity behind them. It makes me wonder if the world I thought I knew would even be possible without the Celestial." I pause, turning over image after fascinating image. "In the Terrestrial, we can't see people's emotions or motives. We just see actions and outcomes, right? In the Celestial, everything is right in front of you: Fear and hatred, love, sadness. Angels, demons. Everything's right there to be seen." My eyes tear through the roof into the office below, splashed with the shocking red of violence, two men dead on the floor. "You can't hide the truth."

"I beg to differ."

We jump to our feet, and Jake pushes himself in front of me. Over the side of the building comes a large hand, followed by another. The speaker heaves himself onto the roof and pulls himself up to his full height. In his hand he holds a dagger of sorts, blood glistening on its blade. He's disheveled, but I have no trouble identifying the man in front of us as Damien.

With the halo still firmly in place, I catch glimpses of the demon's true self as his form seems to morph in and out of focus before me. His wing is severely damaged and hangs awkwardly, feathers jutting out here and there. I wonder if he can still fly.

"Nice to see you again, Brielle." His black eyes roam uncomfortably over my body from head to toe and back again. With a glance at Jake, he sheaths his knife. "Hmm . . . I wonder."

His figure stabilizes in front of me, the human appearance gone, replaced by the totality of his fallen form.

"Brielle?" Jake says, grabbing my hand.

Damien's cloaked himself and transferred to the Celestial, disappearing from Jake's sight altogether.

"He's still there," I whisper. "He hasn't moved."

Damien glares at me, his eyes nearly closed. "So you *can* see me."

I look at Jake.

"Don't," Jake whispers quietly, avoiding my gaze.

Damien grins. It's the most disgusting thing I've ever seen. He grabs my arm and yanks me away from Jake. Jake reaches out for me, but his attempt is useless. I tumble toward Damien, who catches me roughly and spins me so that I face Jake. He is shaking, but still, his flaming hazel eyes are averted. He stares at the ground, at the sky, everywhere but at me.

And I understand.

Damien flashes his talons in front of my face, and before I realize what he's doing, he drags a razor-sharp nail down my cheek. I am screaming, crying out in pain, writhing, trying desperately to get free. Jake can't help himself, it seems, and he turns his face to mine. I know he sees blood, black as night, blossom on my face. I watch in horror as rays of light break through the lush green and deep brown of Jake's eyes, and the pure white of love's greatest expression stares back at me.

Damien purrs and flings me into Jake's arms. I watch as he takes off into the sky. He is broken, damaged, but he manages to hover clumsily above us.

"I'm sorry," I sob.

"No, I'm sorry," Jake says. "I'm so sorry."

He extends his hand toward the gash on my face. He offers healing, but at what cost?

"Don't," I tell him, stepping back. "Leave it. It's what he wants."

Overhead, Damien opens his mouth and releases a sound so intense I drop to my knees, crying out and covering my ears. It's the sound of violence, the hum of hate, the very ring of evil. It is a growl, a roar, a cry of desperation. It is pain. It is death.

"Brielle!" Jake cries. I don't know why he can't hear Damien's Celestial cry, but I'm grateful.

And then it's over.

"It's okay," I say, standing. "I'm okay."

"What was that?" he asks, searching my face.

Before I can answer, monstrous black wings flash overhead. I look up to see another demon, larger by far than Damien and uninjured, descending from the apex of the bridge. I shudder. This is the demon who survived Canaan's sword. This is Maka.

Damien's damaged wing seems to have reached its maximum exertion, and he, too, drops to the roof, faster and with much less grace than his counterpart.

"Jake," I warn. "Another one. Behind you."

Without any visible communication, they both transfer to the Terrestrial, their massive forms side by side. Damien, with his olive skin and jet-black hair, stands arrogantly, his arms crossed, his handsome face smiling. The demon-man next to him is huge, black and muscled, his long hair hanging in braided curtains. Both stare at us greedily with dead black eyes, and after a moment the large one speaks.

"You can see us, then," Maka says, his voice deep and hollow. "It seems Damien was right about you. And you—" He turns his attention to Jake. "You leave your girlfriend there, bleeding. How selfish. In your hand lies an ability so rare, so precious. And yet you refrain. Why, I wonder?"

Jake doesn't answer.

"How do you feel about that, sweetheart?" the ogre asks, turning to me.

A flash of white against the orange sky draws my attention, and my eyes flick briefly away. Behind the two demons, approaching fast, is Canaan. He drops out of sight across the river, and I squeeze Jake's hand. With the two demons standing before me in their human form, I am the only one able to see into the Celestial.

Moments later Canaan resurfaces over the top of an evergreen, and I keep my face as stoic as possible, refusing, like Jake, to answer the question put to me. I try not to appear distracted but watch as Canaan changes course. He approaches from Jake's right-hand side, his arms outstretched.

We're saved!

Any second now we'll be safely wrapped in the wings of our Shield. If my face betrays any sense of this, I'm unaware. But something—my demeanor, fate, bad luck—something causes Damien to transfer back to the Celestial just as Canaan crosses over the ledge of the roof.

With a violent roar Damien steps in front of me and draws his sword. In a jabbing motion he thrusts it at Canaan. It makes contact with one of Canaan's outstretched hands, and he pulls it back in response. He can't reach me now, but he snatches Jake to himself, cloaking him. Maka transfers, drawing his weapon and rising into the air behind Canaan.

And then the air around me seems to disappear, cosmically vacuumed away. I gasp, frantically searching for it. But something heavier fills my lungs. It drips from my nose and my mouth.

I'm drowning.

Air is in limited supply, but there is no shortage of blood. I watch the world of colors and light swirl around me and know I'm dying. I reach out, turning, struggling to find the source of pain. Finally my hands find the hilt of a dagger protruding from my chest. Damien's Terrestrial form stands just feet away, his demonic face triumphant, his hand still extended from the blade toss.

I look around frantically for Jake, for Canaan, but there's no friendly face to be seen. I drop to the roof, spitting and gurgling, wishing again and again for just one more breath.

38

Canaan

Nooooooo!!! Canaan, turn around!"

Jake's cry is one of anguish. Canaan lurches and pulls to a stop.

"Go back, go back, go back!" Jake begs. He's hysterical. "Please go back!"

Canaan turns his eyes to the warehouse, and tragedy breaks through him. Brielle is engulfed in the flames of violence. She lies faceup, the life force bleeding out of her. It leaks down the ridges of the aluminum building with the dirty rainwater, soaking into the ground below.

Maka and Damien stand, in their Celestial forms, next to the dying girl, sneering. Canaan hovers, conflicted, in the sky.

"Canaan! Go back!"

"Jake, if we go back, the odds are against us. I can't guarantee your safety once you leave these wings. For your gift alone, they'll dig their talons in."

"I won't be easily corrupted."

"I know that. But they'll use your compassion against you. Your feelings for Brielle. They do whatever it takes to taint the truth. To corrupt what God has created you to be."

"I don't care," he wails.

"You do care. And you're my responsibility. I have a job to do."

"*She's* your responsibility, Canaan. She's my responsibility. Go back!"

"Jake . . ."

"It's my choice, Canaan. Don't take this from me."

Is he right? Is this good-bye?

"What if it's her time, Jake?"

"That's God's decision, not yours," he argues. "I have to try. Take me back."

Canaan hesitates. This is the child he's watched grow year after year. He's raised Jake the best way he knew, making the boy's well-being his first priority, always. How can he deliver Jake to the lions?

"We're losing time, Canaan," Jake says, watching the flames flickering erratically. "Please, take me back."

He's right. This is his choice.

Canaan slaps his wings hard, tunneling faster than ever through the orange sky glittering with Terrestrial rain, finally landing lightly on the roof. Canaan opens his wings, and Jake emerges. He crosses through the flames and collapses at Brielle's side. Though Canaan is near, Jake loses his Celestial eyes when he leaves the safety of his Shield's wings. Canaan knows his human eyes lie to him—compel Jake to believe he and Brielle are alone in the darkness.

"Drop your sword," Maka's mind demands. He holds his scimitar over Jake's head. It's a threat. Symbolic, of course, but a threat nonetheless. "Now, or we won't wait to see what the boy can do."

Canaan draws his sword and holds it up. Maka jerks his

head to the ledge of the building, and Canaan tosses it over. Maka's scimitar cannot damage Jake's soul, which belongs firmly to the Creator. But human weapons are surprisingly efficient, as Damien's dagger has so aptly shown.

"Whether he heals her or not, you'll take him. Do your best to corrupt him," Canaan says. "What does the girl matter?"

Maka glances at Damien.

"We've all lost something tonight. If Damien is right—if the boy has the ability to heal—then perhaps it's all been worth it. That would be good for Damien. He could use a new charge. A right hand. A human with gifts. We could help him . . . prepare Jake for that task. But if Damien has deceived us . . ."

"Why would I do that? What do I gain by angering you?"

"Nothing but fire."

Damien blanches but does not respond.

"Now go."

Canaan jumps softly and floats away, his eyes on Jake. Tears run down the boy's face, but his jaw is set. Though he no longer sees the forces around him, he understands the consequences of this action. Jake can heal Brielle, but growing old with her is impossible now.

Without his sword Canaan is no match against two armed demons, but if Jake is willing to give his life for Brielle's, he'll do his best to ensure she remains safe. Canaan is certain he can keep one of them from death, and as Jake said, it's his choice.

Jake's hand presses against the knife wound to her chest, and Canaan watches the flames flash unevenly, slowing. He waits impatiently for them to steady, to throb rhythmically to the strong, healthy cadence of Brielle's heart.

But moments pass and the flames move ever slower, more

erratic. Canaan's eyes move to Damien, whose face is contorted in confusion, his good wing twitching involuntarily. Maka stands hunched, his weapon still drawn. The expression on his face shows his confidence has faltered.

Jake's head is bowed, his features hidden from them all. Two bright flashes of crimson light the orange sky morbidly, and the flames still. Jake's body shakes, and his desolation fills the atmosphere. The waters of sadness, murky and gray, wash over him, obscuring Canaan's view and causing him instead to focus on the two demons perched like gothic bookends on his left and right.

Maka roars in anger and turns on his fallen brother. He draws his sword and swings it at Damien. Canaan wraps his wings tightly and falls into a dive. If Brielle's time has come, he can at least save Jake.

39

Brielle

reathing is easier now, or maybe the need has left me. The sky, lively with its sorbet colors, has begun to change, to fade. I watch in wonder as the hues bleed away, leaving Jake's face framed by a pure white sky. I stare up at him, at his sun-kissed face, at his white eyes shining down on me, and wish I could ease his pain. His body shakes, and he leans toward me, kissing my lips lightly and closing my eyes.

I lie here, Jake's body close, and I sleep.

It's possible long days or short minutes have passed, but when at last I open my eyes, Jake is gone. I try to sit up, but I'm unable to move. I know that should frighten me, but it doesn't. Instead, I relax and stare at the white sky above. The longer I stare, the more I can't be sure of what I'm seeing.

A tiny dark spot has begun to form. Soon it resembles a gold coin sparkling in the distance. Larger and larger it grows, losing its distinct shape and rolling like the molten liquid gold of the halo, running like paint down the white canvas around me until I am surrounded by the richness of this glowing liquid.

Light bounces off its surface, warming me. The gold continues to move and bubble, molding itself.

And then before me, angels emerge out of the light, singing in a language I cannot understand. Snowy white wings cover their faces and their feet, and with another set of wings they fly. Behind them, the gold has transformed into a high platform, and I slam my eyes shut.

A light so bright it pains me appears on the platform. I pinch my eyes tighter and tighter, but it's not enough. The light sears, and I want nothing more than to throw my arms over my face and hide, but I can't move. My eyelids are useless—I see the gold and the angels, feel the burning light through the thinness of them.

The singing draws nearer, and I feel someone's presence close by. Layer upon layer of feathery wings cover me, and the pain diminishes, leaving me exhausted. Again I sleep.

When I wake I see the underside of a downy-soft wing, glowing softly with the light from beyond. I listen, the only sense useful to me now. The singing voices are still there, but they're quieter now, hushed, respectfully so. A conversation is taking place among them.

"Will she stay?"

"I don't believe so, no."

"Then she has decided."

"In her heart."

"Has she confessed with her mouth?"

"There is not yet enough understanding."

"So the Father is sending her back."

"Yes, I think He is."

"But then why is she here?"

"Somehow, some way, her physical death serves His purpose."

"And when will He restore breath to her?"

"What is time to an Eternal God?"

"Immaterial."

"Yes, immaterial."

The angels' song floods my ears once again, and a peace washes over me. Whatever His purpose, I understand something now I didn't before. A righteous God isn't bound by time. He has an eternity to make things right. In this moment I know. Even if He never reveals His reasons to me, even if He never explains why He allowed my mother and Ali to die, I'll still fight against the darkness so His light can spread. This God that Jake serves is a good God.

He doesn't owe me an explanation.

I owe Him my life.

40

Canaan

*L*ightning flashes as the demons' scimitars clash again and again. Maka bears down hard on Damien, moving him toward the ledge, trying to force his brother into the sky where Damien's broken wing would severely handicap him. Hostility rips from their throats, challenging the rumbling thunder above.

Oblivious to the bedlam, Jake lies prostrate across Brielle's body. Wisdom begs that Canaan take only Jake into the safety of his wings, but leaving Brielle's body feels like a betrayal—of Jake, of the job he's been given. With the demons locked in their own conflict, could he get away with taking them both, or would they turn and attack?

Having already retrieved his sword, he's now just feet away and makes his decision. He stretches for the star-crossed lovers as a guttural cry, primal and resonant, hits him from behind. A stabbing sensation follows, and four talons come into his line of sight, protruding from his chest. Then they're withdrawn, and Javan soars over Canaan's head, setting himself down on the roof of the warehouse.

Canaan was stabbed through the shoulder, and his wing suffers for it. Escaping with his charges is no longer an option. Carrying one or both of them while injured and pursued by any number of demons would only guarantee Jake's demise. An attempt to flee is not in the boy's best interest.

Victory is.

Canaan draws his sword and lands in front of Javan. The demon clacks his grisly teeth together, taunting. Canaan strikes out, and Javan blocks the attack. But he is weak. His sword arm trembles, and Canaan doesn't hesitate. He plants his foot in the demon's chest and shoves. Javan backs up, tripping over Maka's heel. Canaan advances and drives his scorching blade into Javan's abdomen. With hisses and squeals, Javan dissolves into the light.

Maka turns, infuriated at Javan's intrusion, and seeing the failure of his fallen brother, swings his sword wildly. Canaan ducks under his arm and grabs the elbow of his sword hand. Using Maka's own momentum, Canaan heaves him into Damien, who is ready and waiting. Damien's scimitar penetrates the massive demon's chest, and Maka burns, vanishing in a burst of ash.

Canaan turns to Damien, whose face hangs in an expression of mixed relief and outrage. His plan has failed, but he's survived.

Thus far.

Canaan raises his sword and approaches. Damien has to be returned to the pit. He has to remain there for the duration of Jake's life, or his charge will never be safe.

Maka had backed Damien to the very ledge of the building. Now Canaan closes in, giving him only two choices: he can take to the sky, where his injury will be put to the test against Canaan's, or he can fight. The demon halts, indecisive.

The sound of clanking metal draws their attention.

"Jake? Brielle? You guys up here?"

It's Marco, climbing up the maintenance ladder behind Damien. His head emerges over the ledge of the building.

"I thought I heard—" He catches sight of Jake, of Brielle's body.

"Stop, Marco," Jake cautions. "It's not safe right now."

"What happened to her?" Marco whispers.

In a last-ditch effort to secure his survival, Damien grabs Marco and throws him to the roof in front of him, pressing his sword to Marco's neck. Marco yells and punches at the air, unable to see the force controlling his body.

Damien laughs cruelly. "Drop your sword, Canaan."

"Drop yours!"

Helene appears out of the neon sky. She hovers behind Damien, her healing complete. With a slash of zealous light, she beheads the demon. Damien's form sparks and fumes as it leaves this world, rematerializing in the very fires of hell—his damaged eyes surely the least of his worries.

Canaan beams at Helene, grateful for her endurance and fortitude, and she beams back. She sheathes her weapon and lands lightly on the roof.

"What was that?" Marco asks, struggling to right himself.

Helene crosses invisibly to him, places her dainty hands on his shoulders, and squeezes. Instantly he's asleep, and Canaan's powerful little partner guides Marco gently to the roof.

Canaan transfers to the Terrestrial, Helene following. Jake takes in their two forms, and a cry shakes him.

"It's over," Canaan says, wrapping him in his arms.

Helene walks away, giving Jake the privacy he needs to mourn. Jake buries his face in his Shield's chest and weeps.

41

Brielle

*I*t's the smell of rain that tells me I'm breathing again. It splashes my face and neck. My hands.

My ears seem to be working as well, and over the rain rushing down the corrugated roof, I hear Jake. He's crying. The sobs are loud, but there's something reassuring about that. That a boy who laughs shamelessly weeps that way too.

It's honest.

I hear Canaan.

He's praying. I wonder if he'll teach me.

My eyes open, and I blink against the rain. Kneeling above me is Helene—restored, healthy. She smiles.

Beautiful.

"I like happy endings," she whispers.

Beyond her, I see Jake and Canaan. Canaan holds Jake tight.

"I am so sorry about Brielle," he is saying.

Helene winks and offers her hand.

"What about Brielle?" she asks.

"Yes," I say. "What about her?"

Canaan opens his eyes and yells something unintelligible.

Jake wrenches himself around and chokes. I take Helene's hand and let her pull me to my feet.

"You were talking about me, I think."

Jake walks toward me, slowly, his hand outstretched, his mouth hanging open.

"I can't believe . . . how . . . what are you . . . you were . . ." He reaches out. "Are you okay?"

I laugh. "I am. I really, really am."

Jake blinks and blinks, like he's not seeing me clearly enough. He strokes my face, my hair. "But how? I extended my hand, Elle. I tried. But we all watched you die."

He turns to Helene. "Did you . . ."

"I didn't do anything," Helene says, raising her hands. "She was waking when we transferred. You gentlemen were busy, so I helped her to her feet."

"God knew, Jake," I say. "He knew what I needed. Even with the halo on, my perspective was so limited. I wasn't *really* seeing. Not with the right kind of eyes, anyway. Fear. Guilt. The past. My whole life, really, was standing in the way."

"Brielle . . ."

"And then, there I was—horizontal in the Throne Room, my eyes on fire, and . . . everything changed, Jake. Everything."

The roof trembles as Canaan falls to his knees. "I can't believe I ever doubted," he says. He turns his eyes to us, his smile wise.

"God *chooses* to use us, Jake, but really, He can do it all on His own."

42

Brielle

I twist my fingers into Jake's and watch as Helene drops off the roof. Her white wings fill, setting her down gently.

"Where is she going?" I ask.

"To get Kaylee," Canaan says. "She's been standing watch over one of the men, kicking him in the head whenever he stirs. It's . . . comical, but the authorities will be here shortly. We thought you might like your friend to avoid all that."

Helene returns, laying Kaylee on the roof next to Marco. Her eyes open once and then quiver heavily. Her head lolls, and she drifts back to sleep.

"What are we going to tell her?" I ask, kneeling next to my friend.

"The truth is always a good place to begin," Helene answers. "Though she won't have as many questions as you might think."

"You don't know Kaylee," I say. Helene's never been accosted by Kaylee and her never-ending curiosity.

"There are things the human mind chooses to forget," Helene explains. "She'll remember some things, of course, but her human mind will do everything it can to rationalize what's left. To splinter the things she can't process."

I remember what Jake said about Marco—that he thought Damien abducting us was nothing more than a car accident.

"Not everything will be forgotten. Not everything can be," Canaan interjects. "But when human beings are exposed to the Celestial—to the truth—they make a choice."

"Consciously, she won't understand the decision, but choosing is unavoidable." Helene watches the girl at her feet, benevolence gracing her features. "I'll stay with her as long as I can."

Helene lifts Kaylee into her arms and holds her tight. And then she steps from the roof, her wings pulling them into the buttery Celestial sky.

I look to Canaan. "Unavoidable?"

"Kaylee's mind will either believe everything she's seen— a task nearly insurmountable with fear as its foundation—or she will allow doubt to shadow it," he said. "Doubt works more quickly, needing nothing to substantiate its claim. It will act as a salve, soothing away things her mind would rather forget."

"Shouldn't we want her to believe? To understand the truth?"

"Certainly," Canaan says. "But the mind can't be forced. And belief, well, that starts closer to the heart." He takes my hand in his. "I am so proud of you, and I'm glad the Father saw fit to return you to us. I'll see you back at the house."

He pulls Jake into a hug and then stoops to pull Marco into his arms. As they fly toward Stratus, I step closer to Jake, looking into his white eyes.

"She'll be okay, right?"

"We all have choices to make," he says. "We have to let Kaylee make hers."

I turn his words over in my mind. "Letting other people choose, waiting for them, hoping they make the right choice—that seems almost harder than facing the decision yourself."

"You're telling me." Jake laughs.

I smile, understanding more and more just how difficult this must have been for him. I think of the ring—the wedding ring in Canaan's chest at home—and I realize how much more there is to figure out.

"There's a lot I don't know, Jake. So much I still need to understand."

"I know," he says. "But you're not blind anymore. That'll help."

I hear a siren in the distance, whining, wailing. It's remarkable how alike the sounds of captivity and freedom really are.

"You ready?" I ask.

"Most definitely," he says. I follow him onto the maintenance ladder reaching down to the muddy earth. When we reach the ground we stand there, staring, waiting for the authorities. Waiting for someone to take responsibility for the children inside.

"What are you thinking about?" I ask Jake.

"The truth," he says after a moment.

"The truth we're going to tell the authorities right now, or the truth, truth?"

"Both," he says, smiling.

"And what exactly are you thinking about the truth?"

"I'm thinking it sets you free. If you're brave enough to look for it."

He's right. You have to be brave. Even when you're afraid.

In the shadow of the warehouse, I tug off the wet beanie and remove the halo. I shake out my hair, and we watch as Canaan's gift transforms into a glorified piece of jewelry. Well, I watch the halo. Jake watches me. I feel his eyes on me, on my face. And when I have the halo back on my wrist, I turn my face to his.

The sun won't be up for another few hours, but even now Jake's hazel eyes are warm, inviting the countless questions lining up in my mind. Blood is crusted down his shoulder and across his chest, and his face is pink with the slap of wind and rain.

"So how do you like being the hero?" he asks.

"I'm just glad someone was. I still can't believe stuff like this happens to children. Here. In America. If being the hero means freedom for . . . anyone, I'd gladly do it again."

His face turns serious, and he looks down at my ragged shirt, sliced open, blood still wet. I wrap my hand across my stomach, and he tucks a flyaway strand of hair behind my ear.

"I have a feeling this is just the beginning, Elle."

That's a crazy thought!

"Easing me in, are you?"

He laughs lightly. "I just want you to know what you're in for. You know? Sometimes heroes don't make it."

I slip my arms around his neck. "Tonight they did."

Our faces wet with rain, our clothes soaked with blood, I wouldn't trade this moment for anything. The world around us is alive with noise, I'm sure, but for a minute I'm conscious of nothing but Jake's soft breathing and his heart beating against my chest.

"Now, about that truth," I say, peering over Jake's shoulder, waking again to the sights and sounds of misery around us. "There's a police officer headed this way, and I'm thinking he's going to want some version of it."

"Then we give it to him," Jake says. We turn toward the

cruiser parked just feet from the open warehouse doors. "The truth, the whole truth, and nothing but the truth. Just nothing about angels," Jake clarifies. "People, yes. Angels, no."

The red and blue lights atop the cruiser draw the children like lonely, frightened moths to the flame of freedom. Malnourished and weak, they make their way into the night air and surround the lone officer. As the sea of stolen children swells, the poor man gropes for his radio.

With our fingers stitched together, Jake and I walk toward the group.

"You shall know the truth," Jake says.

"And the truth shall set you free."

Afterword

Jake

Another seven days have passed, and it's Saturday again. Brielle has a thing for numbers, so I'll put it to you this way:

Forty-two days ago Brielle's best friend was murdered. Nineteen days ago I met the girl I'll one day propose to, and seven days ago a knife sliced through her chest, killing her. That very night, God healed both her heart and her mind, and He sent her back to finish out the days He had numbered for her.

And I couldn't be more grateful.

With the constant downpour and school wrapping up for the semester, we've had a considerable amount of downtime. I've been spending it with Brielle. Kaylee joins us most days, recalling terrifying nightmares, most of which actually happened. We listen, waiting for an opportunity to share.

I met Brielle's dad for the first time on Wednesday. It went okay. I can't say he's a fan just yet, but I'm hoping. He did give me permission to take Brielle out next Friday, so that's a good thing. It's funny, but I'm a little nervous about it. Angels and demons are commonplace to me, but dinner and a movie? That's a whole different kind of scary.

And then there's Marco.

After spending a day with Canaan and me, Marco called the one taxi driver in Stratus and had himself driven to the city, where he turned himself in. In light of the children's statements and the overwhelming evidence against Horacio and his men, the district attorney has hinted that the charges against Marco will be dropped. They're still trying to decide what to do about his impossible disappearance from prison, and Marco's explanation has done nothing but muddle the entire affair.

But in an effort to thoroughly clear his name, he has consented to an undetermined period of evaluation at a state psychiatric facility. Brielle and I take turns calling, and Canaan has invited him to stay with us once he's released. I don't know if he'll take Canaan up on the offer, but I hope he does.

There's something there. Something about Marco that continues to nag at my spirit. It's a mystery I'll have to unravel.

One of many, it seems.

"Jake," Canaan called this morning.

I was at the kitchen table, alone, giving Cocoa Pebbles a try for Brielle's sake.

"Could you come in here, please?"

"Sure."

I honestly didn't mind abandoning the mushy chocolate soup, but when I walked into Canaan's room I knew something was wrong. He was standing at the foot of his bed, staring down into the open chest.

"What is it?" I asked.

Canaan didn't answer, which isn't like him at all. A quiet

Canaan makes me nervous. I moved across the room until I could see what had silenced his lips.

And then I dropped to my knees, their strength sapped by the sight.

The jewelry box was gone. The one with Brielle's ring in it. Vanished.

There in its place was Damien's dagger. Dried, crusted blood—Brielle's blood—still marked the blade.

I tried to make sense of what I was seeing. Thinking, rethinking, and still coming up with nothing.

"Has anything ever disappeared from the chest before?"

"No," Canaan says. "Never."

My hand trembled as I reached inside and withdrew the knife.

"What does it mean?"

Canaan shook his head.

"Does it mean I'm not going to marry Brielle? Has the choice been taken from me? Is something going to happen to her?"

My panic moved Canaan to action. He took the dagger from my hand and returned it to the chest. He replaced the lid and pulled me to my feet.

"It means that life is fragile, Jake. That God is wise. That we don't have the whole picture."

My breathing was coming quick and fast. Canaan pressed a hand to my chest, steadying me, reminding me of who I am.

Of who I'm not.

And I am not God.

"It means we wait."

Reading Group Guide

Spoiler alert!
Don't read before completing *Angel Eyes*.

1. Brielle knows what it's like to lose a loved one. Has this ever happened to you or someone you know? How did you cope?

2. At the beginning of this novel, Brielle feels very much alone. In truth, she has a great support system: her dad, Kaylee, Miss Macy, Mr. Burns. Do you have a group of people you can rely on when things get tough? Who are they?

3. Mr. Burns tells Brielle that "It's okay to be broken." Do you agree with him? What does that phrase mean to you?

4. Ali was Brielle's best friend but she was also someone Brielle admired and looked up to. Do you have a friend like that?

5. Ballet is Brielle's creative outlet. How do you channel your creativity?

6. By placing an engagement ring with Brielle's initials on it into the chest, the Throne Room seems to be indicating that Jake and Brielle will marry. Do you believe God orchestrates marriages? Can you think of a biblical example? What do you think happened to the ring at the end of the novel?

7. The halo gives Jake and Brielle different gifts: Jake the gift to heal; Brielle the gift to see. What challenges or responsibilities come with those gifts? Why do you think the halo affects them differently? If you put the halo on, what gift do you think it would give to you?

8. Jake quotes Proverbs 3:5-6. It says, "Trust in the LORD with all your heart, and lean not on your own understanding; in all your ways acknowledge Him, and He shall direct your paths." Do you have trouble trusting what you can't see? Do you have advice for someone who does?

9. Brielle's father is adamantly against anything religious. How do you think he'll react to Brielle's new beliefs? Is there someone in your life who is adamantly against religion? How do you reach out to them?

10. Brielle is attracted to many things about Jake. Can you name a few? What do you look for in the opposite sex?

11. In this story, fear is portrayed as cold and clingy. It is portrayed as a weapon. Do you think this is an accurate representation? Have you ever felt attacked by fear? What did you do?

12. While this story is entirely fictional, the Bible speaks very clearly about the existence of angels and demons. Do you believe in guardian angels? Have you witnessed anything that would lead you to believe in their presence?

13. Brielle struggles to understand how a righteous God could let bad things happen. Have you ever wondered about this? What are your thoughts?

14. Human trafficking is a very real problem both in the United States and abroad. What are some things you can do to help?

Acknowledgments

Shannon would like to thank...

Matt. You make everything better. Everything. This story included. You helped me brainstorm and you talked me through my theology. Thank you for choosing me, for loving me, and for being my biggest fan. I've always been yours. SHMILY.

Justus. My little man. I gave Brielle your eyes and can only hope she'll one day have your passion. You're smarter than any one child should ever be, but it's your heart that wins me over daily. Keep reading. Keep writing. And dream big, kid. God has plans.

Jazlyn. My angel fish. You were there when this story was born and your nose kisses have cured so many things along the way. I hope your desire for buried treasure extends to the Word. Hide it in your heart, baby girl. Keep it there.

Mom and Dad. You introduced me to Christ over Chinese take-out and you've endured my many passions through the years. For loving me and for never rolling your eyes, thank you.

Sharon and Steph. You are my heart and soul. Parts of you are in every beautiful character I write. I hope you see yourselves there.

Jacy. Faded jeans and long sleeve white tees make me think of you. I hope they always remind you of a God who heals and a love with no bounds.

Jenny and Joanne. Randa and Celeste. Team Root. Inspire. Where would a writer be without her writer friends? Because of you, my journey has not been a lonely one.

Alicia and Aaron. Thank you for late-night talks and copious amounts of homemade butterbeer. Both have changed my world. *Lacey and Carla.* Where would we be without you? You are family and I can't thank you enough for being who you are. *Jordan, Ty, and Pete.* Superheroes extraordinaire. Thank you for keeping my husband sane. *The Corringtons, Blacks, and Tubras.* You dropped out of the sky when we needed you most. You'll never, ever know . . .

My Living Way family. Thank you for letting me grow. Thank you for letting me change. Thank you for being my family regardless.

The Lukes and the Callahans, the Dittemores, Masons, and Delks. You're all in here somewhere, in these pages. Your support means the world. I love you all.

A very special thank you to *Jason Pinter* for pulling me from the slush pile, and to *Holly Root* for being the best agent a girl could ask for. You chatted puppets when God-knows you had more than enough to do. I'm forever grateful.

And finally, to *Becky and Ami, to Allen and LB. To Eric and Kristen, to Katie and Ruthie and the entire team at Nelson Fiction.* What can a girl say to those making her dream come true? Words aren't sufficient, but thank you. It's a pleasure to venture into the great unknown with you.

Return to the Celestial as
the battle against evil continues in

BROKEN
WINGS

Available
February 2013

For the latest news about the
Angel Eyes Trilogy, visit

ShannonDittemore.com

Connect with Shannon through
Facebook and Twitter:

f Facebook: Shannon Dittemore – Author

Twitter: @ShanDitty

To learn more about the tragedy that
is human trafficking and ways to
help fight it, visit www.chabdai.org.

Author to Author Interview

Recently, Shannon Dittemore interviewed fellow Thomas Nelson author, Krista McGee, about her novels and her life. We hope you enjoy the discussion.

Shannon Dittemore

Krista McGee

SHANNON DITTEMORE: Tell us a little about your story development. The Esther parallels in *First Date* were a pleasant surprise. I didn't see them coming. Did you set out to tell a story based on Esther or did that happen as you wrote?

KRISTA MCGEE: Esther was my inspiration. Girl from nowhere becomes queen and saves her people from complete annihilation. How cool is that? I've read Esther dozens of times, and for years I kept thinking, "I wonder what that story would look like if it were written today?" God is the same yesterday, today, and forever, right? The same God that called Esther to accomplish his purposes (to save a nation of people!) is working in our lives every day. I want girls to know that. Life can be tough. But God is always with us, working all things together for good for those who love him and are called according to His purpose (Romans 8:28). He may call us to do things or go places totally out of our comfort zone, but His plans are always best! That is the truth taught in the book of Esther, and I wanted to mirror that truth in *First Date*.

SD: Addy is set several challenges as part of the competition. If you were in her place, which one would you excel at? Which one would mortify you?

KM: Worst first – I would stink at golf. In fact, "stink" is being generous. My eight-year-old son can kill me on the mini-golf course. And forget real golf. I can dig an amazing hole with a golf club, but make contact with the ball? Forget it! I'm a lot like Kara, so performing on stage in front of a huge crowd would definitely be my favorite. Bring on the spotlight. I'm ready for my close-up!

SD: **Girl drama is all over this novel. You also focus a ton on true friendship. Addy has some exceptional relationships—girlfriends who are there for her through this ordeal. You're a teacher. You see these types of things all the time. How important would you say true friendship is during our teen years?**

KM: I have an amazing group of senior girls that meet with me once a week for Bible study and sharing. They keep each other accountable in so many ways and constantly encourage each other. I love watching them give hugs and pats on the back, and even a "girl, what are you thinking?" when needed. They have made it through high school with great testimonies and relatively few regrets, and I know that is because of the commitment they have made to God and each other.

SD: **One of my favorite parts of *First Date* was the back-story involving Addy's parents. Is missionary work something you can identify with?**

KM: Yes. Our family had the amazing privilege of ministering in both Costa Rica and in Spain as missionaries. I loved living in other countries and seeing God at work there. Missionaries are my heroes, and I want to highlight them as much as I can in my writing.

SD: Addy is sucked into this reality TV experience quite unwillingly. Can you relate or are you a reality TV fan? Which reality show would love to participate in? Is there a show that would terrify you?

KM: Okay, confession time – I don't even watch reality TV dating shows. I can barely stomach the commercials. All the crying and catfights and "oh, no she didn'ts." No, thanks. I do love *American Idol*, though, and some of the other shows that allow talented, unknown people to have a shot at fame.

SD: What can you tell us about your next novel? Inquiring minds want to know!

KM: I am so excited about *Starring Me*. I had so much fun writing about Kara in *First Date* that I knew I wanted to tell her story when I had finished Addy's. Hers is a modernization of the Isaac and Rebekah story. My "Isaac" is Chad Beacon, teen pop star, who is looking for a costar for a new teen TV show. Kara is picked to audition for the show, but, unknown to her and the other girls auditioning, there's much more going on than just a talent contest.

SD: Dreamy boys, competing girls, millions of viewers, and a message for the ages. Thank you, Krista, for taking time to chat! I'm super excited to see *First Date* on shelves and can't wait to pick up your next one.

About the Author

Author photo by Amy Schuff Photography

S hannon Dittemore has an overactive imagination and a passion for truth. Her lifelong journey to combine the two is responsible for a stint at Portland Bible College, performances with local theater companies, and a focus on youth and young adult ministry. The daughter of one preacher and the wife of another, she spends her days imagining things unseen and chasing her two children around their home in Northern California. *Angel Eyes* is her first novel.